THE FINAL SANCTION

STEVE LYONS

BBC

Published by BBC Worldwide Ltd,
Woodlands, 80 Wood Lane
London W12 0TT

First published 1999
Copyright © Steve Lyons 1999
The moral right of the author has been asserted

Original series broadcast on the BBC
Format © BBC 1963
Doctor Who and TARDIS are trademarks of the BBC

ISBN 0 563 55584 X
Imaging by Black Sheep, copyright © BBC 1999

Printed and bound in Great Britain by Mackays of Chatham
Cover printed by Belmont Press Ltd, Northampton

Chapter One

Zoe Heriot jerked upright, the echoes of an explosion in her ears.

She moaned with a feeling of dread as hands pressed her shoulders back down into the soft earth. But it was all right. The hands belonged to the Doctor. He muttered soothing words and made Zoe feel safe.

'What's going on? What was that?' came Jamie's voice. The sound had woken him too.

'It's nothing to worry about, Jamie,' said the Doctor, although his tone suggested uncertainty. 'Our friends out there appear to have resumed hostilities.'

'Oh, is that all?' said Jamie sarcastically.

'I'm sure we'll all be perfectly safe if we remain hidden. That device went off some way away, you know: across the other side of the minefield.'

Zoe was fully awake now. The depressing weight of recollection settled upon her, chasing pleasant dreams from her head. She sighed at the prospect of facing the problems that sleep had deferred.

She sat up cautiously, aware that if the Doctor had not kept her from obeying her earlier, half-asleep impulse to stand and run she might have been demolished in the crude shelter.

It was still dark. Dark and cold. Beneath her tightly drawn overcoat, Zoe's bones ached. The mud on her left cheek had formed a brittle crust. She felt as if this terrible night had lasted for ever. She wondered how she had managed to sleep, and for how long.

'Do we have to stay here much longer, Doctor?'

'Have patience, Zoe. It should be light soon.'

She felt little cheer at his words. She stared gloomily at the precarious latticework of branches and foliage above her and wondered, not for the first time, why the TARDIS persisted in seeking out the ugliest, least hospitable worlds in the universe.

And where the TARDIS was now.

The Doctor had insisted that, come the morning, they would find his ship where they had left it and wonder how they had not stumbled across it in the night. Zoe knew better.

The none-too-distant crackle of gunfire deepened her misery.

But none of that had happened yet.

As Zoe Heriot took her first step on to the surface of a new world, she was still able to feel optimistic. True, she was greeted by a biting wind and heavy drizzle – true, her booted foot sank into the mud – but the Doctor's enthusiasm for this new locale was infectious.

'An oxygen-rich atmosphere, near-normal gravity, a temperate climate, well, more or less… Oh yes, I should be very surprised if some form of intelligent life hasn't evolved here.' He clapped his hands together gleefully.

'Aye, well, if they're so intelligent, they won't have stuck around long, will they?' said Jamie sourly. He emerged from the TARDIS wearing a blue cagoule, and glared at the overcast evening sky with suspicion.

'Now, now, Jamie,' said the Doctor, 'we have simply arrived at an unfortunate time.' As if to underscore his words, a chill gust of wind shook the skeletal branches of dead trees and found its way into the folds of Zoe's coat. She tightened her belt, with a shiver.

'And in an unfortunate place,' the Doctor added dolefully, as he surveyed their bleak surroundings and beat his hands against his upper arms to warm himself. Zoe wondered how he could possibly be comfortable in his habitual ensemble of black jacket, thin blue shirt, bow tie and checked trousers. 'Still, never mind. Appearances can be deceptive, you know. There could be a marvellous city or a spaceport on the other side of that hill.' He indicated a muddy rise, seemingly at random, and strode cheerfully towards it.

Zoe exchanged a long-suffering glance with Jamie, before they followed him dutifully.

There was no city; just a beach comprised of grey sand, oily stains and a thick carpet of brown seaweed with thorns. But the Doctor reacted as if he had discovered a beautiful oasis. He scrambled towards the beach happily, and Zoe wrinkled her nose with distaste at the thought of having to follow him.

She picked her way down the treacherous slope, grimacing as mud oozed into her boots and dampened the bottom of her coat. Jamie took her arm supportively. As it transpired, Zoe had to support him when he slid on a clump of grass and almost went sprawling. Still, she appreciated his intentions.

'I can't say I'm keen on this place, Doctor.'

'Nonsense, Jamie.' The Doctor was on his haunches, sifting through the prickly seaweed as if expecting to find gold. 'You don't know anything about it yet.'

'Well, I reckon I know all I need to know. It's freezing, for a start.'

'Well, if you will insist on wearing that kilt…'

'It's not just that, though. There's something… something bad about this place. Can you not feel it too?'

'You're probably still adjusting to the gravity. It's a little greater than you're used to. Only a little, mind.'

'It is, isn't it?' Zoe should have realised earlier. Ever since their arrival she had felt as if she was carrying a dead weight, as if this miserable world was grinding her down. She had tried to ignore the sensation. Instead, she should have deduced the logical explanation for it.

Dark water rolled in from the sea. Excited by the wind, it burst into a fine spray before collapsing on to the sand and lapping around the Doctor's shoes.

'What are you looking for, Doctor?' asked Zoe.

'You can tell a great deal about a world from its beaches,' the Doctor mumbled.

'From observing the tides, you mean?'

'Well, yes, there is that – and the action of the tide here does suggest to me that this world has more than one satellite. But, no, I was thinking of something more...' He grunted as he dug into the sand and wrested something free. 'Concrete!' he concluded triumphantly, brandishing a crumbling white brick.

'What's so good about that?' scoffed Jamie.

'Well, Jamie, it proves there is intelligent life here. At least, there has been. This didn't occur naturally, you know – it was manufactured.'

'Then whoever lives here is quite advanced,' said Zoe.

The Doctor beamed approvingly. 'Yes, yes, that's right.' He dropped the brick and stood up, lacing his fingers together and giving his companions a familiar contrite look: apologising in advance for the fact that he was about to get his own way. 'Now, I think it would be rather impolite of us to leave without saying hello, wouldn't it?'

Zoe had had a bright idea once, in the early days of her association with the Doctor. She had asked him why they could not take his remarkable space/time machine back by just a few minutes or hours, why they could not warn their past selves about what lay in store for them.

He had tried to avoid her question. 'We may have had our ups and downs during our little adventures together – but we have done a great deal of good, haven't we? I think it would be rather silly of us to undo it all.'

'Of course it would,' she had insisted, 'but we could make

things easier on ourselves, couldn't we? And then we could save even more lives.'

'I'm afraid this old ship of mine doesn't take too kindly to being told where to go.'

'But we could try!'

The Doctor had sighed then. 'No. No, Zoe, we couldn't.'

'I don't understand. Why not?'

'Well, we haven't met our future selves, have we? So we know that, in our future, we can't meet our past selves.'

'But if we decided to try; if we made definite plans…'

'Some things have to happen, Zoe. There are some rules even I must not break.'

He hadn't wanted to say more, so Zoe had just nodded and internalised the information. One more piece in the jigsaw puzzle. She would see the full picture eventually.

Imagine, though, if she could go back in time. She thought about it now, as she lay in the muddy shelter and waited for light. If only she could go back; if she could catch herself on the beach and just tell the Doctor where they were and why he had to turn back now.

Imagine, if she could spare herself the hell of a frozen night on this battlefield and the churning, sick certainty that worse was to come.

The first explosion caught them by surprise. They froze in the middle of a shallow, muddy valley. Jamie claimed he could smell burning, and Zoe believed him because his senses were sharper than hers. Gentle hills blocked her view in all directions, but still this field was just open enough for her to feel exposed. She knew that running would be difficult too. The ground had tugged at her feet with every step. Combined with the high gravity, the wind and rain and the encroaching darkness, it made for heavy going.

Jamie stated the obvious. 'It sounds as if there's a war going on.'

'We don't know that, Jamie,' said the Doctor.

'Oh no? How come I can hear gunfire, then?'

Zoe strained her ears and thought she could hear it too: the whines and crackles of blaster fire, rather than the pops and chatter of more primitive weapons.

The Doctor's expression suggested that all the misfortunes of the universe were a personal disappointment to him. 'A regrettable by-product of civilisation.' He sighed. 'Perhaps, one day, I shall find a race that hasn't resorted to violent methods to address its problems.'

'Should we help?' asked Zoe, uncertainly.

To her relief, the Doctor shook his head. 'If we have arrived in the middle of a fully fledged war, then I should say the best thing we can do is sneak away and leave them to it.'

'That,' declared Jamie, 'is the most sensible thing you've said all day!'

The Doctor's lower lip jutted out stubbornly. 'On the other hand, this could be an isolated skirmish. We don't seem to be too close to the battle. If I could just climb one of those hills, I might at least see...'

He was interrupted by another explosion. It came from closer by, this time.

'Look, Doctor, I think we should be getting out of here!' cried Jamie.

The Doctor wrung his hands in frustration. 'Oh, oh well, I suppose you're right, yes.'

The simple act of turning back seemed to lift the weight of this world from Zoe's shoulders.

But then the Doctor came to a halt, his expression wide-eyed and afraid.

'I want you both to stand very, very still,' he whispered urgently. His companions knew him well enough to obey without question.

'What is it, Doctor?' whispered Zoe out of the corner of her mouth, not sure if she should even turn her head to look at him.

'Zoe,' said the Doctor, with forced calm, 'I want you to kneel down by my right foot, as slowly and as carefully as you can manage – and I want you to tell me what I'm standing on.'

The words brought a chill to Zoe's heart. She did as the Doctor had instructed, all the time dreading what she would find. His foot had sunk deep into the mud, so she had to reach out and cautiously, oh so cautiously, brush some of it aside.

Something exploded.

Zoe jumped, bit her lip to keep herself from screaming and calmed herself with a deep breath. Again, the sound had come from beyond the hills. She resumed her task.

She saw the red light first, and swallowed dryly. She continued to dig, even more gingerly, until she had revealed a dirty, brown, disc-shaped object, about twenty centimetres in diameter. The light came from an LED display on its uppermost surface. The Doctor had planted his foot across one edge of the disc.

'It's… I think it's a bomb of some kind.'

'Oh dear,' sighed the Doctor. 'That's rather what I was afraid of. Jamie, Zoe, you have to get as far away as you can. Quickly, now.'

'What, and leave you here, you mean?'

'I've no time to argue, Jamie. I can't do anything about this little problem until I know you're both out of harm's way. And be careful: tread only in the footprints we made on our way out here. If there's one mine in this field, then there are likely to be more.'

'Wait!' hissed Zoe. She had noticed something: how the flickering pattern on the display screen grew more frenetic whenever she moved. 'Doctor, I think there's a motion detector on this device.'

Rigid with fear, she put out a hand to keep herself from

rocking on her heels. The mine detected that small movement too, and its screen flared.

'What?'

Zoe gave a frightened shriek, as the Doctor dropped to his knees beside her. 'Doctor!'

Waving away her concerns, he yanked the mine out of the clinging mud and turned it over in his hands. 'Don't worry, Zoe. If this thing was active it would have blown us all to smithereens several minutes ago. You're right, it is triggered by motion rather than by pressure. Very nasty. Very nasty indeed.'

'You mean we're safe then?' asked Jamie. 'That thing isn't working?'

'Not at the moment, Jamie, no,' muttered the Doctor, still engrossed in his find. 'Of course, mines like this would have to be activated by remote control or on a time switch – otherwise they'd be set off by whoever laid them.'

'Remote control?' Zoe echoed worriedly. 'Doctor…'

It took him a moment to catch up with what Zoe was thinking. Then he jumped as if startled, raised his eyebrows to the fringe of his dark hair, dropped the mine as if it was hot and exclaimed: 'Oh! Oh my word!'

An agitated Doctor began to usher his companions back the way they had come. But Zoe had a better idea. 'This way!' she cried, setting off at right angles to his path.

'No, Zoe, the TARDIS is this way!' cried Jamie.

'I know that,' she said, 'but this is the quickest route back to the beach, where it's safe.'

The Doctor looked uncertain for a moment, then he nodded abruptly. Zoe grinned proudly to herself as she led the way. She liked to feel useful. And if there was one thing her training at the Earth School of Parapsychology had given her, it was a good sense of direction.

Her smile faded soon enough, though. As she had foreseen, running was not easy. She felt as if she might fall with any step, as if the planet itself were conspiring to both pull and push her down. She began to pant with effort, but still the hill beyond the beach refused to grow closer. Or so it seemed.

Jamie and the Doctor fared only marginally better. Even so, Jamie, chivalrous to the last, took Zoe's hand when he saw how she was struggling.

But, suddenly, it was too late. A cacophony of electronic bleeps broke out across the field. There were many more mines than Zoe had imagined, they surrounded her on all sides – and they had just been activated. She stumbled to a halt and gave a despairing groan.

'Get down!' the Doctor cried, gesticulating wildly and dangerously. 'Both of you, now!'

Zoe flung herself to the ground, no longer caring about the dirt. It felt cold and clammy against her hands and her left cheek. She heard a wet thud as Jamie landed beside her.

'Keep very, very still,' the Doctor urged. 'Don't move so much as a muscle!' Zoe realised that he was still standing behind her.

And then there was nothing: no sound but for the elements, and even they seemed subdued. The electronic chorus had ended. The mines had been primed.

In front of Zoe, in front of her eyes, was a half-buried mine.

She stared at the narrow red line on its motion detector. She held her body rigid and ignored the sudden, treacherous feeling that her skin was itching all over and her muscles were aching with disuse. She did not dare to close her eyes; couldn't tear her gaze away from the mine in any case. She realised she had been holding her breath. She let it go, as slowly and as gently as she could. She took another breath, shallow and measured. She felt her head sinking slowly into the ground and she gritted her teeth to keep from shivering.

The red line flickered, just slightly.

Zoe closed her eyes and prayed for the Doctor to do something. Soon.

* * *

Looking back on it now, Zoe decided that that was when she had known at last.

That was when, lying paralysed in alien dirt, she had looked into the future and had seen that she would not be sleeping in her own familiar bed in the TARDIS that night. Or, perhaps, for many nights to come.

That was when this world had closed its trap on her.

Chapter Two

When the Doctor had given the order, Jamie McCrimmon had dropped on to his front. But he had put his hands out to cushion his fall and kept his head up to see what his friend was doing. He regretted his curiosity. His arms threatened to shake as they supported the greater part of his weight. They sank slowly into the mud, so that Jamie feared they might splay apart and bring him crashing down. And his neck ached. He gritted his teeth and, with his eyes only, implored the Doctor to do something.

'Just hold still a little while longer,' said the Doctor quietly.

Jamie frowned.

'Don't worry – it's perfectly all right to talk. The mines can't be set off by sound, only by movement.'

'You mean we've got to stay like this until somebody finds us?' croaked Jamie, not daring to speak too loudly despite what the Doctor had said.

'I think it's very unlikely that whoever laid the mines will come back,' said the Doctor. 'And, as for anyone else... well, let's just hope to be left alone for a while, shall we? At least, long enough for me to do something about our predicament.'

'Like what, exactly?'

The Doctor smiled and winked. Only then did Jamie see that his right arm was moving, slowly, very slowly, reaching into his jacket.

'Be careful, Doctor!'

'I intend to be. Don't worry, Jamie, these devices react to changes in light. So long as I keep my arm against my body and move slowly enough, I should be able to reach my pocket.'

Jamie almost nodded as he realised what the Doctor was up

to. He caught himself in time.

The rain intensified; he felt water dripping off his hair and down the back of his cagoule. A blast of wind threatened to unbalance him. He felt sure he had swayed, but the movement could not have been enough to trigger the mine. This time. He scowled and psyched himself into a renewed effort. He tried to imagine that his arms had steel bars running through them.

Where Jamie came from, war was mostly an honourable pursuit. It didn't consist of laying traps for the enemy: weapons that could kill a man before he knew they were there. It didn't consist of lying in a cold, dark field and waiting to die.

He would rather have faced twenty redcoats, alone and unarmed, than this.

The Doctor had eased his sonic screwdriver from his pocket. Jamie didn't really understand what the device did, just that it was some sort of all-purpose magic tool for getting them out of scrapes. Now the Doctor had hold of it, he could get them out of this one.

The long, tubular, silver device emitted a piercing whine. It reverberated in Jamie's ears and bored into his head, like a thin drill piercing his eardrums. The pitch of the whine rose steadily.

The mines began to bleep again. At first the noise, coming so suddenly, caused Jamie's heart to leap. Had something gone wrong? Were they all about to die? Then he realised that, had the Doctor actually set the mines off, he probably wouldn't know anything about it.

The Doctor let his hands drop to his side and gave a grin of pure relief. 'It's all right now, I've deactivated the devices. We can move again.'

'Oh, thank goodness for that!' exclaimed Zoe, rolling over on to her back and relaxing her muscles.

Jamie was equally grateful. He stood and rubbed his arms

ruefully. He had only one complaint. 'Well, why didn't you just do that in the first place?'

'Well, Jamie,' said the Doctor regretfully, 'I couldn't be sure what frequency to set the sonic screwdriver to. I might just as easily have blown us all sky high.'

They resumed their trudge towards the beach, agreeing that they still wanted to leave the deactivated minefield as soon as possible. Ironically, it seemed to Jamie that they covered the distance more speedily now their need was not so desperate. Still, by the time they had mounted the low hill at the edge of the valley the sky had become black. Jamie caught the occasional glimpse of light through heavy clouds, and guessed there were at least three moons in the sky. For the most part, though, they remained hidden.

The sea was a glistening black shroud in the darkness. The sand seemed light in contrast, but still grey and depressing. Seaweed created grotesque, black shapes across its surface.

And there was something more.

Was it Jamie's imagination, or did some of the shapes resemble bodies? Heaps of intertwined corpses? No, surely it was a trick of the shadows and the drizzle.

Or so he could have believed, had it not been for the Doctor's reaction.

'Oh no,' he muttered to himself, 'oh dear, oh dear. Zoe, I think you should turn away now, you don't want to see this.'

The Doctor was already scrambling down to the beach. Jamie followed him without a second thought, as did Zoe.

The shapes were, indeed, corpses. Jamie counted at least two dozen, strewn across the sand. A faint smell of rotting fish reached his nostrils.

The Doctor was examining one of the corpses. Jamie crouched by his side. The body was that of a tall, scrawny man with a thatch of white hair. He was wearing a loose-fitting, one-piece, tan-coloured garment. Jamie thought he was human at first, but his skin was bright pink and each of his hands had just three long, webbed fingers. He didn't seem to have a nose, and his staring eyes were a deep black, although they could just have been reflecting the sky. The Doctor reached out and gently closed the dead man's pink eyelids.

'It's horrible!' exclaimed Zoe, who was standing behind them. Her curiosity sated, she was trying not to look at the bodies any more.

'What is it?' asked Jamie.

'He's a Kalarian,' said the Doctor. 'All the people here are Kalarians.'

'So, are they good or bad?'

'It's not always that simple, Jamie.'

'Perhaps they're fighting each other,' suggested Zoe.

'Aye, well, this lot have lost this battle, that's for sure.'

The Doctor shook his head. 'I don't think there's been any battle here.' He stood up, moved a short way along the beach and stooped gingerly over a pile of four more corpses. 'These people are all malnourished. They're wearing identical, plain overalls. And they've each been killed by a single shot from a plasma rifle to the head.'

Zoe gave an appalled gasp. 'You mean they were prisoners?'

The Doctor nodded, his expression grim. 'Until they were slaughtered, yes.'

They walked along the beach, then, back towards the spot where the TARDIS had landed. After his earlier reluctance, the Doctor seemed positively eager to be leaving. He chivvied his companions along with promises that they would soon be home.

The going was easier on the sand – although the thorny seaweed sometimes stung Jamie's bare legs – but it was now difficult to see further ahead than a few feet.

Finally, Zoe struck out inland. The Doctor looked surprised for a second, then followed her. They climbed a gentle hill, presumably the same one on which Jamie had almost fallen earlier. The incessant rain had made it more slippery than before, and Jamie felt as if he was walking on a treadmill, forever sliding back the distance he had gained.

They reached the top, at last, and waded through the undergrowth, still following Zoe's lead.

And then she stopped and turned to her friends with an expression of dismay. 'It's gone! The TARDIS has gone!'

The Doctor sprang to Zoe's side and put an arm around her shoulders. 'Now, now, Zoe, let's not jump to conclusions, shall we?'

'It was here!'

'Are you positive? It would be very easy to get lost in these conditions. I expect the TARDIS is just through those trees over there, or a little way back.'

'It was here, Doctor, I know it was!'

'I was rather unsure myself when you left the beach like that,' the Doctor cajoled her. He pointed and added, 'I think we should have walked a little further in that direction.'

Zoe shrugged, but Jamie could see from her face that she wasn't convinced. He wasn't sure himself. He wanted to imagine they were only a few steps away from leaving this world, but he had learned not to place too much trust in the Doctor's navigational skills, either inside or outside his ship.

'Come on,' said the Doctor, with what sounded suspiciously like false optimism. 'Let's try a little further on, shall we?'

Three hours later they were huddled together at the base of a tree, listening to the rain as it beat down on a makeshift shelter of branches and whatever plants they had been able to rip from the ground.

They had concluded that it was too dark to continue the

search, but the Doctor had insisted – or kept up the pretence?
– that they would have more success when it became light
again.

Zoe was asleep. She had been too agitated to rest until the
Doctor had spoken to her, softly but firmly, staring into her
eyes. Then her eyelids had fluttered, her breathing had
become shallow and regular, and the Doctor had eased her
gently back on to a bed of leaves.

Jamie sat with his hands around his knees, determined to
remain awake. His friends might have need of his protection
during the night. The Doctor stayed awake too. He sat
between his companions, lost in thought, his back against the
tree trunk.

An hour passed, maybe more, before Jamie broke the silence.

'Where are we, Doctor?' he asked. The Doctor had an idea, at
least; Jamie had known him long enough to see when he was
hiding something.

'I don't know, Jamie,' said the Doctor with a sigh. 'I really
don't.'

'But...?'

'But...' The Doctor cast a furtive glance towards Zoe. She
was still asleep. 'I'm rather afraid we might be on Kalaya. The
Kalarians' home world. I've never been here before, but from
what I know of it... well, the conditions are right.'

'And that's a bad thing, is it?'

'If my suspicions are correct, Jamie, yes, it would be a very
bad thing. I think we might just have landed in the middle of
one of the most pointless, bloody wars in human history.'

'Ah,' said Jamie. 'So those Kalarian people, they're fighting
humans then?'

The Doctor shook his head. 'No, no, the Kalarians are just the
bystanders.' He was playing with his hands, a sure sign that he
was nervous. 'Our only hope is to find the TARDIS and leave
here before it's too late.'

Jamie didn't ask any more questions. He sat up straight and listened for signs of danger. But all he could hear was the gentle rhythm of the rain – and, eventually, of the Doctor's voice, as he started to speak softly to himself in faraway tones.

For a while Jamie strained to hear the words, but then they didn't seem to matter any more. Later, he would be unable to recall a single one but he would, briefly, remember the feeling of well-being and security that had suffused him.

And then he would only remember being jolted awake by the sound of an explosion.

They resumed their search as soon as there was any light at all.

The rain had stopped, but their clothes were still wet and the air was sharp and cold. They fought their way through the stubborn undergrowth, clambering over small hills and pushing aside prickly bushes but finding nothing.

As the day drew on, conditions changed little from the greyness of the pre-dawn hours. When the clouds did afford them a glimpse of the sun it was pale and distant.

They walked further than they ought to have walked, still hoping for a hint of dark blue against the flora but knowing they had strayed hopelessly off course. The Doctor pointed out the curvature of the beach and suggested they might be on a small island. Jamie and Zoe nodded dutifully, but neither was in any mood for a discussion of geography.

They saw and heard no further signs of battle, which came as a small consolation.

It was Zoe who brought the search to an end. 'We've come full circle,' she insisted. 'This is definitely where we landed and it's where I brought us back to last night – only the TARDIS has gone, like I said.'

The Doctor sighed dolefully. 'Yes, it seems you were right after all, Zoe.'

Jamie settled the matter by discovering a shallow, square

depression in the mud. The rain had filled it. They stood around the hole and stared into the brown water, as if it might reflect past instead of present and tell them what had happened to their ship.

'So, now what do we do?' asked Jamie.

That was when seven terrifying creatures burst from the trees.

Zoe screamed. Jamie dropped into an alert stance, but knew he was outnumbered. The Doctor threw up his hands and wailed: 'Oh, oh, oh!'

The creatures surrounded them. They resembled nothing more than giant, armoured, bipedal sharks. They weren't tall, but they were bulky and imposing. Huge tubular guns ran along each arm of their golden casings. Large, pointed fins grew from their backs and slim, black tubes ran from these to the backs of their heads. Their true faces couldn't be seen through their golden helmets, but the fact that those helmets portrayed immobile red-eyed, sharp-toothed expressions of fury said all that Jamie needed to know.

He found himself rooted to the spot, staring helplessly down the barrels of two guns.

'Now,' hissed one of the creatures, in response to his question, 'you are to consider yourselves prisoners of the Selachian Empire.'

Chapter Three

Lieutenant Kent Michaels wondered when it would all end.

The soft, wet earth of Kalaya was almost comfortable, if he gave himself over to its embrace, ignored the cold and didn't think about where he was. He had to remind himself that he had a duty to perform.

Below him, two enemy land-transports rolled along the grey beach. At first glance they resembled huge armadillos, their armoured hides spattered with green moss. They would have come from Ockora, thought Michaels, where the raw materials of technology were grown, not mined. Though not exactly conscious, the transports were alive.

They struggled along on caterpillar tracks. Through dirty windows, Michaels saw two Selachians standing in the cab of the first one. He allowed himself a grim smile. The Sharks had spent decades augmenting their own battlesuits – making use of the knowledge of a hundred species, whether bought, stolen or seized by force – and yet they still couldn't sit down in them.

Surely this campaign would be the last? For him, at least.

Michaels had always considered himself a young, fit man. But his thirty-eight years had begun to weigh on him more than he had ever thought they could. Days of fighting stretched behind him and slowly, insidiously, had become the only life he could remember.

This area of the beach was littered with rubble: the ancient remnants of buildings that the Selachians had razed. The second transport bumped into a hunk of masonry, concealed by spiky seaweed, and shied. Its operators forced it onward over the obstruction, as the leading vehicle pulled ahead.

Michaels made a decision.

He scrambled back a few metres to where his detail of six privates waited. He could see they shared his tiredness. It had been – how long, two months or three? – since the Terran Security Forces had ceased air attacks for fear of harming the native populace and the battle for Kalaya had become a land war. The Selachians had been on the run by then, but they would never surrender. Within weeks, they had entrenched themselves on this island, determined to fight to the end for a world that they had occupied for four generations.

Now, the TSF had pushed their foes back to a small stronghold on the island's western side. The Sharks were resorting to desperate tactics: suicide runs and the execution of prisoners. As the war neared its end it became, if anything, more bloody and frustrating.

When it was over, there would be victory celebrations on Earth and its colony worlds. Not here, though. Here, a thousand people – no, barely three hundred now – would collapse into their billets and just be thankful for their continued survival.

'Change of plan,' said Michaels, pulling his respirator down and away from his face as the troops gathered around him. 'The Sharks have presented us with an easier target.'

He told them what he had seen. He outlined his plan for a lightning attack on the second transport. They would take out two, maybe three, of the creatures, destroy some hardware and perhaps strike a third blow if anything of value was being transported.

It would be a small victory. But then, small victories had become the main aim of this war. Kalaya was being liberated square metre by square metre. Life by life.

Michaels gave the word as the first transport trundled out of sight and the second drew level with him. His people surged over the hill. Some howled like eager young commandos, their fears subsumed in the immediate rush of battle.

Morgan pitched an electro-grenade in front of the target. His aim was perfect. As the vehicle surged forward it struck the arcing device and detonated it. The vehicle's engines – vocal cords? – let out a nerve-rending screech as it bucked alarmingly.

The force of the explosion was such that it kicked up a fine, grey blizzard. The intention had been to buckle the cab, perhaps to trap its occupants within. The transport's hide was too tough. It ground to a halt, but sustained only minor damage.

Reaching the transport, Andrews and Wilson slapped neuro-scramblers on to its side. It sagged and seemed to emit a small sigh.

The Selachian operators kicked open their doors and stepped from the vehicle. Almost simultaneously, a rear hatch sprang open and two more creatures emerged.

The humans were prepared. Michaels aimed his rifle and squeezed off shot after shot. The first two bullets went wild, but he gritted his teeth, told himself to concentrate and scored two hits to an armoured chest. He took several steps back to absorb the shoulder-bruising recoil. He knew that, beside him, his people were doing likewise.

Spent rounds clattered to the ground.

All the time, Kent Michaels was thinking: Damn, damn, damn, I hoped for less than four. The odds are worse than two to one. Someone will die, perhaps me.

The Sharks kept coming. They always did.

The Terran Security Forces trained new recruits to deal with Selachians. They warned them how the aliens used every psychological advantage they could muster. Their armour, their ships' designs, their very name, had all been chosen to inspire fear. Inside their golden battlesuits they bore no resemblance at all to sharks. The recruits were asked to remember that. When the monsters were bearing down on them, with all the strength, determination and invulnerability of tanks, the hapless soldiers were told to picture the scrawny, scared beings behind the disguise.

Eighteen per cent of TSF privates did not survive their first encounter with a Selachian.

And Michaels, though he had been in this situation scores of times before, still felt a surge of primeval fear that made him want to faint or run.

'Fall back!' he yelled, and the others gladly broke off the attack and looked for cover. Fortunately, they were all experienced. Nobody froze, this time.

The Selachians fired back. Jets of plasma erupted from their arm-mounted weapons, and ignited. The edge of one caught Michaels's shoulder and seared his combat uniform. The padding protected him, but Morgan was less fortunate. Three blasts and he collapsed next to the transport's caterpillar tracks with a whimper of pain.

Michaels tore his eyes from the corpse. It was not easy. Morgan was sprawled in more blood than one body ought to have held. The Selachians' weapons were designed for maximum psychological impact upon survivors. They left as big a mess as possible.

Michaels had not known Morgan well. He made a point of not knowing his troops beyond their names and a basic assessment of their skills and traits. The war was more bearable that way. Morgan was just a name, a rank, a number, a face. Michaels repeated that mantra to himself as he dropped behind a pile of rubble and aimed his rifle again.

It wasn't the Selachians' way to conceal themselves. The four creatures stood beside their vehicle, secure in their battlesuits, and blasted away at the half-concealed enemies who surrounded them. They took the brunt of many bullets, but stood their ground and even appeared unconcerned. Michaels knew better. Their desire not to show weakness would be their downfall.

The TSF's weapons had been proved against Selachian armour. Each bullet released a swarm of nanites which, upon encountering a metallic surface, burrowed into it and prised its molecules apart. It was a slow process, but effective. Unfortunately, the Selachians had developed a defence. Their battlesuits now contained nanites of their own, which hunted down and neutralised the invaders before they could do much damage. The humans' only hope was to bombard their enemies with more bullets, more quickly, than the battlesuits could handle.

One creature was staggering. Michaels made it his primary target, as did some of the others. Caught in a crossfire, the Selachian threw up its hands in an uncharacteristic gesture of helplessness. Cracks crazed across its chest and water bled into the sand.

Michaels felt grimly satisfied as the trickle turned into a deluge. The battlesuit fell apart like an eggshell and the Selachian dropped to its knees. It would be unable to breathe now, and dead within minutes.

The victory made one of the humans overconfident. Michaels couldn't see who it was: smoke from Morgan's grenade and from the Selachians' weapons had settled over the battlefield, and the bulky, dark uniform with its face-concealing respirator made identification difficult. What Michaels did see was someone – York, perhaps – leap from cover and run four steps towards the Selachians before lobbing a grenade between their feet.

He was cut down as speedily, as ruthlessly, as Morgan had been. As so many good people had been before that.

The explosive detonated, but only seemed to add to the smoke and the confusion.

The Selachians were advancing again. Another tactic of theirs: when surrounded, pick one target and aim for it. For an instant, Michaels thought they had chosen him. But no, they were bearing down on Wilson. She scrambled away, alarmed. She couldn't go far. The sea lay in her path. She would be the next to die.

While the creatures' attention was distracted from him, Michaels broke cover. He ran for the transport and flattened himself against its soft, warm side. From here, he had a clear shot at the Selachians' backs. He added his own contribution to the volley of human fire.

First one and then another Selachian fell. They must have sustained damage from the explosion, Michaels thought.

But it was too late for Wilson.

And that revelation distracted him, just for a second, despite all his training and experience.

Something – someone; a man – attacked Michaels, pinning his rifle against his chest. The lieutenant hadn't seen the man, didn't know where he had come from. He let his weapon go and made to push the stranger away, but his balance was already lost. The momentum of the stranger's attack carried both men backwards.

An arc of clear liquid crossed Michaels's field of vision as his back hit the ground and his breath was knocked from him. The man was on top of him, but then he was rolling to one side and Michaels realised that he was not the threat.

He picked himself up. The transport had recovered, somehow, from the scramblers. It had dragged its front end tortuously around to face the battle. It had extruded a large nozzle from a casing beneath its windscreen. Michaels flung himself to one side as the transport blasted out a second jet of acid.

In the past, it had been nerve gas. Now that TSF soldiers wore respirators as standard, the Sharks had updated their weapons accordingly.

Michaels saw the neuro-scramblers, lying at the vehicle's side. He leapt for them, counting on the acid gun's recycling stroke to give him time. He grabbed one in each hand and drove them hard into the transport's hide, then threw himself back to the ground. The vehicle sagged again and Michaels raised his head cautiously.

The nozzle had drooped until it pointed downwards. The scramblers had done their work, sending into the behemoth's crude nervous system contradictory impulses that had confused it. But the transport had somehow worked those tendrils out once, in just a few minutes.

The silence was Michaels's first clue that the final Selachian had been downed. He stood, slowly and wearily, and surveyed the battlefield as a hot breeze dispersed the smoke.

Four Selachians lay in the remnants of their own armour. One was still twitching.

Morgan, York, Wilson and now Luqman were dead. It had been an expensive victory.

The stranger – quite a young lad, Michaels now realised; trim, well muscled and healthy – climbed to his feet. Beneath an untidy fringe, he wore an expression of incomprehension. He seemed lost, but he had acted decisively enough a moment ago.

An older man hopped from the back of the transport. He looked like a tramp or a comedian in his baggy, slightly mismatched clothes, but his face was serious and his eyes betrayed a keen glint of intelligence. He hurried over to his friend, and Michaels noticed how they both held their hands awkwardly behind their backs. Their wrists had been tied with the thin but durable rope that the Selachians refined from kelp.

He did not recognize them as TSF men. He wondered how they had come to this world.

'How are you feeling?' he asked the younger man.

'Aye, I'm OK. My coat took the worst of that stuff.' The lad had an odd, lilting accent. Droplets of acid had burnt tiny holes into his thin, blue, waterproof coat. Michaels frowned as he saw that the stranger's legs were bare.

'You were lucky. You also saved my life. Thanks.'

'Well, I think we ought to thank you,' said the older man, effusively. 'Jamie and I were prisoners of the Selachians, you know. I'm the Doctor, by the way, nice to meet you. This is my friend, Jamie.' He made as if to shake hands, then frowned as it occurred to him that he couldn't, and settled on a little bow instead. 'I don't suppose I could trouble you to untie us?'

Michaels nodded curtly to his two remaining soldiers. They produced knives from their belts and sawed through the strangers' bonds. Keep them busy, he thought. There would be time enough to mourn the fallen later.

'Doctor, what about Zoe?'

'Yes, yes,' said the man who had identified himself as the Doctor, 'I'm coming to that, Jamie.' He stretched his newly freed arms appreciatively, then laced his fingers together and gave Michaels an appealing look. 'A young friend of ours is still a captive, I'm afraid. The Selachians took her away in a vehicle just like this one.'

'I saw it,' said Michaels. 'It will have reached their base by now.'

The Doctor's face fell. He looked like a child who had been denied a treat. 'Oh, oh well, we shall have to free her.'

'I've just lost four soldiers freeing you,' said Michaels in exasperation.

'Well, there's no need to take that tone,' the Doctor blustered.

Michaels jumped as the Selachian transport shuddered. One of the scramblers fell from its side with a plop. 'No arguments, Doctor. We're going back to our camp.'

'Well, the Doctor and I'll stay here if you don't mind,' said

Jamie. 'We can rescue Zoe ourselves, can't we, Doctor?'

The Doctor seemed amenable to the idea, but Michaels shook his head firmly.

'You're coming with me. I should think my commanding officer will want a word with you.'

The Doctor gave a heavy sigh and turned to his companion. 'I think we'd better do as the man says, Jamie. He does appear to be rather heavily armed.'

Chapter Four

Zoe didn't dare to move. She lay still, precisely where she had landed when her captors had thrown her into the back of the transport.

The compartment within it was surprisingly small. The walls were uneven and without corners. Had it not been for the feeling of motion, she could have believed she was in a moss-encrusted cave rather than a vehicle. The floor was clammy; Zoe had grown used to feeling as though there was a warm sponge pressed against her cheek. And her wrists were beginning to hurt from being tied behind her back.

One of the creatures stood over her. It was silent and showed no expression. To be more precise, Zoe told herself, it couldn't show an expression through its helmet. It always kept one of its arm-mounted weapons trained upon its prisoner. After a while, she had found it helped not to look at it.

Zoe was relieved when the vehicle shuddered to a halt. Perhaps now she would be reunited with the Doctor and Jamie, at last.

Grey light spilled over her as the guard threw open the rear door. 'Stand up!' it hissed in a voice that sounded thin and slightly tinny. The voice, Zoe realised, was being relayed via speakers in its armour.

She squirmed, trying to obey but discovering that her shoulders ached and she had lost sensation in some of her fingers. Even as she managed to gain leverage against the wall, the creature lost its patience. It took two steps towards her, stooped awkwardly – more of a crouch, really; Zoe noted its lack of flexibility – and hoisted her by the armpits. She squealed indignantly but bit back any further protest.

Zoe turned the push the creature gave her into a little jump out of the back of the transport. She landed on her feet in wet sand and immediately looked for her friends.

She saw another five transports, but couldn't work out which one, if any, had been carrying them. She saw a massive device resembling a wire-frame cannon, which could only have been a weapon of some sort. She saw a pile of what she thought at first were bombs, but they turned out to be upturned crustaceans, each waving a pair of tiny, helpless claws.

And she saw at least ten more of the shark creatures. Each had a purposeful air about it, even if it didn't seem to be doing an awful lot. Some were tinkering with the vehicles or with the cannon or with other contraptions.

This, thought Zoe, must be where they were making their base. She had been brought along the beach to a fairly large, roughly circular area. It was all but inaccessible from inland as it stood at the base of a high escarpment. There were more of the creatures up there – they stood out against the dull sky – and another two were guarding the narrow stretch of beach along which she must have been driven.

'Come,' hissed Zoe's captor, emphasising its command by gripping her shoulder and pushing her again. As it marched her past the front of the transport, the two operators emerged and fell into step beside it.

The prisoner and escorts left the vehicles behind and headed for the water. Suddenly, Zoe felt sharply alone. 'Wait a minute,' she cried. 'Where are my friends?'

'They will join you presently,' one of the creatures said. Zoe didn't feel reassured.

And then there was black water lapping around her ankles and then her knees, and a terrible thought struck her.

The creatures were aquatic: their appearance was a clue, as

was the faint sloshing sound that came to her when they moved. Even if she was wrong, they could almost certainly breathe underwater in their armoured suits. They were taking her into the sea.

'No,' screamed Zoe, 'no you can't!' She pulled back, away from the creatures, but knew that running would be futile at best. She tried to reach them with reason instead. 'I won't be able to breathe down there.'

They didn't seem to care. Two pairs of metal, four-fingered hands seized her arms and propelled her onward.

'I said, I won't be able to breathe. You'll kill me!' She thrashed about and tried to break free, but her captors' grips were strong. The water was around her waist now. Seaweed tugged at her feet and she lost her balance, but the creatures simply carried her along with them as her legs flailed helplessly.

'Doctor!' screamed Zoe, exhausting her last, faint hope. 'Jamie! Doctor!'

Then she was tipped over and thrown forward. She barely had time to draw breath before her face hit the cold water and she lost a quarter of the air in her lungs in the shock of it.

Zoe gave up struggling and concentrated on retaining what oxygen she had.

She had closed her eyes. A distant part of her wondered if her life ought to be playing itself out on the insides of her eyelids. Her job as a resident astrophysicist on a space wheel seemed long ago and far away now, like something she had read in a children's book.

Her lungs were beginning to ache. She opened her eyes and blinked to adjust to the feel of water against them.

The creatures that held her were swimming at a steep downward angle, propelled by the powerful strokes of their free arms. The third was out of sight, presumably behind her.

At first, she could see nothing ahead through the dark, murky water. Then she realised that a huge, black shape was squatting on the seabed. Zoe's heart sank. She stifled a gasp and lost a little more air. It was the size of a row of houses, but it looked like a shark. A real shark, not an upright one like her captors. Was that why she had been brought here? To be fed to some – some horrible sea monster?

As they came to rest at the monster's side, Zoe felt relieved and a little silly. The monster was made out of polished, black metal, and its surface showed the familiar pockmarks that came from travelling through space. She still had only a vague impression of its shape – this close up, it was impossible to see more – but it had to be a starship.

Set into its side at one end was a circular door. One of the creatures inserted its finger into a small depression and twisted it. The door rolled aside and Zoe was carried through.

They came to a halt.

Zoe felt she couldn't hold on much longer. She was almost in convulsions as her lungs cried out for air. Black shapes were beginning to crowd her vision. She clenched her fists and felt her nails biting into her palms. Not long now, she told herself, not long.

It was difficult to see for sure through the dark water, but Zoe thought she was in a very small room. The circular door had closed behind her and she thought she could see another in the opposite wall. An airlock. It had to be.

Or was she deluding herself? Seeing what she so desperately needed to see?

No, thank goodness, the water was receding, being pumped out but not quickly enough. As the level dropped past her ears, Zoe pushed herself upwards, threw back her head and heaved in the deepest and sweetest breath she had ever taken. She fell back into the water and choked as she swallowed some of it, but within seconds it was down to her chest and she was panting and coughing and letting tears fall freely down her cheeks.

As always, her captors gave no acknowledgement of her suffering. As the last of the water gurgled out of the airlock, one stepped forward and used its finger to operate the inner door.

Zoe was still taking deep, grateful breaths as she was propelled into the ship proper, and so the first thing to hit her was the smell of many unwashed bodies.

She was at one end of a surprisingly large hall. It might once have seemed opulent, with its marble floor and its fluted colonnades. Now, however, it was steeped in grime and misery.

The hall was filled with prisoners. Zoe performed a quick calculation, based on her estimate of the floor area and the amount of space taken by each of the occupants, and deduced that there had to be at least two hundred people present. About half of them, maybe a few less, seemed human. The rest were the gangly, pink-skinned beings that the Doctor had identified as Kalarians. All wore the tan, one-piece overalls in which the Kalarian corpses on the beach had been clad. The atmosphere was one of lethargy and hopelessness. Some prisoners milled about lifelessly; others were hunched on the floor.

There were plenty of shark creatures present too. They lined all four walls, standing immobile in their sentry positions. At the far end of the hall Zoe saw a large, water-filled hole, the size of a small swimming pool. An access hatch, she guessed, to lower, waterlogged decks. As she thought about it, she remembered that the airlock door had been quite high in the ship's hull: this had to be its top deck, and the one on which its owners received air-breathing 'guests'.

One of Zoe's escorts marched over to a large, metal chest. It reached inside and produced a set of tan overalls. Zoe felt something give between her hands and realised that another of the creatures had snapped her bonds. The rope fell away and she rubbed her wrists gratefully. Then the overalls were tossed towards her and the order came: 'Change.'

'What, here?' she protested.

Immediately, one of the creatures raised its arm in her direction. Zoe gulped as she stared down the barrel of its gun.

'You will follow Selachian orders without question. This is your final warning. Change!'

Zoe gave no further argument. She peeled off her sodden coat and dropped it on to the floor. The boots came off next, then, a little more reluctantly, the tight-fitting top with its pattern of sparkly threads which she had been so delighted to find in a back street boutique in twenty-first century Manchester.

Zoe felt her cheeks colouring as she stripped down to her underwear. She turned her face away from the other prisoners, though, to be fair, nobody was staring. They were clearly well used to this humiliation of new inmates.

She struggled into the overalls, feet first, as quickly as she could. They were far too big and the fabric felt coarse against her skin. Still, it was good to be wearing something dry.

The creature that had threatened her – the Selachian – lowered its gun. 'You will now join the other prisoners,' it said.

One of its fellows gathered up Zoe's discarded clothes and bundled them through an aperture in the left-hand wall. An incinerator, she guessed. She did not dare to object, but the symbolic destruction of her identity was not lost upon her. She began to understand why everybody else seemed so abject.

The creatures had not even returned her boots, she thought, staring down at her stockinged feet miserably. And, as for the Doctor and Jamie… she could not bear to think about what the Selachians might have done to them.

Zoe shuffled over to join her fellow captives.

Chapter Five

The passageway was dark with shadows. It was lined with stacks of metal barrels, which further restricted Jamie's view. Somewhere a red light blinked, and wisps of cold smoke pulled at his throat.

His feet clanged against the metal surface. He tried to place them more carefully. His hands sweated as they clutched the plastic furniture of his rifle. The muscles in his finger ached to close around the trigger again.

His combat uniform was heavy and restrictive. He had left the bulky jacket hanging open but his legs, used to the freedom of a kilt, felt as if they were encased in rubber.

He peered cautiously around a pile of barrels. Heard movement. Realised too late that it was behind him. Turned. Saw the Selachian. Fired wildly. Missed.

The Selachian's gun barrels flashed.

'You're dead,' announced a lifeless, computerised voice. The lights came up.

'Och,' spat Jamie in disgust, as Lieutenant Kent Michaels strode over to him. 'I didn't hear that thing creeping up on me.' Of course, it had done no such thing. Michaels had explained to Jamie that his targets were not real. It had something to do with the projection of light – like those television gadgets, he supposed. It hardly seemed fair that an enemy could just appear behind him, but Jamie didn't say as much.

'That was the idea,' said Michaels laconically. 'Don't worry, you didn't do too badly. You got two of them before they killed you.'

'Eh? They did what?'

'It's what would have happened in an actual combat situation.'

'Oh, outside, you mean.' Outside, thought Jamie confidently, I'd have heard it coming.

'Quite.'

'So, do I get to fight with you?'

'You still want to?'

'Of course I do. They've got Zoe, haven't they?'

Michaels sighed and patted Jamie's shoulder with the same paternal air that the Doctor often displayed. He seemed genuinely fond of the young Highlander – well, Jamie had saved his life, after all – and indulgent towards his wishes. Jamie, for his part, wanted to prove that he needed neither favours nor guidance, just a chance to rescue his friend.

Michaels seemed older than the rest of the TSF people, even the other lieutenants in charge of the detachments. Partly, thought Jamie, this was due to the fact that he was calmer, more laid back. More sensible, more cautious, more... well, weary. When Jamie looked into the lieutenant's eyes, he got the impression that Michaels was looking back at him from a distance and yet, somehow, still seeing all. His black combat uniform was old, battered and dirty, but it looked comfortable on him.

Jamie would have placed Michaels's age at somewhere in his mid-forties, although he looked good for it. He was tall and athletically built. He had a strong face, short and tidy dark brown hair, thick eyebrows and a full moustache which leant him an air of maturity and authority. His expression never seemed to vary much whatever the situation. Right now, he expressed his concern with a faint relaxation of his facial muscles and a slightly raised eyebrow.

Outside the training room, the décor returned to the bland, grey walls of – it seemed to Jamie – spaceships everywhere. 'I'll be honest with you,' said Michaels, as he guided the young

Highlander back towards the main airlock. 'The simulations test your nerve and determination as much as your combat skills. On that score, you passed. I just don't know if I want to send a lad like you into battle.'

'Look, I'm as old as some of the people you've got out there!'

'I know,' said Michaels regretfully. He sighed. 'You really want to do this, don't you?'

'Yes, I do.'

'Well, I won't pretend we don't need every warm body we can get.'

Jamie grinned. 'So, I'm in, then?'

'We'll have to work on that aim of yours. We haven't got much time.'

Jamie held his rifle like a dear friend. He would learn how to use it, he vowed to himself. He would become a better shot than anybody else. And, failing that, he had found a pocket for his trusty dirk in the leg of his uniform.

When the final push came, those shark things wouldn't know what had hit them.

The humans' ship squatted in the centre of a huge, flattened clearing. Like its owners, it had been in better condition. It was a rusty brown in colour, and its hull was studded with dents. Six spindly legs protruded from its long, segmented body, and were turned earthward by ball joints to rest in the mud and hold the ship's stomach slightly off the ground. The ship resembled a giant, mechanical spider, casting a baleful eye upon the camp site – and the soldiers looked like primitive worshippers, clustered around their god.

They resided outside the ship. Depleted though they were, it wasn't large enough for all of them, and its quarters had mostly been pressed into service as field hospitals. Low, black, dome-shaped, plastic tents stretched as far as Jamie could see. Each was capable of taking eight people, more at a push. He couldn't help but notice that there were many more spaces than there were people to fill them.

That, and the continual presence of armed guards around the clearing, kept him from forgetting how close the enemy were.

Jamie and the Doctor sat side by side on a long, wooden bench at a long, wooden, slatted table, in the shadow of the spider-like ship. The Doctor had retained his own damp and mud-splattered clothes. He looked more dishevelled than ever.

Jamie stared, without appetite, at his tin plate on which lay a few spherical, multicoloured pills. 'Well, it's one way of getting around food storage problems on a long mission such as this,' the Doctor explained. He sounded apologetic, as if the meagre repast was his fault. 'Eat up, Jamie. It may not be very tasty, but it will keep you going.'

Jamie picked up one of the pills and placed it experimentally on his tongue. The Doctor was right. It tasted of nothing.

'I found the TARDIS,' said the Doctor, almost casually.

'What? Great, where is it?'

'These people took it. I gather it's on their flagship.'

'What, that rusty old contraption?'

The Doctor shook his head. 'That's just a personnel carrier. Their flagship is in orbit. I believe they call it the *Triumph*.'

'How do we get back to it, then?'

'Rather more easily, I fancy, than if the Selachians had taken it.'

'Aye, well, there is that.'

Lieutenant Michaels slipped on to the bench beside Jamie. 'How is it?' he asked, indicating the plate. Jamie pulled a face. Michaels's lips curled into a slight smile.

He placed two tin cups on the table. Steam rose from them and gave off a pleasant, fruity aroma. 'Try this. Some of the privates brew it from native berries and leaves. It makes a nice change from vitamin pills. It's good for morale.'

'I can see how it would be,' said the Doctor appreciatively, drawing his cup towards him and warming his hands on it.

'Commander Redfern wants to speak to you two,' added Michaels, prompting a strange expression to flicker across the Doctor's face. 'You've set your chronometers to local time, haven't you? There are 22.5 hours to the day.'

'Oh yes,' said the Doctor.

'The commander T-Mats down for daily inspection at 1400 hours. Be ready.'

As Michaels left, the Doctor rummaged through his pockets and produced a large fob watch. It was bereft of its chain, and the glass across its face was cracked. He held the watch up to his ear, frowned, shook it, listened again and smiled.

'I should say we have, oh, a good few hours at least, yet.'

'What was all that about?' asked Jamie.

'Did you hear what the lieutenant said, Jamie? T-Mat. You remember that, don't you?'

'Aye, I remember it well enough. It's a machine for...' Jamie struggled for the words. 'It takes people apart and puts them back together somewhere else.'

'Almost instantaneously. There must be a terminal on the carrier ship and another on the *Triumph*. Rather solves our little problem of getting back to the TARDIS, don't you think?'

'That's all very good, Doctor, but it's not what I was talking about.'

'I'm not sure I know what you mean, Jamie.'

'Oh yes, you do. This Redfern fellow. When you heard his name, you looked like you had a nasty taste in your mouth.'

'Well,' said the Doctor carefully, 'I do try not to prejudge people whom I haven't met.'

'Aw, here we go – another thing you "try not to do", eh?'

'I'm simply going by the historical accounts of this time and place,' said the Doctor defensively. He took a deep breath and his expression darkened. 'And, according to those accounts,

Wayne Redfern is one of the cruellest and most evil men who ever lived.'

This time, Jamie was ready for the ambush.

He whirled around, dropped into a crouch and fired.

Four photon bullets created explosions of light as they hit the wall of the training room.

'You're dead,' the computer informed him, almost managing to sound smug.

The third Selachian had appeared from his right this time. He barely caught a glimpse of it before the main lights dispelled its flickering image.

'It didn't do the same as before,' Jamie complained as Michaels appeared.

'It's not meant to,' said Michaels. 'You can't predict what will happen in battle.'

Jamie hefted his rifle, miserably. 'I was just getting the hang of this thing too.'

'You don't have to do this, Jamie. You aren't a member of the TSF.'

Jamie presented the lieutenant with a stubborn scowl.

Michaels held up his hands in a placatory gesture. 'OK, OK, we'll run the simulation again. But concentrate this time, Jamie. I told you, we haven't got long.'

The Doctor hadn't wanted to say much until he and Jamie were alone. They sat on low, collapsible beds in the tent that Michaels had assigned to them, and sipped at their second helpings of the fruity drink. It was pleasant and warming. Jamie was just beginning to appreciate how much protection his combat uniform also gave him from the cold air.

'The year,' said the Doctor, 'is 2204. It's almost a century since the Selachians developed their battlesuits and left their home world. They conquered Kalaya in the first six months and three more neighbouring worlds within a year. Since then, they have fought, done business with and defrauded a thousand companies and countless individuals on a hundred worlds. They've built up a legend around themselves, they've created or bartered for many, many weapons and they have become a very powerful force indeed.'

'And now they've started a war, eh?'

'It isn't that simple, Jamie. Both humans and Selachians are proud species. But, yes, they are at war.'

'What for?'

'Well, several things really, but what it boils down to is power. Each wants to be the most powerful race in the galaxy. It's a matter of defence, you see – or that's what they tell each other. They've both been targets in the past. The thought that somebody else could make them targets again frightens them very much.'

'And the Selachians might win, is that it?'

'I wish that was the problem, Jamie, I dearly wish it was. But no, the Selachians are losing this war. The humans have driven them back to their own system. One by one, they have retaken the worlds seized by the Selachians. This world, Kalaya, is the last.'

'So it's nearly over, then?'

The Doctor was gloomy and reflective. 'It's a lot more difficult to end a war than it is to start one, Jamie. If only more people remembered that fact.'

'But the Selachians will surrender, won't they? They'll have to, sooner or later.'

'No, Jamie. As I told you, they are proud people. They won't surrender – and the humans won't be appeased until they do. But, yes, it is almost over.' His expression became grave. 'The Terran Security Forces,' he intoned, as if pronouncing a death sentence, 'have created a new and deadly bomb. In a very short time – just a few days now, I should think – Commander

41

Wayne Redfern will give the order to use it. He will destroy the Selachians' home world, Ockora, completely and utterly. He will snuff out millions of lives.'

The revelation stunned Jamie. He had seen many incredible weapons – barely a trip in the TARDIS passed without him facing some new way of dealing death – but he hadn't considered their use on such a scale before. A whole planet, a whole species, destroyed just like that? It was too big, too monumentally awful, to take in.

But the Selachians were the enemy, weren't they? They were killing innocent people. He had seen the bodies himself. What if it was the only way to stop them?

What if he had had the power to wipe out the redcoats? To destroy them before they had slaughtered a thousand good Highlanders with their cowardly tactics? Wouldn't that have been the right thing to do? To save all those lives?

The thought of using such power made Jamie feel sick. But wasn't he planning to fight the Selachians to the death, for Zoe's sake?

'So we've got to stop them from using this bomb?'

'No, no, that is precisely what we must not do.'

'Eh?'

'This has already happened, Jamie. It's a part of human history.' The Doctor held up a hand to forestall any objection. 'Not your history, maybe, but history nonetheless.' His eyes and voice took on a distant quality as he mumbled, 'And some things have to happen.'

'So what do we do?'

'We rescue Zoe and we get away from this dreadful place before it's too late.'

Jamie was relieved, although he wasn't sure he ought to have been. 'Well, now you're talking! That's why I joined this TSF bunch: to rescue Zoe.' Nice and simple, he thought. Just do what's right and leave. Leave the big decisions to somebody else. And if a few Selachians had to die, if he had to pull that trigger… well, at least it would be a fair fight. Anyway, they weren't people, were they? They were monsters.

'Yes, Jamie,' said the Doctor kindly, 'I know you did. I only hope…' His voice tailed off and he rubbed at his chin thoughtfully.

'What is it?' asked Jamie, suddenly worried. 'Come on Doctor, I know something's up. It's about Zoe, isn't it?'

The Doctor sighed. 'Wayne Redfern's name didn't become vilified just because of the deaths of the Selachians. They were the enemy, after all, and a long way removed from the concerns of most of the people of Earth. No, there was more. Ever since the first days of this war, the Selachians have been taking prisoners. Each time they are forced to leave a planet behind, they take a good number of its people – and their attackers – along with them.'

Jamie swallowed, feeling his stomach sink as he saw where the Doctor was leading.

'By the end, they held over ten thousand hostages on Ockora. They thought it would be enough to save them. It wasn't. Redfern used his bomb anyway.'

'Lieutenant Michaels said…' Jamie could hardly speak the words, but he had to. Just in case the Doctor could disprove his terrible suspicion. 'He said the war here was almost over; that the Selachians would be leaving soon.'

The Doctor nodded solemnly. 'If they take Zoe with them, she's as good as dead.'

Chapter Six

The Doctor had come face to face with infamous men before: tyrants, dictators, killers, power-crazed megalomaniacs. It always surprised him how small they seemed, compared to their reputations. It was as if, despite his vast experience, he still couldn't imagine how evil could come in such a small package as a single human being.

It was like that with Commander Wayne Redfern. He was not a short man, but then nor was he the towering ogre that the Doctor had foolishly expected. He was older and thinner than the holoscans in future history books would make him seem; one step away from gaunt, but still healthy. His cheekbones were prominent, giving the impression that the skin of his face had been stretched thin. He had retained his hair, but it had turned the colour of steel.

Redfern sat behind a real oak desk, in a large office with deep carpets and textured wallpaper. He dressed like the rest of his organisation, except that he had two gold stars on each of his epaulets. However, his black, multi-pocketed uniform was immaculately maintained. The Doctor suspected that Redfern spent most of his time in plush quarters aboard the orbiting *Triumph*. He wondered if he had ever stepped off this carrier ship and into the war that he was conducting.

Lieutenant Michaels saluted smartly. 'James McCrimmon and the Doctor, sir.'

The commander acknowledged the introduction and greeted his guests with a smile that involved baring his teeth rather than flexing his facial muscles. He gestured them towards two seats, while Michaels stood stiffly to attention by the door.

'I understand you're visitors to this world,' said Redfern, as the Doctor and Jamie sank into comfortable velvet cushions. By the twenty-third century, human accents had become mostly homogenised, but Redfern's voice possessed a discernible drawl which placed his origins in what would once have been a southern state of America.

'We certainly aren't Kalarians,' said the Doctor, with a dangerous hint of condescension.

'Then what are you doing here?' Redfern showed his teeth again: a warning, this time.

'I'm afraid we took a wrong turning. Left at Proxima Centauri instead of straight ahead, you know how it is. You lose concentration for a second...'

The Doctor had intended to sound jocular, but he was all too aware that he had belied himself by fixing Redfern with a glare. The commander returned it with equal severity.

Jamie spoke up, breaking the eye contact between them. 'We're not planning to stay. We just want to get our friend back off the Selachians and we'll be off. Well, just as soon as we can get back to the -'

The Doctor faked a brief coughing fit, silencing his companion. 'Our, ah, survival pod,' he concluded apologetically. 'We seem to have mislaid it.'

'Survival pod?'

'Yes, I understand you may have salvaged it? It's an unusual design. Dark blue.'

'Unusual. I'd concur with that.'

The Doctor waved a dismissive hand. 'Oh, well, of course it's nothing more than a... a storage box really. Tents and rations and things, some woolly jumpers. Plus the equipment we need to signal our, ah, mother ship, of course.'

'Of course,' said Redfern indulgently. He leant back in his seat and crossed his hands over his lap. 'We thought it was a Selachian device. We've been trying to open it.'

'Oh?'

'Without success.'

'Well, obviously. You don't have the key, do you?'

'May I borrow the key?' Redfern must have seen the Doctor's face falling, because he added, 'You understand why I need to examine this pod of yours?'

'Zoe has it,' Jamie blurted out. 'Our friend, Zoe, that is. Doesn't she, Doctor?' he added as an afterthought. It was a hopeless lie, but the Doctor had no choice but to bolster it with an enthusiastic nod.

'Oh dear,' said Redfern, his voice devoid of sympathy. 'You do seem to have found yourselves in a difficult situation.'

The Doctor leant back too, and studiously mimicked Redfern's casual pose. 'So,' he said, clapping his hands together, 'is there anything else you'd like to ask us?'

The Doctor reflected on the conversation as he wandered around the camp, hands clasped behind his back. He wasn't sure how he had managed to bluff his way through it. Why hadn't Redfern searched him for the TARDIS key?

He had the unnerving feeling that the commander was playing games with him. Or was he allowing Redfern's reputation – unearned as yet – to influence him?

Another worry came to the forefront of his mind as he saw Michaels polishing his boots at the long wooden table. An incongruous action, perhaps, but the Doctor knew how important routine could be to people in this type of situation. It provided a distraction, and a thin veneer of normality.

He stood behind the lieutenant for a moment, watching as he described tiny circles on the toecaps with a filthy cloth. How best to broach the subject, he wondered? Best to come straight out with it.

'I'm worried about Jamie.'

'You too?' said Michaels evenly, without looking around.

'He insists on wearing this… this combat armour of yours and taking up a gun and making some sort of a foolhardy attack upon the Selachians.'

'Yeah, well, for some of us, that's life.'

'You do realise what might happen to him?' the Doctor cried, angered by Michaels's indifference.

'Yeah. He'll go out to fight and he'll probably be dead within fifteen minutes.'

The Doctor was taken aback by the matter-of-fact statement. He wrung his hands and stammered: 'Yes, yes, and that's precisely why you can't allow him to do it!'

Michaels turned to him. To the Doctor's surprise, there was genuine concern in his expression. It made him more animated than the Doctor had seen him before. 'I know how you feel, Doctor. I like Jamie – and that's not supposed to happen because the average life span of a soldier out here is four weeks; of an untrained one, about four hours. I don't want him to die. But it's his choice. You'll have to talk to him.'

'I wouldn't be able to stop him. Jamie's loyal, but he can be very stubborn indeed!'

'Then what makes you think I can help you?'

'You can order him not to fight!'

'We need all the help we can get. If I turned Jamie away, Redfern would put him in another detachment. Anyway, what do you think he'd do if he couldn't join us?'

The Doctor sighed. In truth, he had known all along. 'He'd fight anyway.'

'Without our protection. He'd go in there on his own.'

'Yes, yes, I suppose you're right. I can see I shall have to think of something else.'

'Then I suggest you hurry,' said Michaels sympathetically, 'because Redfern just gave the word. There's a briefing in half an hour. We're making our final assault on the Selachian base at dawn.'

* * *

48

The Kalarian day, in this season, was short – and, as the night drew in, it began to rain again.

The Doctor didn't sleep. He sat, cross-legged and fully clothed, on his bed, the canvas of which stretched almost to the ground beneath him. He put his recorder to his mouth, but he didn't blow down it. He didn't wish to wake Jamie. Instead, he mimed the notes to 'Three Blind Mice' with his fingers. He imagined that the rain, which pattered against the roof of the domed tent, was his personal percussion section.

Sometimes he could envy Jamie's ability to sleep through almost anything. Though the young Highlander knew what awaited him in a few hours' time, he seemed at peace.

He didn't want to expose Jamie to the horrors of an all-out war against an intractable foe. He didn't want him to be hurt or worse. But he could think of only one way to take the decision out of his companion's hands. A desperate plan, but it might work.

It was time, at last.

The Doctor pocketed his recorder and swung his legs on to the plastic-covered floor. He searched his jacket until he found a discarded chocolate wrapper and a stubby pencil. He scribbled a quick note to Jamie, just in case, and left it by his side.

The rifle was lying there, a sad reminder of why the Doctor had to do this. He stared at it for a long moment, then sighed and straightened and walked out into the night.

Leaving the camp was easy. The guards were only expecting trouble from without. From within, the Doctor could observe their routines, even chat to them, learn which part of the perimeter was the least secure and pick the perfect time to slip across it unnoticed.

Crossing the island was more of a chore. The night was as dark and inclement as the previous one, and the Doctor stumbled many times in invisible undergrowth. He wished, too, that he had Zoe's sense of direction. At more than one point he feared himself lost.

Eventually, though, he tore himself from yet another prickly bush, scrambled over a hill and brightened at the sight of the grey beach spread before him. If he wasn't mistaken, he had found the exact spot at which he and Jamie had been freed from the Selachians.

Or somewhere very much like it.

The Doctor hurried down to the sand, flailing his arms to keep his balance. Brittle, brown seaweed crunched beneath his shoes. He patted down his jacket, worried for a moment that he didn't have the item he needed. He grinned as he produced a white cloth handkerchief from his breast pocket. He unfolded it and frowned at its pattern of red spots. Still, it didn't really matter.

He fished in the sand for a suitable stick. He found one that was thin and about a metre long. He pulled it free, triumphantly, tied the handkerchief to one end with two knots and hoisted the stick like a flagpole. The wind caught the handkerchief and unfurled it.

The Doctor trudged along the beach, keeping the water to his left. This was the direction in which the Selachians had tried to take him.

His plan was simple, but dangerous. He had a history with the Selachians. He figured prominently enough in their records, he would hazard, to be able to bluff his way to somebody in authority. He would offer himself as their prisoner in exchange for Zoe. It wasn't likely to work – but at least he might end up imprisoned alongside her. And the Doctor had every faith in his own ability as an escapologist.

Something moved. To his right and upwards, in the undergrowth. Too big to be an animal. Anyway, the Doctor had seen no animals on this world.

'I've come here as a friend,' he called gingerly, although he could see no one. 'I only want to talk. I think you might be interested in what I have to say.' He waved his improvised flag of surrender, optimistically.

Huge, shambling plants detached themselves from the vegetation.

They took on human form.

To the Doctor's dismay, three TSF soldiers bounded down the incline and surrounded him, rifles at the ready. He recognised one: a young, bearded sergeant. He was sure he had spotted him at the camp just before he had left it.

He gave a wail of complaint. 'You followed me here!' He was just beginning to see how it had been possible. Light rippled across the soldiers' green-and-brown streaked uniforms, and they became a more familiar black in colour. Holographic camouflage fields. He should have inspected the uniform that Jamie had been given more carefully.

'CO's orders,' rapped the young sergeant. 'Looks like he was right too. You were taking information to the Sharks!'

The Doctor looked up at his flag, self-consciously. He let his shoulders sag and his mouth turn downwards. He wasn't concerned for his own predicament. He feared, instead, for Zoe's fate – and for Jamie's too, if he risked his life to save her.

'I don't suppose you'd be interested in hearing an explanation for this?' he said gloomily.

Chapter Seven

Jamie woke, the next morning, to find the Doctor missing.

At first, this didn't concern him overmuch. He had long since noted that his friend required little sleep. He had obviously gone off on some nocturnal excursion and would be back in his own sweet time.

Jamie dressed in his combat uniform and ran through the details of the previous night's briefing in his mind. There was so much to remember – particularly as Michaels had taken him to one side afterwards, to go through some things that everybody else knew already.

Then Jamie found the note. And that was when he began to worry.

The Doctor had wandered into Selachian territory, unarmed. The thought brought a lump to Jamie's throat. He wondered whether to tell Michaels about it. Part of him expected the Doctor to enter his tent at any moment, a grin across his face and Zoe behind him.

He was partly relieved and partly disappointed, then, when Michaels informed him of the Doctor's actual whereabouts. The lieutenant joined Jamie at the slatted table beside the spider-like ship, and they ate a tasteless breakfast of pills in the grey light of the pre-dawn. 'I don't want you to worry,' said Michaels. 'He's been taken for questioning, that's all. He's up on the *Triumph* with the CO. Probably better off out of it, too.'

Jamie tried not to let what he knew about Commander Redfern concern him. 'Look, I am still fighting with you, aren't I?'

'I vouched for you.' Lieutenant Michaels looked doubtful. 'Is it still what you want?'

Jamie nodded vigorously.

'I'd be happier if you'd stay in my detail.'

'Aye,' said Jamie, unwilling to discuss the matter again, 'well it's too late now, isn't it?'

Soldiers bustled around the camp, in a last burst of frenetic activity before the battle. Jamie felt left out, having nothing to do. But then, the soldiers didn't seem to be accomplishing much of use and he suspected that they were just nervous.

Michaels introduced Jamie to his opposite number in the detail that would be going under water: the heavy-set, bearded Lieutenant Marsh. 'You know how to use that thing?' Marsh grunted, indicating Jamie's rifle with a nod.

'I've practised with it,' said Jamie defensively.

'Had experience of underwater combat?'

'A bit,' he hedged, wondering if his adventure in Atlantis counted.

'Stay out of the way, do as you're told and do your best.'

Marsh pivoted and marched away, leaving Jamie to scowl after him. Michaels gave him an encouraging pat on the shoulder. 'Best go on to the ship and get kitted out.'

Jamie fidgeted, impatiently, in the long queue that led along a grey corridor to the carrier ship's equipment store. At last, it was his turn to shoulder his way into the one tiny space left free of metal shelving. He explained to a fresh-faced junior NCO that he was going under water. The young man nodded, reached around Jamie's neck and pulled the hood of his uniform over his head. It settled into place with a click and became surprisingly rigid. The NCO pulled a light, black back pack from a shelf behind him and helped Jamie to struggle into it. He worked deftly behind Jamie's back for a few seconds, pulling cords out of the pack and attaching them to the hood. Next, he slapped a magazine into Jamie's rifle and thrust two more into pouches on each side of his belt.

Outside, Jamie experimented with the respirator that hung loosely around his chest. When he brought it up to his face it slotted neatly into the front of his hood. Although it seemed opaque from the outside he could see through it clearly. A faint pumping sound emerged from the back pack. He could feel that he was no longer breathing fresh air.

Only an hour later Jamie started to have doubts.

They surfaced as he was standing on the grey beach with thirty other soldiers, watching a weak excuse for a sunrise. Marsh delivered last-minute instructions, in an abrasive style that was far from comforting. 'We'll have the advantage of surprise, at first. The Sharks will be concerned with the attack on their land base, but it won't last. Soon as they hear about us, they'll pull back to defend their ship. There'll be reinforcements, plenty of them, and all behind you. You forget to watch your back, you're dead.'

Jamie looked down at his uniform's myriad waterproof pouches, glumly. He couldn't even remember what most of them held.

'The sonoscopes have found the warcraft for us, but we don't know what else is down there. Stay alert. No drifting off to sleep.'

Perhaps he should have listened to Lieutenant Michaels and fought with him further down the beach. At least he would have had less to worry about then. But no, according to the Doctor, the prisoners would be on the Selachians' submerged ship. Jamie had to go there.

Marsh inspected the chronometer in the wristband of his uniform. An age seemed to pass before he looked up and nodded abruptly. 'Move in!'

There was a palpable sense of relief as the soldiers waded into Kalaya's black water. Action, Jamie supposed, was preferable to the uncertainty of waiting. He tried to believe that. He tried to believe that everything would turn out fine if he kept his wits about him. He had been in difficult scrapes before, hadn't he? He possessed a survivor's instinct.

Then his colleagues began to dive and he realised that, with all his other concerns, he had forgotten to put his respirator in place. He performed the task with a little embarrassment and a little more fear at what the lapse said about his state of preparedness. But it was too late to back out now, even if he had wanted to. The oxygenerator whirred into action and Jamie slipped into the twilit world beneath the waves.

The detail swam a small way out, then turned parallel to the shoreline. Jamie was a strong swimmer, but he hadn't allowed for the extent to which his uniform and weapons weighed him down. It was difficult, too, to see through the dark water, particularly as the respirator obstructed his peripheral vision. Jamie struck out with sure but mechanical strokes, just aiming to maintain his formation with the others.

He knew nothing about the ambush until the water in front of him turned red.

Belatedly, words crackled in his ears, through his uniform's communication system. 'They've seen us... four Sharks... two more behind... got Walters...'

For precious seconds, Jamie drifted in a state of bewilderment, struggling to see through a mass of heaving shadows. Then he caught a glimpse of golden armour and knew that the Selachians were upon him.

He untangled his rifle laboriously from its sling. He seemed to be moving in slow motion. Lieutenant Michaels had warned him about that. It took him an age to bring the sights up to his eye and to squint towards his target. The monster bore down on him, cleaving the water with powerful strokes. Jamie's eyes widened, fixating on the shark's-head design on its helmet. He could have frozen then, but he had encountered many monsters in his time with the Doctor. He gritted his teeth, overcame his instinctive fear and pulled the trigger.

Michaels had gone to great pains to explain how the rifle could operate under water. It had been adapted, he had said, in view of the TSF's current foe. An impatient Jamie hadn't cared about that. Even now, he only cared about the vicious but comforting kick of the weapon as it discharged its payload. The pellet cannoned through the water and left a bubbling wake. The recoil sent Jamie hurtling backwards and, he realised too late, over. He came out of an uncontrolled spin to find himself upside-down.

'One shot is never enough to kill them,' Michaels had said.

The Selachian could have finished him off, but he saw no sign of it. Black uniforms crossed his field of vision and he realised that his colleagues had distracted it. They were chattering in his ears about driving the Selachians back. Were the humans gaining the upper hand?

Not yet. As Jamie righted himself, he saw a hapless TSF man held between two Selachians. One drove its fist into the man's stomach, and kept it there. A thick plume of smoke erupted from its arm-mounted gun. A red haze followed it. The Selachians released their victim. He slumped and drifted towards the seabed, leaving a scarlet trail.

Jamie had seen death before, but he was not inured to it. It filled him with anger, with the need to do something to balance the scales.

He shouldered the rifle again, sickened that he had not been able to act more quickly. He fired twice at the murdering Selachian, but missed each time.

Two armoured hands clamped on to his shoulders from behind.

Jamie winced. His hands spasmed open and the sea stole his rifle. He kicked back helplessly and dived, in an attempt to break free. The Selachian's hold was too strong. Jamie started to feel dizzy. He remembered the ill-fated soldier, held in a grip like this one, unable to ward off his killers. He redoubled his desperate efforts.

'Remember,' Michaels had said, 'the Sharks have no great advantage under water. Not in their battlesuits, at least. They're designed for surface use, they're cumbersome – and, without them, the Sharks are helpless.'

Jamie took comfort from those words, but knew too that he was the only combatant on either side who had not been trained for this environment. His only hope was to ignore the pain, to wriggle and kick and squirm and try to unbalance his captor.

Somehow, he managed to wrench his left shoulder free. He twisted around, braced his feet against the Selachian's chest and kicked the creature away with all the strength in his muscles. Above ground, he knew, he would have had no chance – but here, leverage won the day. The Selachian reached for him, but the kick had sent it drifting. It recovered slowly, but managed to swipe at Jamie as he floundered. A heavy fist grazed his collarbone. He thrashed his arms and pedalled his feet wildly. The Selachian raised its guns.

Some distant survival instinct reminded Jamie that he still had pouches and a belt full of Michaels's fancy gadgets. He tried to think back to the briefing, but all he could remember was: 'Their guns aren't optimised for underwater use – they don't have much range – but they'll still leave a big hole in you.'

Instinct told him to reach for his dirk, but what good would that do?

He couldn't tear his eyes away from those twin barrels, so he resorted to patting himself down with his hands, feeling blindly for something, anything, but knowing he would never have time to use it.

The Selachian fired.

Jamie flinched, brought his knees up and rolled into a ball.

The water around him turned hot but, by some miracle, his reflex action saved his life. The blasts missed him.

The reprieve would not last long. The Selachian surged towards him. But, by now, Jamie's questing left hand had managed to pull open a pouch and alight upon something.

He wasn't sure what it was. It felt oily and wriggly. He didn't have time to wonder. He flung it into his attacker's face. It expanded as it left his hand, and spread into an amorphous black shape like an oil slick. It seemed to reach out and wrap itself around the Selachian's helmet. The Selachian flung up its hands and clawed at the obstruction, blinded. Yes, of course – Michaels had briefed Jamie on the Cloak. He had called it a last resort, a tiny chance to make an escape. He had also mentioned that the Selachians had developed the technology and sold it to Earth a decade earlier. Jamie had wondered how such a thing could have happened.

He could have pressed his advantage, could have found another weapon, but his mind was still blank from the fear of his close call. The only coherent plan he could form was to get away from the monster before it could tear the Cloak free.

A red light blinked inside Jamie's respirator mask. Michaels had been particularly insistent that he should remember what that meant. Something had gone wrong with his air supply.

He could hear Marsh's voice, beneath his own heavy breathing. 'Keep at them, we can do this. Only three of them left now. Close in. Don't let them break through.'

Jamie wanted to do something. He cast around for his rifle. He rummaged in his pouches, but remembered that few of the standard-issue devices in them would function down here. He had made a lucky choice earlier. His neck and shoulders ached, he was short of breath and his head was beginning to pound. Why wouldn't that infernal red light stop?

To Jamie, it seemed that less than a minute had passed, but it must have been much longer for, suddenly, the battle was over.

He could hear cries of exultation over his communicator. The Selachians had been defeated; this group, at least. He was glad of that, but ashamed of himself. How long had he drifted, shaken and useless, trying to think of something to do while other people fought and died in his stead?

Lieutenant Michaels had been right. He hadn't been ready for this.

Marsh was by his side. Jamie didn't recognise him at first through his blank mask, but his words came loud and clear. 'You OK, soldier?'

Jamie shook his head to clear it. He didn't want to display his weakness. 'Aye, I think so, I've just got this red light flashing in my eyes.'

'Get back to shore.'

Jamie railed against the unfairness of the command. 'I'll be all right, I just –'

'You're losing air. They've cut the leads to your generator.'

'I can still breathe. I can make it to the ship.'

'Get out of here now, McCrimmon, that's an order!'

Jamie pouted, but supposed he had to do as he was told. Reluctantly, he turned around and swam in the direction that Marsh had indicated with a pointed finger.

Away from Zoe.

A few minutes later, the red light snapped on permanently and a high-pitched whine sounded in Jamie's ears. He took his last deep breath before his respirator filled with water. He tore it from his face and struck upwards, hating to admit to himself that Marsh had been right; that, had he been in the midst of combat and unable to break off when the last of his oxygen leaked out, he would have died.

He surfaced, gulped in air that tasted salty, fresh and almost overwhelming after the recycled oxygen, and sighted the beach not too far away. He paddled disconsolately towards it, until the water was shallow enough for him to walk. A figure rose from the waves beside him, and another behind. Jamie was not the only soldier to have been sent off the battlefield. He smiled wanly at the man to his right, who was dragging his right leg awkwardly and trickling blood into the water.

'They tagged me, the bastards!' said the soldier, almost apologetically. 'I got one of them before they did, though. How about you?'

Jamie hesitated, not wanting to admit to his failure.

Then he heard a noise behind him, like a concentrated blast of wind combined with a ferocious crackling. He whirled around and almost lost his footing. His jaw dropped open in horror.

The soldier behind him – a woman, he thought, though scarcely recognisable as such now – had burst into flames. They burnt fiercely, repulsing Jamie with incredible heat. Again, he was helpless to act. In seconds, the fire had burnt itself out. The charred remains of a human being dropped into the water and broke apart on the tide.

Jamie looked about wildly for the source of the attack. 'What happened?' he cried. 'What did they do to her?'

The other man remained calm – not unsympathetic, but resigned. 'Selachian spores. They must have laid clusters down there. She must have swum right through one without noticing. They cling to you and combust as soon as they're exposed to air.'

Alarmed, Jamie made as if to brush invisible spores from his uniform. 'What if we've got them on us too?'

The soldier yanked off his respirator. His thin face twisted into a humourless smile. 'We'd know about it by now. Or rather, we wouldn't.'

Jamie didn't know what to say. His stomach churned with disgust. He turned away from the spreading ashes of the luckless woman and pressed on towards the beach. He allowed the other soldier to put an arm around his shoulders, and supported him. He had forgotten about the high gravity of this world, but he felt it pushing him down now.

As they reached the grey sand, the soldier collapsed into a sitting position and inspected his open wound. 'Looks like the war's over for us, pal.'

'Speak for yourself,' retorted Jamie. He was already gazing down the beach. Somewhere along there, the other details would have begun their attack on the Selachians' land base. 'I might not be able to go under water, but I can still fight on land.'

'Your decision,' said the soldier, with a shrug.

'I could do with borrowing your rifle.'

'With me a sitting duck like this? No way!'

Jamie nodded, disappointed. He checked his pouches again and found the disc-shaped explosives – the electro-grenades – that looked so much like miniature versions of the mines that had almost killed him two nights ago. He tried not to dwell on the realisation that the minefield had been laid by humans; that their methods were as dishonourable as the enemy's hidden traps. Even so, the reminder that death could come from any quarter in this dirty, bloody war depressed him.

He thought of Zoe, and steeled himself for what he had to do.

The soldier had produced a first aid pack from his uniform. He winced as he bandaged his wound like an expert. He needed no further assistance.

Jamie gave him a farewell nod, closed his hand around the comforting shape of an electro-grenade, tried to forget about his various pains, and set off along the beach at a steady run.

Two Selachians backed, side by side, along the beach towards Jamie. Four human soldiers came after them, rifles chattering. But the Selachians were firing back. The humans dived for cover as multiple blasts tore the ground apart. Jamie remembered the burning woman, and his lips curled into a sneer of anger.

The creatures hadn't seen him yet. He ran towards them.

'Hey!' he yelled. 'Over here!'

They turned. He flung the electro-grenade and dived to the ground.

The grenade hit one of its targets and exploded, releasing a cloud of smoke. The Selachians reeled, but didn't fall. The humans seized their chance. Breaking cover, they pumped more bullets into the creatures. First one and then the other fell. Jamie could have cheered.

And then there was an unnatural silence.

He picked himself up and joined the four soldiers around the remains of their fallen foes. The Selachians' battlesuits had cracked open, and water gushed into the sand. Inside the armour, hair-thin green wires thrashed as if in pain. Jamie could see exposed patches of pink skin: the beings behind the technological façade.

His momentary rush of triumph was quelled, as he realised the beings were dying.

He had arrived at the very tail end of the battle. He picked his way through the resultant debris, not daring to count the scattered corpses of both armies. The humans had won. He could tell that, because some were still standing.

Jamie passed overturned Selachian transports, a twisted wire-frame cannon with its alien operators dead beside it and even an uprooted tree. He had arrived too late – but then, what horrors might he have seen, had he been earlier? The aftermath was sickening enough.

He found Michaels sitting at the base of a high escarpment, in what seemed to be the heart of the Selachians' former base. The lieutenant had pulled his respirator away from his face and was clutching his right side, where Jamie was alarmed to see that that part of his uniform had melted and congealed.

'Let me help,' he insisted. 'What can I do?'

'First aid pack,' grunted Michaels, through gritted teeth. 'Painkillers. Not as bad as it looks – they only clipped me. Hurts like hell, though.' He reached for one of his pouches with his left hand, but winced and thought again. His right arm hung uselessly by his side.

Following Michaels's directions, Jamie found the painkillers for him. As he eased one of the pills between the lieutenant's lips, Michaels croaked, 'What happened under water?'

'I don't know,' Jamie confessed. 'We were ambushed. The Selachians damaged my generator whatsit. I had to come back.'

Michaels nodded his understanding. His eyelids fluttered and closed. Jamie was worried, but the lieutenant's breathing and pulse were still strong.

And then, from all across the battlefield, there rose a collective gasp.

Jamie turned, to see that the surface of the water was bubbling angrily. A second later, a black ship emerged like a giant shark attacking. Its shape was reminiscent of a shark too, sleek and snub-nosed. A row of jagged teeth had been painted across its prow. Jamie found his gaze drawn towards those teeth, as if the ship might suck him into its maw.

It hung there for a second, engines whining, water cascading from its hull. Somebody was yelling at Jamie to take cover, but he was mesmerised and only just beginning to realise that Marsh's detail must have failed in its task. The remaining Selachians were escaping with their prisoners.

The great black ship lurched forward. Jamie cried out in fear and toppled on to his back. But the ship was climbing. It wasn't going to hit him. He scrambled back to his feet as it flew above him, almost close enough for him to reach it with a jump.

It didn't yet have the height to clear the escarpment. It turned and flew along the beach instead. Soldiers leapt out of its path. But one thought rang in Jamie's mind.

Zoe had to be on board.

He had no clear plan. He simply ran, trying to keep pace with the ship as if it might extend a ladder for him. It pulled away, onwards and upwards. As its flat underside passed over him, Jamie was dimly aware that it was punctuated by a row of huge, silver discs. Then, suddenly, he was thrust downwards by a force like Kalaya's gravity but much greater. He landed heavily, and choked on sand. He felt as if he was being crushed.

The pressure relented as suddenly as it had begun. Jamie lifted his head, but could see only the back of the retreating vessel. 'Zoe!' he yelled, hopelessly. 'Zoe!'

Then a pure black beam stabbed out from the ship. Purple fire licked at its edges. It seemed to rip its way through the air. It crackled into the face of the escarpment and, before Jamie's horrified eyes, the rock began to crumble. He dived for cover as pulverised fragments rained around his ears and a cloud rose to suffocate him. The ship redoubled its speed, pulled upwards and receded into the sky. Jamie screamed Zoe's name again, but coughed and spluttered as dust attacked his throat.

His eyes were streaming. He could barely see at all now. He was vaguely aware of shapes through the dust cloud: soldiers running and falling. He thought, belatedly, of his respirator: it might not provide fresh oxygen any more, but its air filter would still work on the surface. He slapped it into position as something heavy landed on his back.

Jamie fell and skidded on to his stomach. He groaned as his muscles surrendered, and the avalanche buried him.

Chapter Eight

On the battlefield, a young soldier lay dying.

He had to accept what was happening, but he found it difficult to believe. Not that the young soldier was naïve: he had lost a lot of comrades, even brothers, to the guns of the enemy. But, somehow, he had never thought death could claim him.

He had told himself otherwise, of course. He had thought himself prepared. He had fought for his people, for his world, for justice. Against all that, he had said, his life didn't matter. He had been ready to risk it for the cause, to throw it away if necessary. He had been proud of his choice. He had thought it brave.

Now, the young soldier lay on his back in sucking mud and stared at the dour sky of an alien world and knew that, had he thought – had he ever truly thought – it might come to this, then he would have done anything to avoid going to war.

The noise and dust from the avalanche settled, and left only a ringing silence.

Snatches of poetry drifted through the young soldier's thoughts. He had been made to read it at school, although he had forgotten most of it. The poets of bygone years had had much to say on the tragedy of his chosen vocation. The lines which, unexpectedly, came back to him now took on fresh poignancy. For the first time, he knew what the poets had been writing about.

He almost wanted to die, almost wished the avalanche had crushed him where he lay helpless. He wanted an end to the anticipation. But he couldn't let go so easily. A voice inside the young soldier cried that he wanted to live, no matter how vain a hope it was.

Blood flowed from his body and stained the inside of the combat suit that should have protected him. Oddly, the hot pain that had felled him had subsided into a cold, distant throb. It didn't hurt much now. He might even have considered standing, but his muscles were unresponsive and he felt as if a heavy weight had settled on to his chest. It was all he could do to take short, controlled breaths. He felt dreadfully hungry.

Had the battle ended, or was it just that he could hear it no longer? Even the rain seemed distant now. The young soldier wondered how long it would be before he was discovered. Too long, he supposed. He put his efforts into a futile attempt to raise his hand, to yell out, to find some way of signalling his presence to somebody. It occurred to him that only the enemy might be left to find him.

The young soldier thought about his family. They would be waiting at home, so far away. They would know what he was going through, what he was risking. He thought of them struggling to the end of each day, with a feeling of relief that no communiqué had been received, that their little boy had not died. Tomorrow, perhaps the day after, their world would be brought to an abrupt end. He imagined his sister's reaction to the news. It brought a stab of pain to his heart. He wanted to be there, to comfort her. He hated the thought of her having to cope with her grief alone.

His mother would be angry, of course. She would rail against the officers who had accepted her poor, precious son into the armed forces against her will. She would blame the government for his death. She would blame them for not finding another way, a better way, to settle their differences. Now, too late, the young soldier saw the point she had tried to make. He felt angry too. Angry that it was him who was lying here, dying, in a war that other people had chosen to fight.

But, for the most part, the young soldier's anger was reserved for the enemy – as he had always been taught. For the monsters who had invaded the peaceful world of Kalaya; whose outrages had been such that they had demanded to be fought; the warmongers who had callously detonated their bomb beneath his feet and broken something important inside him.

The hardest thing to accept was that the monsters had won. They had beaten him.

The young soldier raged against that terrible injustice and, in so doing, found his momentary doubts seared away by flames of righteous fury.

He had been right to fight the monsters, right to throw his life away in exchange for, hopefully, hastening their defeat. He prayed that, some day, somebody would make the monsters pay for what they had done to him.

As consciousness slipped away at last, the young soldier laid a bitter and heartfelt curse upon the entire plankton-sucking human race.

Chapter Nine

The bomb chamber lay at the heart of the *Triumph*.

To Laura Mulholland, that word 'heart' seemed appropriate. The chamber was filled with equipment, which vibrated and ticked and chimed softly. It was a room full of ceaseless, pedantic activity. And, often, its myriad sounds would merge into one relentless, throbbing heartbeat.

The flagship kept its darkest secret close to its heart. It felt, sometimes, as if the mission was driven by that secret. If and when the time came to reveal the secret, then the heart would become empty and silent.

Mulholland spent a great deal of time here at the heart, in the bomb chamber. She would arrive each morning, with her pens and pad and white coat. She would stand in the dim, reddish light and listen to the rhythm of the heart. Then she would test each of the free-standing consoles, noting readings and making adjustments to numerous calibrations. She would check the thick, insulated wiring between each console. And, always, she would end up standing before the twin housings.

A typical inspection would take her about an hour and a half. She performed the task more thoroughly than she had to. Partly, this was because she had little else to occupy her. Partly, it was because just being in the chamber reminded her that it contained her legacy, no matter how she might feel about that fact on any given day. But mostly, it was because she knew, really knew, the power of the weapon that she had created.

Redfern and his soldiers blithely went about their business, passing the chamber several times each day. To them, the weapon was no more than a means to an end. They didn't think, couldn't think, as Mulholland did in creeping nightmares, that it might ever go wrong. That the tiniest error in any one of ten thousand circuit boards or many more intricate connections could tear the heart out of the *Triumph* in an instant.

Heart attack, thought Mulholland, with black humour.

The G-bombs – the only two in existence, the product of her entire life – hung in the great metal housings. Clear shields protected the bombs from the outside but could not protect the outside from the bombs. In reality, they were small – but reality was overwhelmed by the enormity of their function. Their smooth, grey, metal surfaces swallowed up the light. Their shapes seemed almost too perfect: regular oblongs with rounded ends, each angle, each curve, plotted by computer and sculpted by remote manipulator arms.

Their casings were covered in lettering, stamped in cautionary yellow and black. Bold words warned the unwary not to touch the bombs or expose them to naked flames, open communicators, excessive vibrations or variations in light or temperature.

They were suspended above circular holes, the right size to allow them to pass through the bowels of the ship and into space, whereupon internal guidance systems would take over. Mulholland often wondered what it would be like to stand in the chamber as the bombs began their fateful journeys. They would drop out of sight in an instant. A critical moment, passing so quickly.

Each time Mulholland looked at the bombs, she imagined they might suddenly drop before her eyes. And that would be it, they would be gone. Or, upon entering the chamber one morning, she might find their housings empty. The idea always sent a thrill of fear and excitement up her back.

Each of the G-bombs was, of course, secured by nine sturdy, computer-controlled bolts. Mulholland indulged her fatalistic fantasies anyway. She had dreamed, or had nightmares, of every conceivable circumstance in which her creation might receive its first test.

Most of those dreams involved other people. To Mulholland, the bomb chamber had become her personal domain, a place in which everybody else could be forgotten. Nobody but her had been here since the *Triumph* had left Earth almost a year ago. When Commander Redfern and his aides appeared at the door, clutching launch codes, one of her dreams would come true.

She experienced a moment of pure, exhilarating terror, therefore, as she heard a soft footfall behind her.

Redfern? A Selachian? A terrorist, intent upon seizing the G-bombs for himself?

The intruder seemed almost as startled as Mulholland. He took a step back, threw up his hands and stared at her as if she posed a threat to him. She eyed his untidy hair and shabby clothing. 'What are you doing in here?' she demanded, her voice coming out at a higher pitch than usual. 'Who are you?'

The intruder lowered his hands, cautiously. 'I do beg your pardon, I appear to be lost. I'm looking for Commander Redfern's office, I do believe he wants to speak to me.' He made to step forward with a hand outstretched, thought better of the gesture and hesitated, then thought again. His face settled into a friendly smile. He shuffled towards Mulholland, took her hand in both of his and pumped it warmly. 'I'm the Doctor, pleased to meet you.'

'Professor Mulholland,' said Mulholland, weakly.

A shadow passed over the Doctor's eyes. 'Oh, are you now? Well, never mind. I must say, I find these gadgets all rather fascinating. Are they yours?'

To Mulholland's irritation, he regarded the instrument banks – her life's work, and the work of many other talented people – as a child might regard a set of building blocks.

'You should not be in here,' she said tartly. 'You are not

'wearing an anti-static coat.'

'Yes, yes, of course. Well, if you could just, er… oh, I always hate saying this…' The Doctor clasped his hands together and gave Mulholland a look that was pleading, hopeful and apologetic all at once. 'If you could take me to your leader?'

Throughout the trip to the CO's office, the Doctor chattered incessantly. His grasp of the theoretical principles of the G-bomb was uncanny. He must have studied Mulholland's reports closely. If he was a government snoop, then at least he was one of that rare breed who understood what they were snooping into. Still, he betrayed a hint of disapproval that made Mulholland wary of him. She felt as if he considered her accomplishments beneath him, both scientifically and morally.

She peeled off her precautionary hairnet and allowed her blonde locks to tumble to her shoulders. The Doctor surprised her by commenting, disarmingly, on how youthful she appeared for one with such a distinguished record.

The next time he spoke was as they neared their destination. He cut in front of Mulholland as if he had just thought of something urgent.

'It will work, you know,' he assured her.

'I beg your pardon?'

'Your invention, the G-bomb. It will work. You need to stop thinking in terms of giving it its first test run and start thinking about what it might actually do.'

'It is not my decision,' said Mulholland, making to walk past him.

The Doctor blocked her path again. He looked shocked. 'But it has to be! You mean to say you'd be happy if Wayne Redfern used your creation to wipe out an intelligent species?'

'The G-bomb is a last resort. We won't use it unless we have to.'

'And that will make it right, will it?'

Mulholland had had enough of this. She was only doing her job, she didn't deserve to be interrogated. 'You don't know how many people the Selachians have killed!' she insisted.

'I know more about the Selachians than you can imagine.'

'Good. Then you know why we have to fight them.'

'Oh, I know precisely why you're fighting them. I know who pulls the strings of the Terran Security Forces: a powerful cartel of Earth conglomerates, some of whose methods would put the Cybermen to shame!'

'The business sector finances some of our operations,' Mulholland reeled off automatically.

'We both know it does more than that.'

'In the interests of Earth security –'

'Yes, yes, "Earth security" – and Earth is still very nervous after the Dalek invasion, isn't it? So, while its governments are busy trying to pull themselves together and rebuild, in step... well, let's say, certain business concerns. They offer to take on an under-funded, token security organisation that was easily defeated by the Daleks, and to run it properly. Within five years, with full government approval, they're in control of an army capable of mounting a full-scale intergalactic war to suit their own concerns.'

'We have just liberated a planet from Selachian occupation!' Mulholland protested.

'But why? Why do it now?'

'Because it was the right thing to do.'

'No. Because the Selachians were becoming too powerful – and I don't mean their military might, I mean on the galactic markets.'

'They were trading in weapons – somebody had to deal with them.'

The Doctor laughed. 'Oh, your employers have "dealt" with them, all right. They've been dealing with the Selachians for decades, only the Selachians are rather shrewder than they imagined. A few people have had their fingers burnt. The Selachians beat them at their own game, so they've decided to play a more dangerous one.'

The décor of the *Triumph* always put Mulholland in mind of an English country mansion. Deep carpets and sumptuous artwork lined its walls. Grand staircases with wooden banisters swept between decks; bronze statues stood at their heads. In the main atrium, just beneath Redfern's office, there was even a chandelier.

Mulholland hadn't planned to accompany the Doctor all the way to the office. Now, though, she thought it best not to lose sight of him. For the past few minutes, she had avoided his eyes and tried not to think about what he had said. She didn't want to have to agree with him.

Beside the dark oak door, a brass plaque was inscribed with the words 'Request Access'. A button sat above it. Mulholland pressed it and, after a second, the door slid open. She motioned the Doctor through ahead of her.

Redfern rose from behind his desk, with a look of astonishment. As usual, the desk seemed quite empty. It held only a pen-set, a compad, a framed photograph and two novelty paperweights; between them, they covered little of its vast surface area. A water-cooler, a drinks cabinet and a comfortable couch added to the impression that the occupant of this room had time on his hands.

'Commander Redfern,' the Doctor gushed, 'I won't keep you long, I'm sure you must have plenty of things to do, but I did think we might be able to clear up our little misunderstanding.'

Redfern looked past him, to Mulholland. 'Why have you brought him here?'

'He said you wanted to see him.'

'So you let him out of his cell?'

Mulholland just gaped.

'Ah no,' said the Doctor contritely, 'I decided to find you myself, save you the trouble of coming to see me. Professor Mulholland here helped me with the directions.' He grinned like a mischievous child hoping to charm his way out of trouble.

Redfern's thin lips peeled away from his teeth. 'I happen to be busy, Doctor.'

'Well, of course you are, that's what I wanted to talk to you about.'

Redfern looked set to deliver a retort, but then a voice crackled out of the tiny speaker on the flat metal surface of his compad. 'They've made their move, sir.'

Both Redfern and his office were transformed in an instant.

Ignoring his guests, the commander dropped into his seat and punched an enticing red button on the compad. On the wall to his left – Mulholland's right – nine monitors sprang out of oak-panelled recesses and came to life. Some showed straightforward views of the ship's surroundings, others computer-plotted maps overlaid with the positions of traffic. Three of the screens contained scrolling lines of text. A tenth monitor surfaced through a hatch – previously invisible, thanks to holographic imaging – in Redfern's desk. This, Mulholland guessed, would allow him to inspect any of the nine images more closely. The Doctor scurried around the desk to peer over Redfern's shoulder. Mulholland almost did likewise, but stopped herself.

The commander gripped the compad's microphone, twisted it around on its spindly stem and leant forward until it seemed as though he was planning to bite it in two. He operated switches blindly but expertly, with his left hand. 'OK, this is it. You know what to do. Keep on that warcraft. Don't let it jump to hyperspeed.'

He kicked out and sent his chair rolling the short distance to his desk monitor. He looked surprised and furious as it collided with the Doctor.

The Doctor was flustered too. 'You can't be planning to destroy that ship!'

Redfern fumbled for his microphone and rapped, 'Security team to my office.'

The Doctor's agitation grew. 'The Selachians have prisoners aboard!'

Redfern leapt to his feet and loomed over the intruder. 'Are you telling me how to do my job?' he roared.

'Well, I think somebody ought to,' the Doctor returned, with equal anger. 'Perhaps somebody who's had a little more experience of combat than just...' He swung an arm to encompass the plush office, 'Just sitting in comfort on some faraway, well-guarded flagship and taking decisions based on graphics on screens as if war was nothing more than a, a computer game!'

His tirade over, the Doctor subsided, panted and looked up at Redfern for a response.

The commander's mouth was set into a grim line. 'I have no proof that the Selachians have live hostages. What I do know is that, after blocking their communications for weeks, I am not about to let them take information back home!'

The Doctor seemed to be fighting to keep himself from shaking. In deliberate, stressed tones, he stated, 'There are human beings on that ship!'

Redfern sat down again. 'Wars always have casualties.'

He didn't seem to care. But, then, his voice had always seemed incapable of expressing any emotion – other than anger, which he tended to convey by volume.

Two privates swept through the open door and marched towards the Doctor. 'Take him back to the brig!' ordered Redfern, without looking up.

'History won't forget this,' the Doctor blustered, as the guards seized his arms and almost carried him away. 'How does it feel that your legacy to this universe is to be remembered as a callous, misguided fool?'

Redfern didn't react. His attention was reserved for his monitor. On the centremost of the nine screens that Mulholland could see, six tiny blips converged upon a larger shark icon. She stared at the image and felt a chilling sensation sweeping across her whole body.

With the Doctor gone, she became acutely aware that she had no business in here. Backing out into the corridor, she eased the door closed. Her throat was dry and her head was spinning with thoughts.

Kalaya had fallen. The last of the Selachians' conquests had been wrested back from them. Now, they had only their home world left.

One way or another, the war was about to be won.

One way or another...

Chapter Ten

Zoe screamed as the floor tipped beneath her. She spent a futile second attempting to retain her balance, then gave in and fell like everybody else.

The ship came out of its steep bank, but lurched in the opposite direction. As Zoe slid along the marble floor she reached desperately for a handhold.

John Paterson gripped her hand in his. She gazed into his solid, craggy face and believed he could protect her. He had been her greatest source of hope throughout this ordeal. But then the ship rolled, the laws of gravity surrendered and Zoe was hurled into the centre of a flailing, bruising mass of limbs.

A significant volume of water had escaped into the hall from the lower decks, through the open hatchway. As the ship righted itself with a bump, the water hung in the air for an instant, then came down hard.

Drenched and sore, Zoe dragged herself from the heap of bodies, on all fours. Suddenly, she felt an intense, but thankfully short-lived, pressure in her stomach. The ship, she surmised, had undergone a phenomenal acceleration.

'You all right, miss?' asked Paterson, as he helped her to stand. 'We jumped to hyperspeed. Feels like your guts are trying to escape through your spine, doesn't it? Don't worry, it should be smooth going now, for a couple of hours at least.'

Zoe brushed down her crumpled overalls, ruefully. 'What happened?'

'I'm guessing we were intercepted by fighters.'

'Your people tried to rescue us?'

'Something like that.'

'But we're at hyperspeed now. Does that mean they've failed?'

'It just means we got through the blockade and away from Kalaya. Whoever's flying this crate pushed it to its limits and beyond.' Paterson sounded as if he admired the pilot. 'Doesn't look like it upset the Sharks too much.'

The Selachian guards had retained their positions. It seemed that, through the turbulence, they had remained unshaken. Perhaps they had magnetic clamps in their boots, Zoe thought, although she detected no metallic content in the marble floor. They could be using static electricity, she supposed.

Now, the Selachians moved forward as one, as if they had received simultaneous orders. They waded into the mêlée of battered prisoners and began to haul them roughly to their feet.

To some, this further mistreatment was too much. One Kalarian man fought back, pulling himself free from a Selachian's grip and pounding on its armour with his fists. Three humans joined him, faces twisted by anger. Perhaps they had not seen what Zoe had seen. Perhaps they expected the Selachians to be as shaken as they were.

Their actions stirred a quiet revolt. All across the dry part of the deck, people clambered to their feet. Some joined the fight, but not many. Most hung back, unsure, and many more watched in open-mouthed fear or tried to distance themselves from trouble.

One man took hold of the Selachian's arm. He forced it around so that its gun was pointing at its own head. Only then, it seemed, did he realise that he could not activate the weapon. The confidence drained from his expression and, in a desperate attempt to rally support, he cried out, 'Well come on then, help me! Help me!'

Zoe started forward. She was stopped both by her own nerves and by Paterson's hand on her shoulder. She turned to look at him, feeling puzzled and, in a small way, let down. He shook his head solemnly. He didn't seem frightened, just sad.

Three Selachians marched to the aid of their comrade. The rest of the guards didn't even bother. Weapons blazed, and the rebels were shot down with neither mercy nor preamble. Zoe watched in horror, as the man who had cried out was hoisted into the air by his would-be victim. He squirmed in its grasp, and screamed as it flung him to the floor. Without pausing, the Selachian turned its guns downwards and fired them into his stomach. His blood splashed the nearest of the onlookers, most of whom were backing away as far and as fast as they could through the heaving, panicking crowd.

In seconds, it was over. Six people lay dead, and the mood of the crowd had changed again, all notions of resistance crushed. Zoe saw now what Paterson must have known: that the attack had been both futile and suicidal.

'We will get out of here,' he whispered, as if sensing her need for reassurance. 'Just not yet.'

'How?' she asked.

Paterson's dark eyes twinkled as he winked at her. 'They can't be everywhere at once,' he said, nodding towards the nearest guard. Zoe found herself smiling, despite herself; trusting him, although she didn't know why.

John Paterson was short, almost as short as Zoe, but twice her age and quite heavily built. His hair had been cropped, but not severely enough to disguise its natural tight curl. His face was of the sort that Zoe had heard described as 'lived in'. Its features looked as if they had been squashed together. Behind a jutting nose that was prominent rather than large, his eyes and mouth gave the impression of being slightly sunken.

Most of all, he exuded an air of authority. His harsh, gravelly voice almost sounded wrong at normal speaking volume, as if it were used to barking orders – although he had told Zoe that his rank in the Terran Security Forces was merely that of private. Perhaps what he actually possessed, she thought, was a great deal of experience and confidence. Whatever it was, it was infectious. When Zoe was around Paterson, she felt as she often did with the Doctor: that nothing could harm her, because he would find a way to stop it. She didn't know what had made him take her under his wing – actually, she just didn't want to admit that she could have seemed so vulnerable – but she was glad of his protection and his practical advice.

'This ship has to drop down from hyperspeed eventually,' said Paterson, taking Zoe to one side. 'Now, Redfern isn't the kind of guy who gives up on anything – I'm guessing he'll have people on its tail for when it does. We're gonna be in for a bit more turbulence, I'm afraid.'

'Oh,' said Zoe, not relishing that prospect.

Paterson smiled, and nuzzled her chin with the back of one rough finger. 'Don't worry about it, miss. This time, we'll be ready.'

The next hour passed at an interminable pace.

Paterson moved slowly among the prisoners, pausing to mutter quiet words to the selected few. Some nodded, others waved him away with fear in their eyes.

Eventually, he faked weariness and lowered himself to the floor. Zoe sat by his side, a hundred questions in her mind. They had settled close to the water-filled hatchway, but not so close as to be conspicuous.

'You're not planning to go down there, are you?' she whispered.

Paterson put a finger to his lips.

His recruits joined them over the course of a good twenty minutes. They sidled over in groups of two or three, each careful to appear to the guards to be aimless wanderers. They acknowledged Paterson with no more than slight, furtive nods. Each group sat apart; one struck up a subdued conversation about past glories. Zoe began to think she would explode if something didn't happen soon.

The groups merged, one by one, their body language suggesting that the arrangement was incidental. At last, there was just one group of ten people, Zoe and Paterson included. Some lay on their backs, while others sat half-turned and inspected their fingernails as if they weren't paying attention. In reality, all waited eagerly on John Paterson's briefing.

The plan was a simple one. Simple but dangerous. Zoe began to wonder how she fitted into it. The rest of the group were all male and were older than her, fitter, more muscular and evidently more experienced. But then, thought Zoe, this was true of most of the prisoners – the humans, at least. She was probably the only non-Kalarian civilian.

She attempted to demonstrate her usefulness with comments like: 'If we could find a way to break the electrostatic connection between the Selachians' armour and the floor...' and: 'I wonder if we could poison their water supply?' The others made it clear that they wouldn't be fighting their captors, at least not unarmed. Nor was it practical to organise a mass break-out. They were aiming at nothing higher than a small escape bid.

It almost sounded selfish, but Paterson assured Zoe that they would help everybody by taking information back to the Terran Security Forces. Many of the prisoners, representatives of failed and lost missions, had plenty to tell about Selachian tactics and weaponry. 'I doubt if Redfern knows they're even shipping all these people back home,' said Paterson. 'He'll have written most of us off as dead on the ocean floor.'

Zoe nodded eagerly. 'It will certainly help if I can contact the Doctor and tell him where we are. He'll sort the Selachians out.' It wasn't the first time she had mentioned her friend.

'Listen, miss,' said Paterson, seriously, 'are you sure you want to do this?'

'Of course I'm sure. As I said, if I can contact the Doctor...'

'I don't want to leave a girl like you with the Sharks,' he interrupted, 'but this could be dangerous. Not all of us are going to make it.'

Zoe's cheeks burnt with humiliation. 'Are *you* sure you want to go?' she asked. Paterson was too taken aback to reply. 'Good. Then so am I.'

The soldier smiled thinly – but did his dark eyes betray admiration for her spirit, or simply concern for her life?

Zoe's stomach churned again, as the ship returned to normal speed. She tensed. Looking into Paterson's eyes, she saw worry there too. She almost wanted to back out after all, to take her chances here.

Then the ship lurched as, presumably, it came under fire again.

This time, the prisoners were better prepared. Some held on to the marble pillars around the hall, but there were too many people and too few handholds.

Zoe clung to Paterson. She counted to ten. They made their break for the water.

They almost didn't make it. The ship changed direction and, suddenly, Zoe was sliding away from her goal. She recovered, found Paterson's hand again and leapt with him.

She seemed to hang in mid-air for an eternity, expecting to feel gunfire on her back. But the Selachians, faced with chaos, were slow to react to the surprising sight of ten prisoners diving for the lower, waterlogged deck.

Zoe almost exhaled in shock as she felt cold water in her face. The water was choppy, dark and filled with particles of green silt. Her eyes stung and she had to close them. She floundered for a long time, getting nowhere and worrying about the possibility of pursuit. Perhaps, she hoped, the Selachians couldn't follow. Perhaps they couldn't take a step without sacrificing their balance.

But there would be Selachians down here too.

The water began to settle. Paterson had predicted that this fight with the Terran Security Forces would be briefer than the last one. The Selachians' propulsion systems were more efficient than those of the TSF. Outnumbered, the warcraft would be screaming towards its home world, with Redfern's fighters on its tail.

The would-be escapees needed to find the ship's escape pods before it got there.

Zoe forced her eyes open. The others had studied the standard layout of these vessels; they knew where they were going. She did not. Fortunately, they had not abandoned her. Paterson was still there, motioning her on through giant green shapes that looked like sleeping monsters but which, on closer inspection, turned out to be banks of instruments.

Zoe's lungs began to ache. She wondered how much further she had to go.

That was when the creatures attacked.

She thought they were Kalarians, at first. They had the same spindly build and pink skin They had narrow black eyes, thin, straight, lipless mouths and no noses. But, in place of hair, they had white, wavy crests. Zoe counted four of them, but there could have been more. They appeared from nowhere, each leaping on one of the escapees.

Three tapered fingers reached around Zoe's head from behind and clawed at her face. Another creature. She struggled, but it was surprisingly strong. Fortunately, Paterson had seen her plight. He swam to her with three sure strokes, and prised her attacker away. Zoe gasped and lost most of her air. She watched the ensuing battle, noticing with detached interest the rows of gills down each of the creature's sides and the golden nodules down the centre of its back.

She threw herself at it, hoping to wrest it from her friend. She couldn't do much, but she did provide the distraction Paterson needed. He caught the creature in a choke-hold. It fought back for a moment, then went limp. Paterson pushed it away and beckoned urgently to Zoe.

She tried to follow him, but black shapes appeared at the edge of her vision. Blood pounded in her ears. Her chest and stomach ached from the effort of not drawing breath.

Paterson took her arm and dragged her along. She felt like a limp rag. She tried to recall the concentration techniques she had learned at school, to forget her discomfort and just swim.

She wasn't aware of what had happened to the other escapees. She didn't know where the pink creatures were, nor whether any Selachians had pursued her. She only knew that Paterson had brought her to a circular door and that he was turning its locking wheel. The mottled, fleshy door rolled open, as did an identical door behind it. Zoe almost collapsed through both of them.

She found herself in a tiny, spherical compartment, surrounded by control panels. As Paterson closed the doors behind them, she realised there was no other exit. They had made it to an escape pod – and the pod was full of water.

Well of course, she thought dimly, it would be. Why hadn't she thought of that?

Then Zoe surrendered to the inevitable and blacked out.

Chapter Eleven

Kent Michaels wondered if he would see the tunnel of light again. Surely it was time by now.

But no. The blackness in which he found himself was populated only by vague shapes, elusive silhouettes thrown up by a brain half-aware of its unconscious state.

He saw the social worker who had come to inform him of his father's death, although he couldn't recall his father's face. No wonder, when he had seen so much more of his fists.

He saw the sneering, self-satisfied thugs at the euphemistically styled juvenile care centre. They had taunted him because he was different, withdrawn. Some evenings, to appease them, he had roamed the streets with them. They had played baseball in the rubble or hot-wired antique cars or pooled their credits and pleaded with strangers to buy them beer.

At least three of them were dead now.

Mostly, Michaels had just wanted to be left alone. He had had little time for other people. After all, other people had seldom made time for him. He had enjoyed reading, playing puzzle games or working out in the gym where a friend of his father let him use the equipment for free. Joe McTavish had not been a talkative man, which had suited young Kent. Sometimes, though, as Joe watched him sparring with holographic opponents, a tear had come to his eye and he had commented on how proud Michaels's parents would have been. Their little boy had grown into a fine, strapping young man.

Kent Michaels hadn't cared. His parents were just names on a birth certificate that he had burnt after his first and last meeting with his dipsomaniac mother.

His new athletic build had mostly kept the bullies away, but their sniping had continued from the sidelines. One day, William Butcher had pushed him too far. Michaels remembered the unique, inexplicable feeling of something that had been coiled tightly inside him giving way like a dam, releasing a flood of adrenaline and hot blood.

It had been a joke about his mother that had done it.

A team of carers had dragged the incoherently raging fifteen-year-old boy from his victim. Through the darkness, now, Michaels saw a stark image of that moment. Butcher on the floor, whimpering and bleeding; the other kids cowering away in fear and, though he still hated to acknowledge it, with new respect in their eyes.

Three days before Kent Michaels's sixteenth birthday, before the centre had cast him out to fend for himself, Butcher had taken his revenge in typical cowardly fashion.

The only thing Michaels remembered about that day was the tunnel of light.

Today, though, the tunnel didn't come. The darkness receded, and he blinked as the harsh, white lights of the carrier ship's infirmary seared his retinas. He twitched a hand experimentally, then used his elbows to lever himself into a sitting position in his bed. His head ached, but he was not wired up to anything. This time, it had not been serious.

'The Sharks did a good job, sir,' said one of the grimy, tired privates who had been pressed into service to treat the occupants of thirty beds and as many more mattresses and trolleys. 'Too good. They pulverised the escarpment. The fall looked bad, but it was all silt and pebbles. Plenty of people buried, but not many seriously hurt.'

Michaels wasn't interested in the details. There were always details.

William Butcher, he recalled, had cracked his head open with an industrial spanner. He should have died then, too.

The surgeons had put his failure to do so down to willpower or, as one had put it, sheer obstinacy. The tunnel had opened for him, dispelling the darkness, and he had taken a few faltering steps along it. Then he had stopped and begun to wonder what was waiting for him at its end.

Michaels was not a religious man. He was rational and cynical enough to have put his vision down to a dream born of delirium, given form by countless telepress and television reports of similar near-death experiences. Even at the time, he had recalled the breathless recollections of those who had almost slipped away; how they too had seen the tunnel and, beyond it, the beckoning forms of loved ones who had passed though it before them.

For Michaels, the tunnel had been empty. There had been nobody to greet him. So, he had simply turned away and gone back home.

The private handed Michaels a painkiller, which he swallowed gratefully. He put his hand to his side, remembering the gash that had been torn there. Plastiflesh had been applied to the wound. The synthetic covering purported to emulate skin in all respects, including the fact that it would be shed as a new layer grew. Its patent-holders boasted that it even felt natural. To Michaels, it felt as though a lump of plastic had been grafted on to his ribs. It had already hardened, so he gladly – if a little painfully – gave up his bed.

Another battle over. Another battle survived.

It had to happen some time. He knew that whatever force had chosen to spare him two decades ago would let him go eventually.

Death held no terror for Michaels, just an abiding sadness. His tunnel would still be empty, next time. Now, however, he would at least enjoy the camaraderie of like-minded people on its far side: many, many soldiers alongside whom he had fought, although he had barely known most of them.

And the occasional one who, through an accident of circumstance and emotions, he had come to know too well.

Outside the ship, a wet mist hung in cold air. There were depressingly few soldiers around. Most were nursing wounds or reflecting on lost friends, while others had made a half-hearted start on collapsing the dome-shaped tents. More carriers would arrive soon. They would take the remaining troops back to the fighters, to await instructions. Perhaps Michaels would find himself on Ockora in a few days' time. Perhaps he would be sent elsewhere.

Jamie sat at the long, wooden table next to the ship, staring distractedly into the distance as he chewed on a vitamin pill. Michaels felt a rush of relief as he saw him, but fought to deny it. It was still probable that he would outlive Jamie. He couldn't afford to like him too much.

He sat down beside the lad and gave him a pat on the shoulder. To his concern, it was almost paternal. 'You OK?'

Jamie acknowledged him with a watery smile and waved his right arm, the lower portion of which was encased in a healing tube. 'I'll be fine, as soon as I get out of this thing. What is it, anyway?'

Michaels was only slightly bemused that Jamie did not recognise such a basic piece of kit. The lad's naïvety, whilst faintly endearing, was a puzzle. Perhaps he came from Agora or somewhere, one of those colonies whose people had eschewed technology – but that didn't square with the idea of somebody who had casually jumped into a spaceship and gone exploring with his friends, only to end up stranded in a war zone.

He took Jamie's arm, operated the tube's diagnostic sensors and checked the read-out on its display screen. 'Looks like you've broken a bone in there. The tube says it'll heal in thirty-two hours. You're stuck with it.'

Jamie sighed and became glassy-eyed again. 'You heard about Lieutenant Marsh?'

Michaels hadn't – he had deliberately not asked about anyone – but he could guess.

'The whole detail, gone. The Selachians must have killed them.'

'Or taken them prisoner,' suggested Michaels, without believing it.

'Oh no, they were fighting for keeps down there.' Jamie clenched his fists in frustration. 'I should have been with them!'

'What for?'

'I might have been able to help.'

'Or you might have died.'

'I could have done something!'

Michaels shook his head, then wished he hadn't. The motion made him feel dizzy. 'Listen, you can't afford to think like that. You have to forget about it and move on.'

'How can I?'

'Because you have no choice!'

'How can you be so cold about it?'

'I'm being practical.'

'Now look, I've seen people die before, but all this…'

'This is war,' said Michaels. 'What else did you expect?'

Jamie didn't respond.

Sergeant Cosgrove marched proudly into the clearing. Behind him came three privates and, between them, a water tank floating on an anti-grav cushion. A scrawny, pink-skinned creature lay still within the tank. The water had been clouded by violet blood.

'Looks like we've hooked us a Shark,' said Michaels, approvingly. The capture of a Selachian was a rare event: it meant the alien was alive but too badly injured to operate the termination protocol in its battlesuit. 'I don't suppose it'll tell us more than the others did.'

Jamie stared at the unconscious creature. He kept on staring after it had been taken on to the carrier ship. He was silent for a minute or more. Then, still without a word, he got to his feet and walked briskly into the forest, head bowed and fists still clenched.

Michaels watched him go, but didn't follow. The lad was suffering from shell shock. He just needed time. Anyway, Michaels was used to people leaving him, one way or another.

Irene had left him, after only a month. Citing callous indifference on her husband's part, she had had their marriage annulled under new 'cooling off period' rules.

Michaels had let her go without a struggle. In truth, he had not been upset. He had met Irene whilst shovelling fries for a burger chain. She had been lonely, and perhaps he too had thought that he might need somebody. That month had taught him what he really wanted – and it wasn't to go through the motions of life.

When Kent Michaels had joined the Terran Security Forces, it had felt right. For the first time, he had felt as if he belonged somewhere. Moreover, he was doing something positive, making use of the extra time he had been granted. At first, he hadn't even had to think too hard. He had done as he was told, and had made lives better in the process. He had risen quickly through the ranks – partly because of his quiet confidence and efficiency, partly because many people who were more qualified had died around him – and had been surprised to find that the role of an officer in the field suited him. He didn't mind making tactical decisions and giving orders. He had the experience to do so. And, so long as he could remain detached, so long as he didn't think of the soldiers under his command as human beings, then it was still just a job.

Kent Michaels now had a solid reason not to form personal attachments. It suited him well.

'Lieutenant Michaels! Over here, quick!'

Michaels jumped to his feet, alarmed by the urgency in Jamie's voice. He raced after the lad, through the trees, and found him only a few metres away. He was staring, wide-eyed, at a creature that Michaels could only have described as a green blob. Over a metre high, and half as wide, it advanced with a painstaking shuffle. It possessed no facial features, but it was making a quiet gurgling sound to itself. Briefly, Michaels wondered if it was an indigenous life form, but he had not seen its like in all the time he had been on this world.

The creature had all the hallmarks of the Selachians' organic technology.

Jamie looked nervous, but he stood his ground. He had unsheathed the long dagger that he had insisted on keeping at his side. He hefted it threateningly, but the blob drew nearer.

Then Michaels realised it was not alone.

Some way behind Jamie, another blob was shambling towards the clearing. Michaels whirled around and caught a glimpse of a third, behind him.

Of course – the Selachians had left one final trap. These bio-engineered monstrosities had probably been lurking on the seabed for weeks, waiting for their masters to activate a signal as they fled. How Cosgrove and his men had missed them, Michaels didn't know – probably too caught up in their find, he supposed, and of course nobody was expecting trouble now – but the creatures had already surrounded the humans' camp and they were closing in.

Which meant that, logically, they had to have offensive capability.

'Get away from it, Jamie,' warned Michaels. Too late.

It seemed, for an instant, that the creature's head – if it truly had a head – had exploded. Slimy, wriggling tentacles – ten of them, at least – burst outwards, thrusting towards Jamie. Caught off guard, he was ensnared by three of them. He cried out, more in indignation than fear, and tried to lift his weapon, but his right arm was pinned to his side. As Jamie struggled helplessly, the other strands wrapped themselves around him.

Then something else emerged from the blob: a shorter, thicker appendage, blood red, with a pulsating end that tapered to a sharp point. It hovered, flexing this way and that like a snake taking aim, then it struck with lightning speed and embedded itself in its target's forehead.

The entire attack had taken no more than two seconds. Michaels hesitated for just that long. He ought to get back to the camp and sound the alarm.

But Jamie was screaming.

Michaels dashed to the lad's side. He pulled at the tentacles and managed to yank one free. Immediately, it snapped around his wrist and held it tight.

Jamie fell to his knees. The long dagger dropped from his hand. Michaels made a lunge for it and hacked savagely at the red tentacle. The blade cut deeply and emerged with violet stains. The blob shrieked and quivered and lurched backwards. Its damaged tentacle snapped and left its pointed end buried in Jamie's head.

The other tentacles went limp. The creature sagged. Jamie toppled on to his face.

Michaels heard the sound of gunfire.

The other creatures had reached the camp. They had attacked without warning. To protect Jamie, he had risked many other lives. He was ashamed of himself.

There was nothing he could do for the lad now. He couldn't even afford the time to check if he was dead or merely unconscious. He had lost his rifle during the avalanche, but he still had Jamie's blade. He gripped it in both hands and raced back to the carrier ship.

Doing his duty, as usual.

Chapter Twelve

Zoe lay on her back, sank into the soft surface of the escape pod and allowed the sun to dry her baggy overalls and warm her face.

The sky was a beautiful azure in colour, and perfectly clear. The sound of water lapping against the pod infused Zoe with a feeling of calm. In other circumstances, she could just have lain here and dozed happily. But the idyllic setting was belied by the circumstances in which she had come to it.

She had woken in the pod with a stomach ache and a fire in her lungs. Immediately, she had coughed up water and taken several deep, wracking breaths.

'Easy, easy, you're OK now,' John Paterson had assured her.

She had sat up awkwardly, bracing herself against a console but flinching from it as she realised it was warm and seemed to have a pulse.

Pools of stagnant water had gathered in every crevice. Zoe had tried to ask a question, but found herself coughing again. Still, Paterson had seemed to know what was on her mind.

'I drained the water.' He had grinned then. 'You didn't think we'd have to hold our breath 'til we got rescued, did you?'

'Of course not. But how did you do it?'

'Just pressed a switch. We must have left quite a trail of ice behind us.'

'Why would a Selachian pod contain a system for draining out water?' Zoe could never be satisfied until she knew exactly how and why things worked.

'The Sharks aren't totally nuts, you know. If they can negotiate for what they want, they'll do it. They bring air-breathers on to their ships all the time – and a lot of their technology is alien and won't work under water. You'll find most of their vehicles have evac systems, just in case. Lucky for us.'

Her curiosity sated, Zoe had asked, 'What happens now?'

'We wait. With luck, one of our side will see us drifting and reel us in. Unless…'

'Unless what?'

Paterson had sighed. 'Unless the warcraft got too close to Ockora before we jettisoned. If it did, the pod will have latched on to it. We'll be on our way down there.'

Zoe had been dismayed at this revelation. She had wondered what terrors might await her on the Selachians' home world. Still, she had resolved to make the most of her respite. Settling back, she had listened to the steady whirr of the pod's oxygen-generation unit and remembered how glad she was to be able to breathe at all.

She wondered how many of the other would-be escapees had made it.

Unfortunately, the pod was as small as Zoe had remembered. Even she could barely have stood upright in it. She had found it hard to settle into a comfortable position, particularly as she had suddenly felt the urge to stretch every one of her tired muscles.

Paterson had grinned ruefully. 'I'll say one thing about the Selachians: without their battlesuits, they're flexible buggers.'

Zoe's memory of her confinement was uncomfortable. Now she extended her arms and legs gratefully, and felt her muscles unknot. She was still a little queasy, though. The bobbing motion of the floating pod didn't help, nor did its spongy surface – like that of the transport on Kalaya – which felt somehow greasy despite having been badly scorched. Zoe felt as if she was lying on a giant, mouldy, overcooked meatball – and sometimes she felt it contracting and expanding, as if breathing.

She stole a glance behind her, shielding her eyes against the sun. They were still on course for the island. At the current rate of drift, another twenty minutes should do it.

She remembered what Paterson had said about the Selachians. It discomfited her now as much as it had then.

It had not occurred to Zoe, when the pink creatures had attacked her during her escape from the warcraft, that they were what lurked beneath the Selachians' armour. It should have done, she thought. She ought to have realised that the golden studs on their backs were surgical implants, allowing them to plug their nervous systems into their battlesuits.

The idea appalled her. When Zoe thought back and imagined the creatures without their simple faces twisted by hatred, she realised how frail, almost delicate, they must have been. But that same hatred had driven them to mutilate themselves. According to Paterson, they even amputated their tails in favour of their battlesuits' artificial legs.

The people of Ockora had crippled themselves in their natural element for the sake of attaining manoeuvrability, power and a fearsome new image above water.

Zoe could no longer think about the Selachians without being sickened, for a whole host of reasons. So she had felt a wave of nausea when Paterson had inspected the pod's instruments and announced, unhappily, that it was descending.

With a sigh, Zoe had said, 'Then we did all this for nothing.'

'It's a big old world down there,' Paterson had told her. 'Just 'cos we're landing on it doesn't mean the Selachians have us.'

'Won't it be an aquatic world? We'll be stuck in the pod, surely?'

'I've set the buoyancy controls. We'll float to an island. There are plenty of them.'

'But then what can we do?'

Paterson had leant closer to Zoe and lowered his rough

voice, as if afraid that somebody might overhear him. 'The Sharks don't know it, but we put four T-Mat terminals on Ockora months ago. If we can find one, we can 'mat straight up to the flagship.'

'That's wonderful! Do you know where the terminals are?'

Paterson's face had fallen then. 'It's a big old world,' he had repeated, with a shrug.

The pod had become awfully hot upon contact with the Ockoran atmosphere. Zoe had not needed the extra discomfort, but had had no option but to bear it. Having a good idea of the amount of heat generated by re-entry, she had just been glad that the tiny vessel's shielding was strong enough to keep her alive.

Even so, the descent had seemed to take for ever. She had found it difficult to breathe in the increasingly stifling atmosphere.

The pod's gravity stabilisers, on the other hand, were very efficient. Zoe hadn't felt as though she was dropping at all. She had only become aware that the pod had landed when its circular door rolled open automatically and stark, bright light flooded in.

As Paterson had predicted, they had found themselves adrift on an ocean. Cold water had splashed into the pod and swirled around their feet. Zoe had tasted it experimentally and, detecting no salt, had leant out of the door and taken a long, much-needed drink.

She had been disappointed, though, to learn that there was no way to propel the pod or to steer it. 'It's only designed to get us to the nearest planet,' Paterson had explained. 'Most of its systems were frazzled in re-entry. Now we're here, we're supposed to rely on being picked up. Don't worry,' he had added quickly, 'I've disabled the beacon.'

Paterson made Zoe feel like an old-fashioned damsel in

distress. No matter what the situation, he always seemed to have solved their problems before she could even work out what they were. He must have seen her as a burden – he had almost said as much on the warcraft – and she hated that. She was bright and resourceful, if only she could have the chance to prove it. But she didn't have Paterson's experience, or his knowledge of this time and place.

Of course, it was the same with the Doctor sometimes – but he took pains to explain the basics to her, allowing her to work the rest out for herself. And he was prone to making mistakes. With the Doctor, Zoe felt useful.

'Ockora is dotted with small islands. We'll have to run into one of them, sooner or later.'

Desperate to escape from the confines of the pod Zoe had clambered on to its roof, to discover that Paterson had been right. The horizon was a long way distant in all directions, and she could see at least twenty small islands. The pod was drifting directly towards one of the larger ones. At first, it had seemed close – no more than two kilometres away – but the distance decreased with painful slowness.

Zoe looked at the island again, longingly. Its shore of golden sand seemed doubly welcoming after Kalaya's grey equivalent. Beyond that there was a barrier of lush green trees, not unlike the palm trees of Earth. Zoe saw them as a source of heat, of shelter and, if they were lucky, of food. She began to feel that, if they could reach them, they would be safe.

'We could even collect wood and make a raft,' she had suggested, 'and I'll bet we could rig up a sail. We'd be able to explore the other islands and look for a T-Mat terminal.'

Paterson had smiled indulgently, as if that had been his plan all along.

'Hey, Miss Heriot! Zoe!'

Zoe jerked awake, and almost slid off the pod in the process.

She threw out her arms to steady herself. 'What is it?'

Paterson was hauling himself on to the roof. He had something between his teeth: some sort of cord, but slimy and dark. Zoe felt cold. The sky had darkened, and a chill breeze was blowing. The water was disturbed and the pod was rocking quite violently. How had she managed to sleep? She must have been more tired than she had thought.

With a sudden, terrible fear, she turned to look behind her. 'Oh no,' she moaned.

They had been knocked off course. The island was close, so temptingly close – just under three hundred metres away, she thought. But the pod was drifting away at an angle to it.

Paterson sat beside her and pulled the cord from his mouth. Zoe recognised it as the sort of brown rope with which the Selachians had bound her. It trailed over the edge of the pod behind Paterson.

'We aren't gonna get any closer,' he said. 'We've got two choices. We can stay here and wait 'til we bump into another island, but it's getting late.'

'And the Selachians might see us at any moment.'

He nodded grimly. 'I reckon we swim for it.'

Zoe swallowed as she looked at the seemingly vast – and increasingly threatening – expanse of water between pod and island. It wasn't that far, she told herself, not really. But she was tired and sore.

'I can go by myself,' offered Paterson. He waved the end of the rope. 'This is tied good and tight to a console inside. I don't want to leave this thing drifting for the Sharks to find – once I get to the island, I'll reel it in. You too, if you like.'

'No,' said Zoe definitely. 'I'll come with you.'

Paterson didn't argue. 'I could do with your help,' he said.

For the first time since embarking on this insane escape bid, Zoe smiled.

* * *

By the time she had swum ashore – taking longer than Paterson, but determined to reach the island without help – the sun had begun to dip below the horizon. The temperature had dropped, too. Zoe shivered in her wet overalls, missing the warm top that the Selachians had destroyed. She pulled off her drenched stockings and was pleased to feel that at least the sand had retained some of the sun's heat.

She was forced to ignore her discomfort. Paterson needed her to help drag the escape pod on to the beach, against the current of the water. The task was more difficult than Zoe had imagined, even though she was aware that Paterson was doing most of the work. She fell more than once as the brown rope slipped between her fingers. But, finally, the great green sphere ran aground.

Paterson wanted to haul it further, until it was out of sight – but Zoe forgot her pride and confessed to being exhausted. Paterson seemed almost ready to drop too. 'OK,' he said, 'I suppose it can't do much harm here for one night.'

'Good. I don't think I could do anything now but sleep.'

'Not yet, I'm afraid. We need to build a fire.'

'Won't the Selachians see it?'

'We'll be in more trouble if we don't. It gets cold here at night. We'll go into the forest – it should be thick enough to keep most of the smoke in.'

Zoe sighed and prepared herself for a trek.

'When was the last time you ate?' asked Paterson, as they crossed the tree line.

Zoe shrugged. The Selachians had neglected to feed their prisoners, at least while she had been among them. Her last meal had been in the TARDIS, just before it had landed. Disconcertingly, she had no idea how long ago that had been. It was night-time now on Ockora, but it could have been mid-morning on Kalaya.

Paterson stopped and hunkered down beside a bush that

sprouted maroon-tinged, star-shaped leaves. 'The Sharks had me for over a week. They brought out some slop when they could be bothered to remember us, but it wasn't what I call food.'

Standing up again, he opened his hand to reveal ten tiny, violet berries. Zoe took one and placed it in her mouth. It fizzed and dissolved on her tongue, leaving a pleasant taste like bitter cherries. As she swallowed its juice, she felt a pleasant warm rush to her stomach.

'Here,' said Paterson, 'take them.' He tipped the rest of the berries into Zoe's hand, then crouched down to collect more.

Zoe ate the berries gratefully. They must have contained some type of stimulant, as they made her feel invigorated. She worried briefly about what she might be putting into her body, but she really had little choice in the matter.

She followed Paterson a short way further inland, until he stopped at a point that looked like all the others and announced, 'This'll do for tonight. We don't want to be too far from water. Why don't you go find some more berries, while I see what I can do about a fire?'

'OK,' said Zoe, surprising herself with her keenness.

'Don't go too far,' Paterson warned. 'We don't want you getting lost.'

'Oh, don't worry,' Zoe said breezily. 'That won't happen.'

Over the next twenty minutes, Zoe became very grateful for her sense of direction. Ockora seemed to have no moon and, though plenty of stars shone in its clear sky, the canopy of the forest blocked much of their light. Zoe's eyes adjusted to the dark as best they could, but even she had to stop every hundred paces or so to reassure herself that she could find her way back to Paterson.

Fortunately, the distinctive maroon bushes seemed plentiful, although she sustained a few scratches in the process of feeling for them. She picked as many berries as she could hold, ate half of them and then searched for more.

The island was smaller than Zoe had calculated. She had set off on a course parallel to the beach on which she had landed, but now she could hear the ocean ahead of her. It was time to turn back, she decided.

Then she heard movement through the trees, as though something was being dragged. Somebody was there – somebody who didn't care about being heard.

Zoe's heart leapt, but she calmed herself quickly. It had to be Paterson. She almost called to him, but caution got the better of her. What would he be doing here? Why would he make so much noise?

She crept forward, flattened herself against a broad tree trunk and peered around it.

She stifled a gasp.

Barely fifty metres away – much closer than Zoe had thought – she saw an Ockoran native. It was using its thin, pink arms to pull itself along the forest floor. Behind it, a glistening, scaled tail flapped uselessly. Zoe wondered if the being had been washed up somehow – but no. It wore a transparent, water-filled mask, from which a hose snaked to what looked like a small, green, octopus-like creature, clinging to its back. The Ockoran's movements were awkward but purposeful. It came to a stop, and Zoe realised that it had found one of the maroon bushes. Like her, it was collecting food. It gathered the violet berries and dropped them into a grey sack that hung from a cord around its slender neck.

Zoe was both terrified and mesmerised.

The creature turned, and stiffened, and emitted a sound that was very much like a gasp. Its eyesight must have been keen. It had seen her.

She didn't know what to do. The creature looked harmless enough, but then so had the unarmoured Ockorans on the warcraft.

John Paterson appeared, wielding a thick branch. Zoe cried out as she saw what he was doing, but too late. He brought the weapon down on the Ockoran's head. It whimpered and tried to roll over, to face its attacker. Paterson hit it again. It collapsed, with a pitiful mewling. He reached down and ripped the pack from its back. The mask came with it. Water gushed into the soil. The Ockoran began to thrash its arms and tail.

'No!' cried Zoe, dropping her berries as she ran on to the scene. 'No, leave it alone – it wasn't doing any harm!'

Paterson stepped back, nonplussed. Zoe leaned over the Ockoran and tried to pick it up. 'What do you think you're doing?' bellowed Paterson.

'I'm taking it to the water. At least it might stand a chance there.'

He grabbed her by the arms and dragged her to one side. 'Are you insane? Do you know what that thing is?'

'Of course I know what it is – it's a living being!'

'And this is a war! Do you want it to bring reinforcements?'

Zoe didn't, but neither did she want the Ockoran to die. 'You can't just kill it in cold blood!'

'It would have killed us without a thought.'

'It doesn't even have implants – it can't ever have worn a battlesuit!'

'They don't need armour to hate us!'

Paterson relaxed his grip then, and Zoe felt a dreadful plunging sensation in her stomach as she saw that the creature had ceased its struggles. It didn't move even when Paterson nudged it tentatively with his toe.

'We didn't have a choice,' he insisted.

Zoe thought she would never sleep that night. She lay in the dwindling glow of the fire, beneath a blanket of bracken, and saw the Ockoran's face – the downward turn of its narrow mouth – each time she closed her eyes.

She had trusted Paterson, believed in him. She would not have thought him capable of such a brutal killing. And yet, he had seemed to genuinely regret the necessity for his action – and perhaps he was right, perhaps it was necessary. After all, he knew this world and its people far better than she did.

Paterson was just a soldier, surviving the only way he knew how.

But the Doctor would have found another way.

At last, exhaustion took its toll, and Zoe slept deeply. When she woke, she was choking on black smoke, and Paterson was standing over her, shaking her.

'The Sharks – they're here on the island!'

'What? How did they find us?' she asked blearily, scrambling to her feet.

'I dunno. Perhaps they saw the escape pod.'

'Or perhaps they came to see what had happened to their friend!'

'Whatever,' said Paterson, taking Zoe's arm and dragging her away from the camp site. 'They're here!'

She had barely taken ten steps before she started coughing again. A thin haze hung in the air, and she heard the crackling of flames. 'What are they doing?'

'Smoking us out.'

Zoe renewed her efforts to keep up. Whenever she flagged, Paterson pulled her along. They changed course once, suddenly, and Zoe caught a glimpse of an armoured Selachian through the trees. Its arms were extended as it shot flames into the undergrowth, setting it alight. Zoe felt a chill at this reminder of the creatures' ruthlessness. They were prepared to raze the whole island to find their enemies.

'Where are we going?' she cried.

'To the beach.'

'What for?'

'We've got no choice. We're gonna have to swim for it!'

'We can't do that – we'll never reach another island!'

'We can't stay here, miss!'

Paterson was right, Zoe knew it. His plan was suicidal, but she could think of nothing better. 'This is the quickest way,' she said resignedly, pointing.

They passed numerous fires, and knew that the Selachians had been this way. Zoe's lungs hurt and tears dripped from her eyes. She was beginning to feel light-headed. Fortunately, they were nearing the forest's edge.

They reached it and froze, afraid of stepping into the open. Paterson looked from the ocean to Zoe to the ocean again, weighing up his options.

Zoe shook her head, breathlessly. 'I can't do it, I can't!'

Paterson's gaze lingered on her. Then he nuzzled her chin with his finger and grunted, 'I'll come back for you, miss!'

He left Zoe's side, too quickly for her to stop him. She wasn't sure if she even wanted to. Had she been able to, she would have held her breath as Paterson raced across the beach.

Halfway to the water, the ground exploded beneath him. He was hurled through the air, landing heavily on his back.

Zoe almost went to him, but she stopped herself. She turned to run back into the forest, but she couldn't do that either. Smoke billowed from within it and forced her back.

And then it was too late to do anything, as Selachians burst out of the trees on each side of her. She screamed and backed away from them. They herded her on to the beach. Zoe saw that six more of the creatures were approaching from all sides. One had even emerged from the water and was wading ashore. How they had done it, she didn't know, but they must have been aware of their targets' location for minutes.

She found herself by Paterson's side. He stood painfully, and they clung to each other as the monsters closed in around them.

As one, the Selachians raised their weapons.

Chapter Thirteen

Jamie dreamt of blood and smoke and of friends slipping through his desperate grasp. The dream went on for the longest of times, but he could not make himself wake.

When finally he did, he was short of breath and studded with beads of sweat. His heart was racing. He reached out into the empty air and called Zoe's name.

The Doctor was beside him, calming him as always. He wiped Jamie's forehead with a handkerchief soaked in cold water. It felt blissful. Accepting that the dream was over, Jamie relaxed and let his head sink back into a deep pillow.

Part of what the Doctor was saying finally registered. 'You're on the *Triumph* – the TSF's flagship, remember?' He grinned impishly and pointed. 'The TARDIS is only a few hundred metres behind that wall.'

'The TARDIS, aye... the *Triumph*...' Fragmented memories were falling into place. Jamie frowned at one unpleasant recollection and lifted his head, to assure his befuddled mind that the Doctor was really there. 'They took you to their ship. That Redfern, he took you away from me. And Zoe – what's happened to Zoe?'

'It's all right, Jamie, I'm here.'

He felt the handkerchief on his brow again, and the Doctor's hand squeezing his hand.

'I think you should rest now. You've had a nasty experience.'

'Aye, rest.' Cold water dribbled on to Jamie's eyelids and seemed to hold them closed. His worries and questions melted away as he was enfolded in a comfortable, warm, dark shroud.

This time, there were no bad dreams.

* * *

Jamie woke only once in the next eight hours. His head was clearer now, though he was still tired and washed out. He blinked several times to adjust to the gentle lighting and, for the first time, he got an impression of his surroundings.

The dark-stained, wood-panelled walls came as a surprise. He saw a watercolour picture of a riverside scene, hanging beside a tall wardrobe with ornate brass handles. The head of his bed was made of brass too, fashioned into spiral patterns. A grandfather clock ticked softly to itself by the door.

Jamie had no doubt, though, that he was in a hospital. Something about its smell gave it away, as did the feel of crisp, slightly abrasive sheets and the emergency cord which hung by his left ear.

Somebody had dressed him in pink-striped pyjamas.

There were two more beds to his left. The furthest one was empty, but the nearest had had its mattress removed and a water tank put in its place. Beside the bed stood a trolley containing angular lumps of machinery. From these, wires led into the tank and connected with its occupant. Jamie felt a shiver of both fear and loathing at the sight of the captured Selachian.

Fortunately, the Doctor was there too. He sat in a chair to Jamie's right, a large hardback book resting on his lap. Engrossed in his reading, he didn't seem to have noticed that Jamie had woken. As he lifted the book to turn its page, Jamie saw its title: *Moby Dick*.

Secure in the Doctor's presence, he allowed sleep to overtake him again.

An indeterminate time later, Jamie was sitting up in bed and gulping water from a beaker. By the time he had drained it, his throat had begun to feel normal again. 'I needed that!' he exclaimed. 'I don't think I've ever been so parched.'

'Well, that's not surprising, Jamie.' The Doctor had laced his fingers together and was playing with them nervously. Jamie steeled himself to hear bad news. 'You see, you've been living off injections of water and essential vitamins for some time.'

'Eh? I don't get it.'

'You've been unconscious for just over three days.'

'What?' Jamie stared blankly at his friend. The claim seemed nonsensical. 'But I can't have been. I don't even know what happened to me.'

The Doctor seemed about to tell him, but Jamie was struck by a more urgent thought. 'What about Zoe? Have you rescued her yet?'

'I'm afraid not.'

'Well, what are these people doing about it?'

The Doctor chose his words carefully. 'Unfortunately, Commander Redfern won't believe me when I tell him the Selachians have prisoners.'

'You mean he thinks they've killed Zoe?'

'He's wrong, of course,' said the Doctor, quickly allaying Jamie's fears. 'But then, he doesn't share our, ah, historical perspective, does he? Don't worry, Zoe will be quite safe for the time being. The Selachians won't harm a valuable hostage.'

'I suppose not,' conceded Jamie. 'Hey, how come you're walking about free, anyway?'

'Oh, I think the commander appreciates I'm no threat to him now.'

'Ah, you mean he knows we're on his side?'

'Let's just say he has changed his opinion of my motives.'

'But he doesn't believe you about Zoe.'

'No, Jamie. Still, I've been working on him with my diplomatic skills.'

'Oh no,' groaned Jamie, 'you haven't!'

'He did agree to have you brought over here – although, actually, I think your friend, Lieutenant Michaels, had a great deal to do with that.'

'Lieutenant Michaels?'

'Yes, yes, he's stationed on the *Triumph* – well, he's been made the senior lieutenant on the mission now. He's been to see you several times. Incidentally, he saved your life on Kalaya. A particularly nasty breed of thinker weapon had attached a probe to your brain. It was shutting it down, one neural pathway at a time. Michaels stopped it, with seconds to spare.'

'I see,' said Jamie thoughtfully. His memory was hazy, but he did recall an ugly green blob shambling through the forest towards him. He shuddered at the image.

'There were more casualties, I'm afraid, before the thinkers were halted.'

'Oh,' said Jamie, realising that the thought of yet more nameless corpses had only a numbing effect upon him.

To take his mind off it, he directed the Doctor's attention towards the room's other occupant. 'And what about that thing? What's that doing here?'

'Ah.' The Doctor's tone and expression suggested disappointment at the audible distaste in Jamie's voice. After all the Selachians had done, Jamie found that irritating in itself. 'He's Commander Redfern's other VIP patient.'

'Has it talked?'

'I don't think he's in any state to say anything yet.'

'What's with all this "he" business?'

The Doctor feigned mild surprise. 'Oh, I'm fairly certain he's a "he". The female Ockorans have darker crests, you see, and their gills are a slightly different shape.'

Jamie sighed. There was rarely any point in arguing with the Doctor. 'What happens now?' he asked.

'Right now, this ship, along with Commander Redfern's fleet of fighters, is in orbit around Ockora.'

'The Selachians' home planet? Hey, that's where Zoe will be!'

The Doctor nodded. 'Redfern has asked the Selachians to surrender. He's given them one Ockoran day to consider it –

that's twenty-six hours, give or take a few minutes.'

Jamie remembered what the Doctor had said on Kalaya. At the time, his predictions had been worrying, but comfortably far-sighted. Now, Jamie felt that time had been stolen from him. In a quavering voice, he said, 'They're not going to, are they?'

The Doctor shook his head solemnly. 'In about four and a half hours, Wayne Redfern will discover that the Selachians won't surrender to anybody. His reaction will make history.'

Chapter Fourteen

The Doctor wandered the carpeted corridors of the *Triumph*, occasionally dabbing at his forehead with a handkerchief when thoughts of what might have happened to Jamie caused him to break out in a sweat.

He had not told his companion half of the danger he had been in. For three days, he had been unbearably worried about the possibility that the thinker weapon had inflicted brain damage. Fortunately, the McCrimmons were a hardy clan. Still, the Doctor was mortified that his own foolishness had kept him from being around when he was needed.

He had left Jamie to rest, feeling liberated by the prospect of his full recovery. But, of course, he wasn't free yet. Zoe, too, had fallen victim to the Doctor's curiosity. She was trapped by history.

He had two choices. He could travel to Ockora and rescue her – though not in the often unreliable TARDIS – or he could change what was to happen. If he dared.

Either way, the same obstacle barred his path: Commander Wayne Redfern.

Finding himself at the door to his quarters, the Doctor decided that a short rest and, perhaps, a tootle on his recorder would refresh his mind. He pressed the access button. Identifying his fingerprint, a sensor sent an electronic impulse to disengage the lock.

Only a basic compad and accompanying screen broke up the retro, wood-panelled look of the guest room. It was no less opulent than the hospital and Redfern's office, although it was much smaller than either. The bed took up two-thirds of its floor area. The Doctor sat on it, cross-legged, and scowled at a copy of the *Mona Lisa* which hung over the washbasin. 'A computerised reproduction, I see. How anyone can claim not to see the difference baffles me.' He dug his recorder out of his pocket. 'I shall have to ask old Leonardo what he thinks, the next time I see him.' He raised the recorder, but paused again. 'Or young Leonardo, of course – you can never be sure with the TARDIS.' Satisfied, he put the instrument to his lips at last, and drew breath.

He was interrupted by a brief squawk, reminiscent of a cat in distress.

'My goodness me, what on earth was that?'

The sound came again.

'Oh. Oh, er, come in?' The door slid open to reveal that the Doctor had guessed correctly. He had a visitor. 'Come in,' he repeated, more effusively.

Professor Mulholland stepped over the threshold, but advanced no further. Sensing her continued proximity, the door remained open.

'I'd like to speak with you.' The request sounded like a mild threat.

By human standards, Laura Mulholland was probably a beautiful woman. Her full, blonde hair was immaculately sculpted so that it curled over one eye and cascaded on to her shoulders. Her eyelashes were carefully groomed, and an emerald pendant was visible above the rounded neckline of a darker green top. Fastidiously plucked eyebrows maintained a quizzical arch; beneath these, Mulholland's blue eyes were at once deep and penetrating. Combined with her perennially pursed lips, they gave a constant impression of cold appraisal. She rarely seemed to blink.

'By all means,' said the Doctor, expansively.

'You don't approve of my work, do you?'

'My, my, you're a very direct young woman.'

'Well, do you?'

Thinking carefully about his response, the Doctor put his recorder away, clasped his hands together and rested them on his lap. 'I just think it's a shame,' he said slowly, rolling his eyes upwards and staring sightlessly at the *Mona Lisa*, 'that somebody should squander such a great intellect as yours on an attempt to cause as many deaths as possible.' Only when he had finished speaking did he look at Mulholland, to gauge her reaction.

A nerve flickered beneath her smooth, white skin, pulling at her mouth. Mulholland wasn't as good at maintaining a passive front as she tried to be. Somewhat stiffly, she said, 'The G-bomb is the first great scientific advance of the twenty-third century.'

'I'm not disputing that – but it's science without conscience.'

'I do not decide how to use the bomb. It has nothing to do with me.'

'You don't believe that.' She really didn't – that alone enabled the Doctor to rein in his anger. Even so he stood up, raised his voice and attempted to pace up and down in the limited space available. 'You can't just open Pandora's box and, and blame somebody else for looking into it!'

'What would you have me do?'

The Doctor halted and turned to Mulholland sharply. She had made the question sound rhetorical, almost condescending. But he saw something in her face: a slight straining of her muscles as she held them still, a quiet desperation in the blue pits of her eyes. She was nervous, worried, in need of approval or perhaps of a way out.

The Doctor had encountered Mulholland several times over the past three days. Each time, he had made some cutting comment or passed on words of wisdom. He hadn't appreciated the effect he was having.

Mulholland was not a public figure. For years, the Doctor knew, she had been working in secret as the head of a project backed by the same consortium that financed and controlled the TSF. Her spectacular success had been one of the factors that had convinced the consortium to start this war. It would certainly end it. The bomb's inventor was not destined to achieve the same notoriety as the man who would order its use. Still, the history books would record her name; therefore, the Doctor knew it well.

And he knew – should have known all along – that Mulholland had a conscience.

'What do you think you ought to do?' he asked.

'I think it's too late to do anything. It's out of my hands.'

'Redfern can't use the bombs without you. He wouldn't know how.'

'But I can't disobey him. I could be prosecuted for breach of contract.'

'Well, if that's all you're concerned about…'

'I'm not some monster, Doctor! I was engaged to do a job. All right, you might say I should have turned it down, but they would have found somebody else.'

'But somebody as brilliant?'

'Our theoretical findings have other applications.'

'Ah, but your employers were only interested in one, weren't they?'

'They told me it was a deterrent. It still is.'

'And what if Redfern uses it? What then?'

'I don't know.' Mulholland's eyes met the Doctor's. For an instant, it seemed she was appealing for help. Then the instant passed. Anger melted her icy restraint, as if the Doctor had forced her to reveal a shameful secret. 'I don't know, all right?'

A heavy silence hung between them.

The Doctor felt more sympathy for Mulholland than he would once have thought possible. A pet hate of his was scientists who didn't consider the consequences of their work, who tried to absolve themselves of responsibility. But then, he knew from experience how easy it was to get caught up in the joy of discovery, to pull at an enticing thread until you knew more about the nature of the universe than you had ever intended to learn. A little knowledge was a dangerous thing, so the proverb went, but it could also be an intoxicating thing. And how much more dangerous could knowledge become, when circumstances forced you to share it?

Mulholland saw that. With a small push, she might even do something about it. She might deprive Wayne Redfern of his super-weapon and spare the Selachian race.

At that moment, the Doctor had the power to make it happen.

But power was a dangerous thing too.

The Doctor was thinking of changing the entire course of history – changing it for the better, maybe, but changing it nonetheless. Time had been remarkably tolerant of his tinkering thus far, but it wouldn't hold with interference on such a grand scale. The consequences of a few hasty words now would be unimaginable, almost certainly apocalyptic. The Doctor couldn't do it, not even to save Zoe. There had to be another way.

So, he let the moment pass – he let the hope fade from Mulholland's eyes – and he returned to his original plan. He would bring about a smaller change, one for which Time would probably forgive him.

He couldn't save the Selachians, but perhaps he could delay their fate – and save some of their prisoners in the meantime.

'Will you at least talk to Redfern for me?' he asked.

'Why can't you talk to him yourself?'

'He won't listen to me. He thinks I'm some sort of... of...'

'Trouble-making, bleeding-heart lunatic,' said Mulholland, probably quoting verbatim. 'What do you think I can say to him?'

'Any moment now, the Selachians will turn down Redfern's

demands. They will claim to have over ten thousand hostages, mostly human, in prison camps all over Ockora.'

Mulholland gave an unattractive snort. 'Your hostages again?'

The Doctor wrung his hands. 'I'm telling the truth!'

'Commander Redfern thinks...'

'I am well aware of what he thinks! But it would be a terrible tragedy if he was proved wrong, wouldn't it?' Calming himself, the Doctor adopted his best pleading expression. 'All I'm asking is that he investigate the Selachians' claims instead of simply dismissing them.'

'Very well,' said Mulholland, 'we shall go and see Redfern together – but I can tell you what he will say. There is no evidence that the Selachians have more than a few hundred prisoners at most.'

'There might be, if anyone was prepared to look for it.' More evidence, thought the Doctor, than futile searches for lost corpses on war-ravaged plains and, eventually, DNA traces detected amidst the fragments of rock where once a world had been.

Driven by the determination that none of those traces should belong to Zoe, he pushed eagerly past his visitor and out of the guest room. As he reached the corridor, he turned back to Mulholland with a frown. 'And precisely how many hostages do you need to find evidence of, before you'll agree that something ought to be done?'

'Let us see what Commander Redfern has to say.'

Mulholland set a measured pace towards Redfern's office, leaving the Doctor to fairly skip with impatience beside her. She didn't even look at him. She seemed to have recovered her cold composure. But the Doctor had seen beneath her dispassionate veneer – not only in his quarters, but in the documented history of events that had not yet happened.

In six months' time, Professor Laura Mulholland would be dead.

The police would find her, eventually, in the drawing room of her secluded mansion. She would be hanging by the neck, hoist by a length of rope refined from alien kelp. A hastily scribbled note would reveal the guilt felt by the noted physicist-turned-recluse, and her fear that her invention was out of her control; that it might kill again.

I was arrogant and blinkered enough to open Pandora's box, she would write. *I cannot live with the demons I have released*.

Chapter Fifteen

Zoe bit back a scream as the back of an armoured hand crashed across her face.

'I've told you, I don't know what you're talking about!'

The Selachian hit her again. 'Your pain will continue until you confess. Only then will you be allowed to die, as an example to the rest of your miserable kind.'

Zoe wanted to show her defiance, to repeat her lie. But she was terrified. She remained silent, and wondered how long she could manage to do even that.

It had been two days since her capture. She remembered how one of the Selachians' armadillo-like transports had climbed out of the ocean on its caterpillar tracks. The creatures had opened its rear doors and allowed water to flood out. Then they had prodded their prisoners into the newly evacuated compartment.

To Zoe, the worst thing had been a dispiriting sense of *déjà vu*. It seemed that all her dreadful experiences since her capture on Kalaya had been for nothing. Still, as the transport had lurched into motion she had pictured it rolling beneath the waves and had been grateful, at least, that she wasn't expected to hold her breath and swim again.

Now, there was a fresh, stinging cut on her forehead. The blood from it trickled on to her lips. She savoured its warm, salty taste, glad of any distraction from the awful reality of the moment. 'We are questioning your accomplice,' hissed the interrogator. 'If you do not talk, then he will. He will suffer less than you. His corpse will be more aesthetically pleasing.'

Zoe wondered if that was an example of Selachian humour.

The interrogator struck her again. Her head snapped back

with the impact of the blow, and her neck ached.

'This is only the least of the ways in which I can hurt you!'

Zoe felt dizzy. She wanted to put her hands to her head, but they were tied behind her to a barnacle-encrusted ring which seemed to grow out of the wall. Not that she could have escaped, in any case. The interrogation cell was only four metres wide, and four Selachians stood between her and the door.

She remembered the long journey to the internment centre, feeling the guns of two guards upon her, wondering all the while if they might find an excuse to use them.

After two days in captivity she had begun to feel relatively safe from such threats. The Selachians had little regard for their prisoners but she had begun to think that, if she kept her head down, she would not be singled out.

Then, this morning, Zoe and Paterson had been summoned by name.

'Did you see an Ockoran native on the island on which you were arrested?' It seemed like the hundredth time she had heard that question.

'No.'

'A young female.'

'No, I've told you, no!'

'She was a musician, and the chosen mate of the son of an associate leader in the Selachian Corps. She was to be impregnated in three days' time.'

Zoe sniffed, and tried to hold back more tears.

'Her name, in your tongue, was "She Who Tends to the Injured and Swims with the Lonely". You killed her.'

'I did not!' Whenever Zoe thought of the pink-skinned creature – the young Ockoran woman – pulling herself along the forest floor with spindly arms, she felt heartsick. She didn't want to hear that Paterson's victim had had a name, a family, a life. The sickening crunch as the soldier had brought his stick down on the young woman's head reverberated through her mind.

'She was murdered in a cowardly attack from behind.'

'I wouldn't kill anybody, you've got to believe me!'

'The deceitfulness of your race is well known.'

'I'm telling you the truth, I swear it!'

'You saw the young woman.'

'I didn't!' The lie became more difficult with each telling.

'Then your accomplice saw her.'

'I don't know – I don't know what he saw.'

The interrogator aimed another slap. Zoe tried to duck, but the Selachian's steely fingertips glanced off her skull. Shapes danced before her, out of focus. She thought she might pass out.

'I will ask you one final time to confess. I will not kill you before you do – but I can destroy you piece by piece in the meantime.' To Zoe's horror, the interrogator turned an arm-mounted gun downwards, aiming at her right foot.

It was too much. A sickly feeling rose in Zoe's stomach. It seemed to connect with the buzzing pain in her head and, between them, they overloaded her nervous system. She felt almost relieved as consciousness fled.

For a blissful minute, she drifted in safe, warm darkness.

She was snapped back to the real world, the cell, gasping for breath as icy cold water dripped from her face.

She was being held upright by two of the Selachians. Her knees were sore. She must have fallen. The water had come from the gun of the remaining onlooker, presumably re-routed from the reservoir in its battlesuit.

The interrogator had not moved. The fake eyes on its helmet bore into Zoe's head, their blankness seeming to confirm that the creature was unfeeling enough to carry out its threat.

'Did you kill the Ockoran woman?'

'No,' sobbed Zoe.

'Did your accomplice kill her?'

This wasn't as easy as it looked in old war films. Zoe knew what she ought to do: just stick to the lie and make it seem like the truth. But the interrogator was prepared to really hurt her. She wouldn't be able to cope if it maimed her or worse. She didn't want to be weak, but the thought of it scared her stupid.

'Did your accomplice kill her?' Zoe could hear the interrogator's gun charging up, with a whine like a dentist's sonic drill.

She remembered arriving in the main holding area, to find all but two of Paterson's would-be escapees from the warcraft. Paterson had asked hopefully after the missing soldiers. The answer had come in resigned, matter-of-fact tones. They had not survived the attempt.

She and Paterson were going to die, anyway. Best to get it over with quickly.

'Yes.'

'I did not hear your answer.'

'Yes!' The first time, Zoe's throat had balked at her cowardice, reducing the word to a whisper. This time, she almost shouted it. 'Yes, he killed her, all right? And he didn't want to, but this is a war and she would have led you to us and, and I didn't agree with it, but you're the ones who held us prisoner, we wouldn't even be here if it wasn't for you!'

Her outburst over, Zoe wept freely.

The interrogator gave a curt nod of satisfaction. 'You confirm your accomplice's story.'

'What?'

She felt drained. She couldn't fully comprehend what she was hearing.

'You mean… you mean you knew?'

The Selachian didn't answer. It motioned to its colleagues on each side of her. They reached behind Zoe and snapped her bonds, easily. She swayed and almost fell to the floor again.

So, Paterson had told them. Of course he had. He had been thinking of Zoe, doing what he could to spare her, while she had done nothing but betray him in turn.

In a daze, she allowed the two Selachians to escort her out of the cell. She wondered if they would take her back to the others, or if they would simply execute her. She thought she had resigned herself to such a fate. She bowed her head as she stumbled along the uncomfortable, slippery ground, wishing she had been allowed to keep her boots.

The prison complex had been hewn out of a large rock formation. Its corridors twisted off at illogical angles and sometimes turned back on themselves, its diggers having presumably shied away from harder deposits. Its larger caverns were bizarre, asymmetrical shapes. Lichen created green patterns everywhere and provided food for strange, amphibious, beetle-like creatures, which lurked in the darkest corners. Every few metres a circular patch of fungus clung to a wall and gave off a bright green glow. Like the back of the transport, the complex smelt musty. It had presumably once served another purpose – but now it had been dried out and given the task of holding almost a thousand of Ockora's air-breathing enemies.

The corridor began to slope upwards. With a start, Zoe realised that she had not been brought this way before. A blade of terror plunged into her stomach. She wasn't resigned to this, after all. She didn't want to die.

'Where are you taking me?' she cried.

'Be silent!'

Zoe faltered, half of her wanting to turn and run, the other half recognising the suicidal nature of that plan. She was at the bottom of an alien ocean.

The Selachians took her arms and dragged her along between them. Zoe screamed and kicked and fought, but hardly slowed them down.

'Be silent, or you will force us to dispose of you!'

Zoe swallowed her fear. So, the Selachians were not planning to 'dispose of' her already? She prayed not.

Then she heard somebody else screaming too.

And she recognised John Paterson's voice.

It made sense now. The Selachians were returning her to the holding area, but they had taken a detour. They wanted her to hear this. She felt herself crying again. She shook her head and muttered, 'No, no, no,' but she couldn't block out her friend's cries.

The Selachians slowed as they reached an iron door. Zoe found her eyes irresistibly drawn towards it.

There was silence for a moment. She feared that the door might open, that she might be forced to see her friend's corpse, might even take his place in the cell. But, then, the staccato, roaring blast of a plasma weapon rang out, and Paterson screamed again.

And Zoe was hauled onwards.

The internment centre offered little more in the way of facilities than the warcraft.

Individual cells were reserved for the disobedient, who would be confined to tiny, dark closets with no food and barely room to sit. For the most part, the prisoners congregated, ate and slept in the same vast, high-roofed cavern. Support pillars and stalagmites divided the area into uneven sections. There were only ten guards, two to each of the five exit passages. Though Zoe was often grateful for the lack of Selachians, it was a stark reminder that the underwater complex was considered secure without them.

Several unfinished passages had been gouged out of the walls, some little more than holes, others extending for metres to provide private alcoves. Whether by accident or by design, Ockora's cold, clean water cascaded through one of these and gurgled out through a sinkhole. Zoe made for this makeshift shower now, needing to bathe her wounds, moisten her burning throat and swill the blood from her face.

If only her memories could be washed clean so easily.

After that, her body wanted no more than to sleep. Her mind, however, was furiously active, still obsessed by what she had heard and by the gory pictures she imagined to go with the sounds. She wandered around the holding area as if she had a purpose, as if this could take her mind off the day's events. A few people asked what had happened to her. Most didn't want to know, or were too inured by their captivity to feel concern.

Some people had spent months here. Their weak, thin bodies offered evidence that, despite the Selachians' claims, the prisoners' daily meal of diluted nutrient paste – a concoction not unlike porridge in its taste and consistency – was insufficient. The Kalarians seemed particularly affected, though perhaps that was because they were so thin to begin with. A few more races were represented too, albeit in small numbers. Zoe steered clear of the single Ice Warrior, although it spent most of its time in morose contemplation.

She wondered when the Doctor would take her away from this.

Paterson was brought back almost an hour later. Any joy that Zoe might have felt at his survival turned to horror when she saw him. His face was a mass of burns and bruises. One eye was swollen shut. His hair was matted with blood. His overalls were torn and stained. As two Selachians pushed him into the cavern he took three limping steps, dragging his left foot, and pitched on to his face.

Zoe was among those who rushed to help him. Paterson was feverish and only just conscious. He moaned and shook his head. The prisoners carried him into an alcove and propped him against a wall. They had nothing to offer him except water but this duly arrived, in the dishes from which they ate or soaked into rags that had been torn from overalls.

Zoe was appalled at what the Selachians had done to Paterson. And only a tiny part of her wondered if it was any worse than what he had done to one of them.

Hours passed.

Zoe spent the time with Paterson. Mercifully, he slept, although his eyelids twitched and his nightmares made him whimper and occasionally cry out. She dozed for a time herself, overtaken by fatigue again.

When she had first arrived here, she had set herself to observing the routine. She had planned a score of escapes in her mind and, though she had dismissed each one as impractical, she had felt confident that a chance would present itself. Now, Zoe accepted the crushing truth that she might be here for a long, long time. She could only resign herself to the hunger, the mistreatment and the mind-numbing boredom and concentrate on getting through it. At least, she thought, the worst of her ordeal was over.

She was wrong.

'The prisoners Paterson and Heriot will report to us.'

The same words as before, delivered in the same amplified voice.

Zoe could not move. Her brain, her muscles, her body had all frozen.

Then the message was repeated, and she knew an even greater fear. She had seen one man shot down for not responding to a summons.

She walked out of the alcove, all eyes upon her, her own gaze locked upon the two Selachians that awaited her. She felt as if her legs were not her own, as if they betrayed her by leading her to this fate. 'I'm Heriot,' she said, her voice emerging as a timid squeak.

'Where is Paterson?'

'He's unconscious. He can't walk.'

'The prisoner Paterson will be woken and brought to us.'

The order was addressed to the assemblage in general. Somebody must have obeyed because, thirty seconds later, John Paterson lurched into view. He was barely able to stand but, although his friends surrounded him, nobody supported him. His choice, Zoe guessed. He was showing his captors that he was not defeated.

One of the Selachians turned to its comrade, and a silent exchange seemed to pass between them. Then the second Selachian pointed to a nearby prisoner, apparently at random. 'You will replace him. Come with us.'

The startled young man didn't dare to object.

For a fourth time, Zoe was marched through the labyrinth of corridors. By now, she was familiar with the creeping dread that came from not knowing what the Selachians would do to her. Surely, if they were planning further punishment for the Ockoran woman's death they wouldn't have spared Paterson?

She was thrust into what appeared to be a communications room. Five squat, organic workstations faced a large screen, which was set into the rock wall. Four Selachians were grouped around the foremost, largest console. She noticed that their battlesuits were decorated, perhaps to show rank. Three had blue stripes painted across their armoured torsos from top left to bottom right. The fourth had a black stripe, edged with red. Zoe's escort addressed the black-striped creature.

'The prisoners, Supreme Leader.'

Without any sort of acknowledgement, the so-named Supreme Leader turned to the instruments and operated them.

The screen activated, to show a middle-aged man with steel-grey hair and tight skin. 'Redfern here,' the man rapped. Zoe's heart leapt: Redfern was the name of Paterson's commanding officer. 'I take it you're ready to talk terms?'

'Indeed,' said the Supreme Leader, 'but the terms will be ours. Ockora will not surrender.'

'You're making a bad decision. We have the firepower...'

The Supreme Leader interrupted angrily. 'And we have many hostages!'

'Many?' Redfern scoffed. 'I doubt it.'

'I am in one of our internment centres at present. It holds one thousand, one hundred and twenty-one prisoners. There are ten other facilities of similar size, spread across our world. Any attack upon Ockora will jeopardise your own people.'

Redfern struggled not to show a reaction, but Zoe saw a flicker of doubt.

'And so, it is the turn of the Selachian Empire to offer an ultimatum. You will withdraw all personnel and equipment from our solar system, and allow us to retake the worlds of Molinar and Kalaya.'

'I have fighters in orbit around your planet,' Redfern blustered. 'You're in no position to dictate to me!'

'Allow me to demonstrate that I am. For every one of your hours that you delay acceptance of our terms, I will have two hostages killed.'

Zoe's heart plunged into her stomach as she realised why she was here.

'I will start with two vile creatures who have taken the life of an Ockoran non-combatant.'

The young prisoner looked terrified as the escorts pushed him forward. 'Please,' he begged, 'please, don't – I've done nothing wrong, it wasn't me!'

Zoe realised now why Paterson had been left behind. The Selachians had realised that his injuries were too visible. They couldn't risk letting Redfern convince himself that their hostages might be better off dead. But she was sickened by the cruel and arbitrary nature of his replacement's fate.

The blue-striped Selachians stepped back, to allow the

Supreme Leader to do its work. It gripped the young man by the front of his overalls, and swung him around until he was backed up against the workstation, presumably in Redfern's view.

The Supreme Leader shot the young man in the stomach. His scream was abruptly truncated as his smoking corpse sprawled backwards across the workstation.

'No! No, wait, you won't solve anything by more killing!' Another man – a familiar man – had appeared on the screen, at Redfern's shoulder.

'Doctor!'

Zoe's joy at seeing her friend was short-lived. He was thousands of kilometres away – and the Selachians had seized her now. They propelled her towards her executioner.

The Doctor's eyes widened, and he hopped with agitation. 'Zoe! Oh... goodness, no, you mustn't! No! Zoe!'

The Supreme Leader treated Zoe with the dispassion it had shown for her predecessor. Thrown against the workstation as the young man had been, she could do no more than stare as the Selachian prodded its gun into her stomach.

'Doctor!' she screamed.

Chapter Sixteen

'Doctor?'

'No, Jamie, it's me.'

'Lieutenant Michaels!'

Jamie was confused, then startled by the realisation that he must have been sleeping. How could he? Where was the Doctor?

'Hey, easy,' warned Michaels, as Jamie tried to sit up.

'How long was I asleep? What's happened to Zoe?'

'As far as I know, nothing.'

'The Doctor?'

'He's in with Commander Redfern.'

Jamie relaxed a little. It wasn't too late, then.

'How are you feeling?'

'I'm fine,' lied Jamie. He felt as if his insides had been sucked out. His body wanted nothing more than to drift back to sleep. 'I don't know why everyone's making such a big fuss.'

'You nearly died, that's why.'

'Aye, well… The Doctor says it's you I can thank for saving my life.'

Michaels shook his head. 'I didn't do anything.'

'But you did!'

'No, Jamie. I didn't.'

Jamie frowned. Perhaps the lieutenant was uncomfortable with compliments. Still, Michaels wasn't his concern right now. He couldn't lie here while Zoe was in danger.

'What do you think you're doing?' cried Michaels, as Jamie kicked back his sheets and made to stand.

'I'm going to find the Doctor.'

'Listen, Jamie, the best thing you can do now is rest.'

'I'm fine – but Zoe isn't. I should be out there, helping.'

His mouth set into a determined line, Michaels stood, pushed Jamie down on to the bed and pulled the sheets back over him. 'You need to learn to obey orders.' Jamie opened his mouth to protest, but Michaels waved a stern finger beneath his nose. 'But nothing. You'll be no good to your friends or to anyone else if you knock yourself out again.' Jamie wanted to struggle, but he was held down not just by Michaels' firm hands but, more so, by the unusually intense look in the lieutenant's brown eyes. 'Listen, Jamie, if you let your emotions get the better of you, you're finished. Take that from me.'

Jamie nodded dumbly. He wanted to shiver, but he wasn't sure why.

Michaels rose and regained his old detachment, if not his equanimity. He sighed heavily, and avoided Jamie's eyes. 'I should be on duty. I only came by to check how you were.'

'Sure,' said Jamie. To fill the leaden silence, he added, 'I heard you'd been promoted.'

Michaels shrugged. 'It's easy enough. You just have to survive. I'll drop in again, if I can.' So saying, he strode abruptly out of the room.

Jamie stared at the door for a full minute after it had closed behind his visitor.

Then, shaking his head, he leapt out of bed with all the energy he could muster. He felt tired, but he could overcome that if he tried. First, he had to find clothes. He crouched and looked under the bed, but there was nothing there and the movement made him dizzy. He closed his eyes, breathed deeply and rose again slowly.

His eyes alighted on the tall wardrobe at the foot of his bed. Of course.

He yanked it open, and was pleased to see his tattered and filthy combat uniform hanging within. Better still, his own clothes had been cleaned and pressed. They were lying in a neat pile, wrapped in clear plastic, at the bottom of the wardrobe. Jamie grinned at the sight of his trusty dirk, laid beneath them.

As he stooped to retrieve it, the dizziness hit him again. This time, it was worse. He felt unsteady on his feet. He clutched at the wardrobe door for support, sure that without it his legs would have given way.

The sensation passed. But Jamie could sense it lurking in his head, ready to pounce again. He felt weak. He let go of the door and staggered back to his bed, falling forward and supporting himself against it as soon as he was close enough. He was sweating profusely, and panting as if he had just come from a battle.

Michaels had been right.

Why? Why did his body have to fail him now, when he was needed?

Jamie collapsed on to the bed, but refused to lie down in case he dozed off again. He held his head in his hands, and allowed the ticking of the grandfather clock to soothe him as he tried to will himself back to health.

Perhaps he had just taken things too quickly.

When his breathing and his pulse rate had settled, he tried standing again. He swayed a little and felt delicate, like an eggshell, but nothing he couldn't cope with. He decided to try taking a few paces, just walking around the room.

It was no use. Blood rushed to his head. His legs trembled, and he was forced to reach for support again, almost crying with frustration.

It took Jamie a few seconds to realise what he had reached for.

He was leaning against the injured Selachian's water tank, both hands on its glass rim. The tank was open-topped; the lid was propped against the bed on which the tank sat, beside the discarded mattress. Curiously, Jamie peered into the water.

He gasped at the unexpected sight of the Selachian's wide, black eyes, staring back at him.

They locked gazes.

The creature didn't move. Nor did it blink. Jamie frowned. Perhaps it couldn't blink? Perhaps it had no eyelids? Despite appearances, it could have been asleep.

He moved slowly around the bed to get a closer view. He had not seen the Selachian properly before. It was difficult to equate this thin and seemingly inoffensive being with the murdering, armoured monsters with which he was more familiar.

He found himself at the head of the tank, across from the humming life-support equipment. He looked into the Selachian's eyes again, as if he might be able to see through them and into its alien dreams.

Its hands shot out of the water, towards his throat.

He reacted too late. The Selachian's fingers were long: they interlocked at the back of his neck. Jamie seized its arms and tried to pull it off him, but it was stronger than it looked – or he was weaker than usual, or both. He struggled for breath, and the pain in his head built up until he felt it would explode.

He blinked away stars and stumbled backwards. The Selachian came with him. Jamie's fall dragged it halfway out of its tank, until it was forced to let go. He landed on his back. His vision had tunnelled and the ceiling seemed a mile away. Then the ceiling was replaced by the Selachian's face. Its dark eyes and slit of a mouth were oddly incapable of forming the expression of rage that Jamie felt ought to have been there.

With a wet slap and a faint odour of fish, the Selachian landed on top of him. Jamie lashed out, and threw it off with surprising ease. He rolled as far as he could. His questing hands found the brass rail of the room's third bed. He pulled himself up, half-blind, not knowing where his foe was, expecting it to attack at any moment.

No such attack came.

As Jamie's vision cleared, he saw the Selachian lying where it had fallen, thrashing wildly like a... well, he thought, like a fish out of water. He watched in horrified fascination. Only now did he see that its contoured body came to an abrupt halt just below its waist. It looked as if its legs – or a tail? – had been amputated. Because of an injury sustained on Kalaya?

The Selachian let out a nerve-rending, keening wail. One thing was clear: it was dying. Good, thought Jamie. Teach it to attack me.

But it seemed in such agony, and so helpless.

The Doctor would have wanted him to save it.

Jamie couldn't lift the creature, not by himself, not in his condition, even if it would let him. He felt his way gingerly around the spare bed, not trusting his legs to support him fully. He reached the head of the bed, fumbled for the emergency cord and yanked it hard. Where the cord connected to the ceiling, a red light began to blink.

Within seconds, the duty nurse charged into the room. He wore a dark blue version of the standard TSF uniform, with a red cross sewn on to a breast pocket. He took one look at the situation and slapped something on his belt. A siren wailed, outside the room.

The nurse tried to lift his alien patient, but it fought against him. Jamie wanted to help, but somehow, without noticing it, he had slid on to the floor.

Fortunately, two soldiers appeared in response to the alarm. They manhandled the struggling Selachian back towards its tank. In the meantime, Jamie succumbed to the overpowering temptation to rest his eyes, just for a few seconds.

As he drifted off to sleep again, one thought haunted him. The Selachian had struggled. It hadn't wanted to be rescued. It had chosen death before dishonour.

Why did its ability to make that choice disturb him so much?

Chapter Seventeen

Wayne Redfern had never been angrier in his life.

It wasn't that the Selachians had refused to surrender. No, when the Supreme Leader had made its proclamation he had almost been pleased. Almost. The war, he had thought, would soon be won, anyway – and part of him wanted the decisive victory that a G-bomb drop would bring. But the Sharks had been despicable and cowardly enough to take hostages. And that complicated things.

They had held him back for so long already. How dare they delay him further?

Redfern thought furiously. Surely, he didn't have to believe the Supreme Leader's claim? Yes, yes, it made sense – it had to be a bluff. An exaggeration, at least. Sensing imminent defeat, the Sharks had taken a few people with them from Kalaya, that was all.

But then there was the Doctor. He had barged into Redfern's office again, just minutes earlier, with Professor Mulholland, spouting the usual pacifistic garbage. Could Redfern dismiss his story so easily, now the Selachians had backed it up?

The Supreme Leader was about to kill a second prisoner. The young girl's scream rang out of the speaker in Redfern's desk monitor: 'Doctor!'

Redfern bared his teeth in a contemptuous sneer. 'Do your worst – you won't make Earth back down. You'll pay for every death, you jumped-up dolphin!'

'No, wait!' The interruption came from the Doctor. He was behind Redfern, waving his hands agitatedly. 'I'm the Doctor! Don't you recognise me?'

The Supreme Leader hesitated. It released its grip on the girl.

With a whimper, she slipped away from it and out of sight of the Selachians' camera.

Redfern turned to the Doctor, surprised. The little man had drawn himself up to his full height and was clutching at the lapels of his jacket. His expression was stern. His brow was furrowed and his eyes were blazing. His head was tilted back at a haughty angle. All of a sudden, the petulant clown had been transformed.

'Yes, yes, that's right, Supreme Leader. You do know me, don't you?'

'Your face appears in our records,' hissed the Selachian.

The Doctor's façade slipped, just for a moment. 'And I imagine it's not the only one,' he muttered to himself. Aloud, he snapped, 'I'm sure it does. Who else has thwarted your greedy and power-crazed schemes as often as I will… I mean, have?'

'You have committed great crimes against our people. You will die for them!'

'Oh, I don't think so. You can threaten your poor prisoners as much as you like, but you don't have any power beyond Ockora, not any more.'

The Doctor had enraged the Supreme Leader – but then, that had never been difficult. The Selachian smashed an armoured fist into its own console. It must have loosened a connection, for the picture on Redfern's screen broke up for a second.

'What do you want, Doctor?'

The Doctor dropped his authoritative demeanour, as if it had been too much of an effort to maintain it. He leaned over the monitor, eagerly. 'I want to talk.'

The Selachian didn't respond. Like Redfern, it was probably trying to work out what this bizarre little man was playing at.

'You see, I don't think it's too late to end this war by negotiation.'

'We do not negotiate. Our enemies will be crushed.'

The Doctor wrung his hands, and the pitch of his voice rose. 'You've got to accept reality. You've been ousted from Kalaya, from Molinar, from… from everywhere. You can't win by force of arms.' His tone became persuasive. 'I'm offering to meet you, Supreme Leader. Face to face, on your world. There's only one condition.' And now, his expression darkened again. 'You must let the girl go. There will be no more…'

Redfern slapped his hand down on his compad, ending the transmission. The monitor went blank.

The Doctor recoiled, startled.

'No deals!' snarled Redfern.

'You… you idiot!' the Doctor cried, shaking with rage. 'I was trying to save Zoe's life!'

'How? By offering yourself up to them? What good would that do?'

'More good than your threats. If I'd left it to you, my friend would be dead by now. She might well be, for all you know.'

'So, you think you can ask the Sharks nicely and they won't hurt her?'

The Doctor looked uncertain. 'It… it was all I could think of, at the time.'

'There's only one way to deal with Selachians, Doctor.'

'Oh? And have you tried any others?'

'I'm in charge of this mission,' Redfern barked, 'and I won't let you go down there!'

'You really are the most illogical and obstinate man…'

Redfern leapt to his feet and towered over the Doctor. 'This is the second time I've had to stop you from going to the Sharks. I think you might be a spy, after all!'

'We weren't exchanging pleasantries, you know!'

'But the Supreme Leader recognised you. Everything else could have been an act.'

As Redfern and the Doctor glared at each other, Mulholland stepped forward. Redfern had almost forgotten about her. She had been hovering by the door, quietly watching.

'What about the hostages?' she asked.

Redfern didn't take his eyes off the Doctor. 'What about them?' he returned evenly. 'We can't be sure they exist.'

'Oh, for goodness' sake!' the Doctor exploded.

'We have only the Sharks' word for it.'

'And mine – I warned you about this days ago!'

'Yes, Doctor, you did. And exactly how did you know about the Selachians' claims before they made them?'

The Doctor's eyes narrowed. 'You *want* to use the G-bomb, don't you?'

'Answer my question!'

'Oh yes,' said the Doctor scornfully, 'you're itching to input those activation codes, to prove your power, to go down in history. To commit genocide. You don't believe in human hostages – what about Ockoran civilians?'

Redfern bristled. He had heard this argument before, from spotty students whose idea of fighting for justice was to parade their own views on placards outside the White House. 'I'll use the bomb if I have to. It will be the Selachians' choice, not mine.'

'Well, don't let me stand in the way of your moment of glory. But think about this: if the Supreme Leader is telling the truth – if I'm right, even a quarter right, about the real number of hostages on Ockora – you won't be welcomed back to Earth as a hero. You'll be court-martialled, vilified, perhaps even imprisoned. You'll become a scapegoat for the real power behind the Terran Security Forces. Think about that, Commander Redfern. I don't expect you to care about the people you intend to slaughter, but you might want to be a little more concerned about your own miserable destiny!'

Redfern stalked the carpeted corridors of the *Triumph*, unable to rest.

He didn't know what to do. It galled him to admit that to himself, so he would never have confessed it to anyone else. But since the Doctor had stormed out of his office Redfern had thought of little else but his harsh parting words.

Only a day earlier, things had been going well. He had contacted Vera Kennedy on Earth, to report that he had taken Kalaya. She had approved. For the first time in their professional acquaintance he had detected a hint of excitement in her normally immobile features. Unless it had just been a glitch in his imaging software.

He couldn't let it all slip away. This was his first major campaign as head of the TSF. He needed to distinguish himself if it was to be his last one. When this war was over, when he had crushed the enemy, he expected plaudits aplenty. He expected his peers to welcome him back to Earth, to admit they had misjudged him, to scramble to offer him the best positions available.

Why couldn't the Selachians accept defeat and get it over with?

Vera Kennedy would be expecting an update. She had agreed with Redfern that, if a surrender was not forthcoming, he would request permission to employ the final sanction. But whose idea had it really been? Whose responsibility? He was no longer certain.

Had it not been for the Doctor, he would surely have taken the next step by now. The end of his exile would have been a tangible prospect. Damn the man for shattering his confidence.

But what if the Doctor was right?

Redfern couldn't trust Kennedy. He couldn't trust any of them. None of his so-called friends, the old network, had defended him over the Interbank scandal. Oh, there had been plenty of words: how they were working behind the scenes, how they would support him. But he had seen no evidence of such efforts.

Redfern shivered as he remembered the court case, the headlines, doors slamming in his face. The bankruptcy hadn't been his fault. Incompetent underlings had acted without his authorisation; he had not seen vital papers; the board had schemed against him. But none of it had seemed to matter. He had been accused of fraud; of neglecting his duty, at least. Bloody-minded officials had wasted millions of dollars in an attempt to ruin him. He too had emptied his account, to employ a lawyer skilful enough to construct a defence around technicalities.

By the end of the year-long trial, the pressure had torn him apart from Annabelle, expelling him from the comfortable world into which he had married. He had always imagined that the urgings of mutual friends had prompted her decision to leave him. Those same friends had been full of grand promises, but had rarely returned his calls.

Redfern had tried to appear pleased about the TSF assignment. When interviewed, he had talked about cost efficiencies and training schemes, adding jingoistic rhetoric about the need for Earth to have an effective defence for the twenty-third century. But, privately, he had thought the appointment an insult, a way of shunting an embarrassment and a pest off-world. It was not even a job to which he was well suited. Much had been made of his army background – but his year of service, as a young man in the wake of the invasion, had been spent mostly on clean-up details. His real experience was in the boardroom and the golf club.

Redfern's one consolation had been the outbreak of war, and the prospect that the right performance on his part might heal the scars and make people forget. But, for the past year, he had lived with a secret fear – and the Doctor had just encapsulated it in a single sentence. The sentence was burnt into his mind now.

You'll become a scapegoat for the real power behind the Terran Security Forces.

It was all too horribly plausible. Redfern had half suspected it himself. The Doctor had simply thrown a spotlight on clues that had been there all along. He had reactivated all the nagging doubts that Redfern had ever tried to put down to paranoia on his part.

It wasn't fair. He had been on the verge of reclaiming his life. Now he could only wonder whether, instead, he was being set up for the ultimate betrayal.

Fifty-five minutes after his conversation with the Supreme Leader, Redfern was back in his office. His master monitor remained on his desktop, ready. As he had anticipated, it attracted his attention with a soft chirp. Its display told him that a message was arriving from Ockora, on his personal priority channel. He waited for a measured fifteen seconds, then accepted it.

The Supreme Leader was no longer at the internment centre. It had returned to the familiar surroundings of its office. It stood, hands clasped behind its back, at a high lectern which looked as if it had been sculpted from moss. Selachian weapons rested in brackets on the rocky wall behind it. The picture distorted as water rippled before the camera lens.

Surprisingly, the water did not muffle the creature's voice. Perhaps it had patched its battlesuit directly into its communicator.

Its words, as ever, were both pithy and predictable. 'I am about to order the execution of two more hostages. Do you agree to my terms?'

Redfern sighed and rested his fingertips on his eyelids, faking weariness. He took a deep breath and said, 'I can't give you an answer yet.'

'Then I will carry out my threat.'

'Wait! Please, let me have more time. I'm waiting for instructions. You know what Earth's government is like.'

'Indeed,' said the Selachian. 'You come from a planet of bureaucrats.' There was a note of triumph in its voice. It was revelling in the defeat of its foe. 'However, I set you a deadline.'

Redfern spread his arms in appeal. 'I'm doing all I can. I beg you, please don't kill any more of our people.' He leant closer to the monitor and gave the Supreme Leader what he hoped was an earnest look. 'Believe me, my superiors will be more amenable if you don't.'

'Terms are being negotiated?'

'As we speak.'

'Then I am prepared to give you the length of time that you offered us: one Ockoran day.'

'Thank you,' said Redfern, almost choking on the words. He gritted his teeth and forced his mouth into a smile. Thankfully, Selachians were not adept at reading the more subtle non-verbal signals of other races.

'However, there is now a further condition.'

'What is it?' Redfern almost snapped the words.

'The Doctor. He must be handed over to us.'

'He is not within my jurisdiction.'

'We have his companion. He will want to come here. You have only to facilitate it.'

'The girl isn't dead?'

'She is useful to me alive.'

Redfern nodded curtly. The Doctor would be pleased. Oddly enough, so was he. For too long, the deaths of those under his charge had just been statistics on daily reports. It felt surprisingly good to claw one back.

'You have one day,' the Supreme Leader reminded him, terminating the communication.

Redfern released the hatred that he had been holding back. He scowled and swore at the blank screen. He hated the idea of the Selachians thinking he was defeated, even if it wasn't true. He ached for the time when he could disabuse them of that notion, forcefully.

He brightened a little – or, at least, found something to savour in his dark mood – at the thought of what Vera Kennedy would say. He imagined her tight-lipped disapproval. But what could she do? If she ordered him to use the G-bomb – gave him an unequivocal, on-the-record order – that would be fine. Somehow, though, he didn't think she would.

A voice crackled out of his compad. 'Sir, computer core here. We've detected a tap on your system.'

'A tap?'

'Looks like it's been running for days, but it's been cleverly concealed. We've only just discovered it. We've traced it to the guest quarters, and sent a security team.'

Redfern smiled. 'Belay that, Corporal. I'll deal with it.'

He paused outside the guest room, wondering how the Doctor had become such an important figure in his life. He no longer suspected him of collaborating, not really, but he allowed him to stay around, even indulged his unconventional views and his righteous outbursts. For some reason, Redfern felt a need to earn the Doctor's respect.

He pressed the access button with his right thumb. Had he wanted to be polite, he would have used a finger and waited for the Doctor to voice-activate the lock from within. His rank gave him the option of circumventing that process.

As the door slid open, the Doctor leapt back from his communications screen.

'Oh, oh, Commander Redfern, how nice to see you, I was just…'

'I know what you were "just" doing, Doctor.' The Doctor's behaviour didn't surprise him. What did surprise him was that he wasn't annoyed. 'So, you overheard my conversation with the Supreme Leader. Can I take it you approve?'

'Yes, yes,' said the Doctor, his expression suggesting that he could hardly believe his luck. Then his eyes narrowed and became more alert. 'Exactly what are you planning?'

'We traced the earlier transmission. We have several T-Mat terminals on Ockora – as I expect you know.'

The Doctor at least had the decency to look abashed.

'We'll find this so-called internment centre and expose the Selachians' lies.'

'And if they're telling the truth?'

'Then…' Redfern paused and thought, before continuing, 'I'll report to Earth.'

'I'd like to join the detachment.' Redfern must have let his disapproval show, for the Doctor hurried to persuade him. 'Well, the life of a dear friend of mine is at stake – as is my own, for that matter. And I have a great deal of experience with Selachians.'

Redfern sighed. 'Very well.'

'Wonderful!' The Doctor clapped his hands together in enthusiasm. 'So, when do we leave? You can lend me a diving suit, of course? Who will be in charge – Lieutenant Michaels?'

'He will take command of the *Triumph*.' Redfern wasn't sure where this latest decision had come from, although he realised now that he had been considering it all along. Perhaps he wanted to prove to the Doctor, and to his former friends, that they were all wrong about him. Perhaps he didn't want his strange guest to seem like the better man.

Or perhaps he just didn't want to let the Doctor out of his sight.

'I'll be leading this mission myself.'

Chapter Eighteen

'Come on, Doctor, pick up the pace!'

The Doctor wailed in protest as Redfern gripped his shoulders and steered him into the small room which housed the T-Mat equipment. He dropped his rifle and stooped to retrieve it, nursing the weapon as if it might go off in his hands. Redfern had insisted that he carry it, despite his objections. The Doctor was also, through necessity, clad in a TSF uniform with an oxygenerator pack. He wore most of his own clothes beneath it, but there had been no room for the jacket. However, he had retrieved a ball of navy blue wool, two screwdrivers – one normal, one sonic – his recorder and a green apple from the pockets. He was fumbling for empty pouches into which to fit them.

The Doctor didn't appreciate being made to display military insignia. He wished he had had time to dig one of his lightweight wetsuits out of the TARDIS. But Redfern had moved the preparations along hastily, and he had not been able to get to his ship unseen.

He had slipped the TARDIS key into one boot of his uniform, for safekeeping.

The reconnaissance team numbered nine all told. Also present in the crowded room were two console operators and Lieutenant Michaels. 'Ah, Lieutenant,' the Doctor beamed, 'I wonder if you might do me a favour? I didn't have time to say goodbye to my friend, Jamie.'

'Doctor!' Redfern was glaring at him with disapproval.

The Doctor looked back at Michaels, hopefully. With a glint of amusement in his eye, the lieutenant gave him a slight, furtive nod.

'All right, men,' barked Redfern, 'move out. First two to the cubicle.'

Still juggling his possessions, the Doctor stepped forward. Redfern placed a steadying hand on his arm. 'Not yet, Doctor.' The Doctor smiled wryly to himself. Redfern probably expected him to run to the Selachians, given the chance.

Two privates stepped into the clear-fronted T-Mat cubicle, almost filling it between them. They stood back to back, rifles at the ready.

'I must say,' said the Doctor, cheerfully, 'it was very clever of you to smuggle T-Mat terminals on to Ockora under the Selachians' noses – ah, metaphorically speaking, of course. I wonder if they even know you've brought the old system out of mothballs? I do hope you've addressed some of its problems.'

Lights flashed and machinery whined and, suddenly, the cubicle was empty. 'Splendid!' The Doctor tried to clap his hands together, but aborted the gesture as his apple almost rolled on to the floor. 'Now, who wants to go next?'

Nobody answered. Everybody was still staring at the cubicle. The Doctor frowned and craned his neck for a better view.

The cubicle whined again, apparently of its own volition. Nothing else seemed to happen.

Redfern yanked open the door, went down on one knee and picked up a flat, white disc. He displayed it briefly to the rest of the room before flipping it to Michaels, who caught it.

'Ah, I see,' said the Doctor. 'A signal that the first party found no surprises down there.' He found a pocket for his recorder, and balanced his rifle against the crook of his arm so that he could chew thoughtfully on a thumbnail. 'I suppose it's safer to communicate this way than to attract attention by employing a second type of carrier wave. Let me guess: you've disguised the T-Mat wave as cosmic radiation, am I right?'

Redfern scowled at him. The Doctor grinned impishly in return.

Redfern marched into the cubicle next, along with Lieutenant Klavar, who was to be his deputy for this mission. Klavar had blonde hair and freckles; she could barely have been more than twenty years old. As the pair disappeared, the Doctor motioned the remaining four soldiers ahead of him with a polite 'After you.'

When his turn came, he paused at the cubicle door, turned and scurried over to Michaels. 'I wonder if you could hold on to these for me?' He bundled the contents of his arms into the surprised lieutenant's grasp. Michaels found himself holding a rifle, a knife and a pile of electro-grenades, with an apple balanced on top. The Doctor patted down his uniform, frowned, then saw the apple, grinned and took it back.

'Now, you will look after Jamie for me, won't you?' he said, giving Michaels no chance to speak as he skipped backwards into the cubicle and closed the door.

He waved to the operators through the transparent plastic, and took a hearty bite from the apple.

The Doctor blinked – and, though the cubicle didn't appear to change, the world around it did. He tucked his half-eaten apple into a pouch and, munching thoughtfully, stepped on to alien soil. He was greeted by Redfern, who stood alone. He must have sent his troops ahead.

'You took your time,' growled the commander. 'Come on, the water's this way.'

'Yes, yes, just give me a moment to find my bearings.'

The Doctor had not been to Ockora before. However, he had heard and read of its beauty. The clear, azure sky and the fresh, still air seemed to bear that out. But the colourful and delicate flowers of the planet – of this island, at least – had been stifled by rubble. There had once been a development here, but it had been quite thoroughly destroyed – many decades ago, if he was any judge. Of the buildings, only the occasional wall remained even partially intact. The T-Mat cubicle and its control console stood in a corner formed by two of these, concealed as well as they could be, but still incongruous.

The Doctor surveyed the ruins, unhappily. Too little remained for him to guess what the buildings would have looked like. However, he recognised the white bricks from which they had been formed: Kalarian materials.

'All you need to do,' snapped Redfern, 'is follow me. Where's your rifle?'

'Hmm? Oh, well, I shouldn't think I'll be needing that.'

'Where do you think we are? This isn't a holiday camp, Doctor!'

The words sparked a deductive leap in the Doctor's mind. He clicked his fingers with enthusiasm, ignoring the bared-tooth look of anger on Redfern's face. 'Yes, yes it is. Of course, that's exactly what this place is. A Kalarian resort! At least, it was. Ockora was a popular tourist destination, once upon a time. The Kalarians built hundreds of hotels and camps and second homes on its islands. Well, you can hardly blame them, can you?' He looked at Redfern, and was perversely pleased to see the commander's exasperated expression. 'I'm sure you must have noticed what a wonderful world this is. I expect you're glad to have had a chance to see it, before you utterly destroy it.'

'Do you want me to have you taken back to the *Triumph*?'

'No, no, of course not. We have work to do, don't we? Come along.' The Doctor trotted eagerly across the rubble, in the direction that Redfern had indicated. Even as Redfern joined him, cautiously relieved, he stopped and turned back. 'If only the Kalarians could have stayed on the islands,' he sighed, 'and left the oceans to the indigenous population.'

'Doctor!'

'You know, you're a very impatient man, Commander Redfern. You're about to create the future here – how can you do that, if you won't learn from the past?'

'I know what I need to know about the Sharks! You can't justify what they've done.'

'Oh, I'm not trying to. I'm simply intrigued by how a once-peaceful people could feel so ill-treated and helpless that they could renounce everything they believed in, create great weapons of destruction and cripple themselves for the sake of protection.'

'What the Kalarians did was a long time ago.'

'Not to the Ockorans. They're rather long-lived, you know. Some of them still remember the culls. Many will have lost their mothers, and for what? Their skins aren't valuable, the Kalarians don't eat them. No, they were murdered for sport.'

'Nobody knew they were intelligent – they showed no signs of it.'

'You mean they couldn't speak your language. Have you heard Ockoran speech-song, unfiltered by speaker systems and translation equipment? They have beautiful voices.'

'They're also ruthless killers! Are you suggesting we give in to them?'

'Not at all. You're right: the Selachians have become ruthless, paranoid and without conscience. But that doesn't mean we shouldn't try to understand why – why the Ockorans felt they had to create their battlesuits, to leave their oceans and fight back; to flatten settlements such as this one.' The Doctor raised his eyebrows, spread his arms and added mildly, 'If you don't understand your enemies, how can you hope to defeat them?'

Redfern gave him a penetrating look, as if suspecting that he was being ridiculed. The Doctor returned it, levelly, and began to see a flicker of understanding.

Nobody was beyond redemption.

The Doctor was pleased with his work – but he couldn't afford to do more. He had interfered quite enough already. He was standing on a world which, by now, should no longer have existed, with a man who should never have come here. He could almost feel Time shifting and working around him, desperately trying to repair the anomaly. He was relying on Time to put things back on course. But too big an anomaly would make that impossible.

The Doctor needed Redfern's help to rescue Zoe – but, after that, the commander still had to fulfil his destiny. The Doctor couldn't let him understand too much.

He broke eye contact with Redfern and clapped his hands, affecting a jaunty air.

Well, let's see if we can find these prisoners, shall we? I expect your troops will be waiting for us.'

He led the way to the beach.

Chapter Nineteen

One day, the Great Mother swam with her children.

She showed them the World, and it was beautiful indeed. They admired its crystal spires and coral mountains. They waved in cheerful greeting to its happy people.

But then, one of the smallest children - a mere hatchling - found she could go no further. A web closed around her, pinning her arms to her sides and binding her tail. The hatchling wailed as the other children swam away from her, without seeing what had happened.

As Jamie woke, his stomach sank again.

He was still in the hospital.

It reminded him of Zoe's situation, and of his own helplessness. He felt as if he had been confined to this bed for weeks, rather than days.

He blinked, to focus his eyes upon the grandfather clock. He had only dozed for a couple of hours, this time. Lieutenant Michaels had told him of the Doctor's mission to Ockora; Jamie didn't suppose he would have returned yet.

He didn't feel too bad. Perhaps he might be able to walk now. Or perhaps he should sleep a while longer, to be sure of being strong when the Doctor returned. He might be needed, then.

Jamie rolled on to his side - and saw a monster on the next bed.

The Great Mother saw the hatchling's plight. Urging her to be still, she severed the web and freed her. The hatchling rejoiced, and the other children laughed at her foolishness. But the Great Mother warned them all to be wary.

* * *

Jamie started, kicked back the sheets and swung his feet around on to the carpeted floor.

The monster didn't move.

It was humanoid in shape, clad entirely in black. Its blank mask was punctuated only by two clear eyepieces and by a thin, white seam, which bifurcated it to give the vague impression of a nose. The monster lay awkwardly on its mattress – the water tank had been taken away – propped up by a back pack which Jamie recognised as an oxygenerator unit. For a second, he thought it might be human, that he might have over-reacted to its strange attire – but then he looked into its eyepieces. Through a thin film of water, the black, pink-rimmed orbs of his Selachian roommate stared back at him.

The Great Mother told her children of the Second World, which lay above the World they knew. Into this Second World passed the souls of the wicked. No living Ockoran could travel to that barren place. But, in the dry hearts of its denizens, there festered a vile hatred for the brightness and purity of the children.

'Well might you be afraid,' the Selachian hissed. 'If I were free, I would have killed you by now – you and all your loathsome kind!' It reached out towards Jamie, as if it could take hold of his throat again and strangle him. But Jamie saw now that it was handcuffed. A thin, black chain connected its wrists to each other, and to the brass head of its bed.

'Aye, well, you're not free, are you?' he bragged. 'We beat you!'

The Selachian cocked its head to one side and spat, 'How can you speak in Ockoran?'

'What are you talking about? I'm talking in English, like you.'

'You insult me! When we come to power, the dominant language of our galaxy will no longer be that ugly, illogical, stilted human tongue!'

Despite its harsh words and the muffling effect of the mask, the creature's voice had a pleasant, undulating tone. It contrasted sharply with the usual guttural snarls and barked demands of its race. Jamie suspected that, for the first time, he was really hearing Selachian speech. Briefly, he wondered how, indeed, it was that he understood it; why language barriers had never been a problem on his travels. The Doctor, he supposed, must have worked some kind of magic. For Jamie, that was explanation enough.

'Now hold on a minute, who says you'll be coming to power anyway?'

'Air-breathers are weak and will be defeated.'

'Oh aye, and I reckon you're doing a fine job of that so far!'

'We shall prevail in time. Right is on our side.'

Jamie snorted derisively. 'On your side?'

'It was human warmongers who invaded Kalaya and massacred our troops.'

'You had no right being there in the first place!'

'The Kalarians attempted genocide against us. We had to protect ourselves.'

'And what about me, eh? Your lot have tried to kill me three times – and you've taken my friend hostage. She's done nothing to you!'

'She will be treated better than I have been.'

'Eh? How do you make that out?'

'On Ockora, we have dried-out facilities for housing your kind. We do not force them to wear – what would be your term? – wetsuits, nor confine them to tanks.' The Selachian flexed its wrists, drawing the chain between them tight. 'I have been bound and stranded in an unfamiliar element. I cannot even communicate, except when your officers use the translation equipment from my own battlesuit to interrogate me.'

Jamie remembered how lost he had felt under water.

'Your treatment of prisoners is barbaric – but then, what should I have expected? The cruelty of air-breathers is proved by history. Had your treacherous attack not caught me unawares and crippled me, I would have destroyed myself rather than allow you to take me.'

Much time passed. Despite the Great Mother's warnings, many innocent children fell into the webs of the Evil Ones and were dragged into the Second World before their time. The Ockoran fathers asked the Great Mother why they could not fight back. However, the Great Mother was wise. She knew that such an action would despoil the First World for ever.

The Selachian turned away, its vitriol exhausted. And Jamie was struck by an image of the creature beneath the black suit flapping helplessly on the floor.

'I thought so – you were trying to do yourself in!'

The creature didn't answer. Jamie thought it was ignoring him. But then he saw that it was shaking, as if straining to keep itself under control.

Jamie stood up, carefully. Feeling no ill effects, he padded over to the next bed and around it, until he could see its occupant's masked face again. He stayed out of its reach, though.

He almost expected to see tears in the Selachian's eyes – but they were as wide and blank as ever. Perhaps it couldn't cry.

'I will never see Ockora again,' it moaned. 'I will never see my mother, my brothers, my sister. I will never gaze upon the crystal spires, nor hear the songs of our fathers. I will never impregnate a female, never do my part to propagate our species.'

'Hey, what are you talking about?' cajoled Jamie. 'This war won't last much longer, you know. I'm sure the commander will let you go, as soon as…'

His next words caught in his throat as he remembered what the Doctor had told him. This creature was right: it would not see its world again. It would have no world to return to.

'I can never regain my life. Weapons-masters and surgeons have desecrated my pure body. Even if I returned to the water, I could not truly swim. I am suited only to combat.'

'Why did you let them do it to you?'

Again, hate corrupted the Selachian's singsong voice. 'It is you who have done it: the air-breathers. You forced me to fight to protect my family, to reclaim my people's dignity.'

'What,' began Jamie hesitantly, 'what did the Kalarians do to you?'

The Evil Ones became more sneaky and greedy. They stole ever more children with each passing day. At last, the Great Mother knew that, whatever the cost, something had to be done. She told the fathers to build a great workshop. There, they laboured night and day, to produce magical armour that could defend the children against their terrible foes.

The Selachian stared at Jamie for a long time. Then, slowly, awkwardly, it pulled itself into a sitting position and turned away, to stare sightlessly at the far wall.

'I will tell you a story that our fathers told us. Your translation equipment will strip much of its meaning away – the emotion and the poetry of the song will be lost upon you – but perhaps it may stir your primitive feelings.'

So intrigued was Jamie that he didn't rise to the insult. He pulled up a chair, sat down and listened, as the Selachian embarked upon its tale.

Suddenly, a monster appeared in the First World.

The children thought it to be alive, but the Great Mother knew that the monster was a hellish construct of the Evil

Ones. It dragged the children of Ockora into its maw, and swallowed them many at a time. It approached the workshop, and it seemed all was lost.

Then the Great Mother swam in front of the monster, taunting it. So taken were the Evil Ones with her beauty that they turned the monster around to pursue her.

She swam as fast as she could, but the monster was faster. Ockora mourned the Great Mother's death. But her sacrifice had not been in vain – for the fathers had had time to complete their protective armour.

And so, the children emerged from the First World, into the Second. The Evil Ones fled before their righteous wrath, and many were made to regret their misdeeds. But the children were not yet safe – for, above the Second World, was yet a Third, and into this did the cowardly Evil Ones flee.

'Was… was all that true?'

'Of course it is true,' the Selachian spat, scornfully. 'I am still young. Do you think I would have given my body and my life to the Selachian Corps, were it not?'

Jamie nodded dumbly, able to think only of the impending fate of the Selachians – the Ockorans. He hadn't considered the full horror of it before. His race was about to commit genocide. Yet one more injustice would be heaped upon a once-peaceful people.

He reminded himself of all the Selachians had done – he called to mind Zoe's plight – but he also remembered how fiercely the Highlanders had fought the attacking redcoats. Didn't these aliens, too, have cause to take up arms?

After all, the Highlanders had lost their war. The humans on this ship might have come from Jamie's world, but that didn't make them his people. They were more likely to be descended from his bitterest enemies.

'I'm Jamie,' he said quietly. 'What's your name?'

The Selachian replied in an equally subdued tone. 'It would not translate into your language.'

'You could try.'

So the Selachian told Jamie his name. And he was right: Jamie could not have understood it, nor even have stood a chance of repeating it. It was a name that couldn't have been formed by a human larynx: a haunting, beautiful symphony, compressed into a second but with a resonance that would live for an eternity. The sound transported Jamie to a fairy-tale, underwater land. But, to his dismay, his imagination churned up the water and filled it with spreading stains of blood.

The Doctor had said they couldn't stop it.

'They're going to win,' he blurted out. 'The humans – they're going to kill you all!'

'Weak air-breathers will never subdue the Selachian Empire.'

'No, no, you don't understand – they've got some newfangled bomb. They're going to use it to destroy Ockora!'

Now, the children's sad fate stood revealed. They could not be free, until they had mastered all the worlds in which the Evil Ones could travel. The Great Mother could not guide them in this venture, but, in their haste, her enemies had left their secrets behind.

'What trickery is this?'

'It's no trick, I swear.'

'Where is this bomb?'

'It's here, I think – on the ship.'

'I will find it,' vowed the young Selachian, straining at his chains with renewed vigour. 'I will not let this happen!'

'Can you not talk to your king or something – get him to surrender?'

'We will not surrender.'

'But they're going to kill you!'

'Death would be preferable to defeat.'

Jamie's thoughts were a whirlwind of possibilities. He knew what the Doctor had said, but he couldn't sit by and do nothing. The Doctor would understand – he would want Jamie to do the right thing, wouldn't he? But, if the Selachians wouldn't surrender…

The children vowed to resist the Evil Ones, to avenge the Great Mother's death and to restore beauty and tranquillity to the First World, as she would have wished.

Their quest continues to this day.

Chapter Twenty

The low, green, fungus-generated light of the main holding area never varied.

With his body clock seriously out of kilter, Paterson had become used to snatching brief periods of sleep whenever he could. He lay on the hard floor, arms folded beneath his head, and always woke a mercilessly short time later, cold and with aching muscles.

Sometimes, as now, there was a strangulated scream in his throat, a reaction to nightmare images of his ordeal at the Selachians' hands. He sat up, swallowed hard, brought his breathing under control and reassured himself that it was over.

Then he felt the throbbing mass of pain in his body and the dizziness in his head. He remembered where he was, and he knew that it wasn't over at all.

'I've searched the holding area,' reported Zoe, as Paterson used his elbows to lever himself into a sitting position.

'But you found nothing.'

'No.'

'And you're surprised? If the excavators had to leave those tunnels unfinished, I don't see you getting further with your bare hands!'

'I know,' she said defensively. 'I just wanted to be sure, that's all.'

'Trust me, miss, the only way out of here is past the Sharks.'

'Then that's just what we shall have to do.'

'Are you kidding me?'

'There are hundreds of prisoners and only ten guards. We can overpower them!'

'No. We've got numbers, but we ain't got the guts. They'd slaughter us!'

'You could do it!'

Paterson frowned. 'Do what?'

'Motivate the others. Make them fight.'

'Yeah, sure, they'll commit suicide on my say-so!'

'If the Doctor was here…'

'But he ain't here, is he? And you're not gonna change that by rattling on about him!'

'Well, I never thought I'd hear you admit defeat!' said Zoe, indignantly.

'I'm admitting nothing, miss. I'm just telling you, if you want out of here you'll need something a bit more practical than these fairy-tale schemes of yours.'

'Then why don't you suggest something?'

Paterson rested his head against the wall, sighed heavily and closed his eyes until she had finally gone away.

He began to regret his rudeness.

He couldn't blame Zoe for her optimism, however misplaced. He had felt the same himself, at first. He had searched the cavern too, when she had been asleep, not long after they had arrived. Not long before the Sharks had summoned them. He had investigated each unguarded opening, following half-dug passageways to their abrupt conclusions and testing the walls at the end of each. He had drawn some curious looks from other prisoners but, mostly, his efforts had been noted with disinterest. At one point, alone and unseen in a darkened alcove, he had been thrilled to find a wall that had crumbled at his touch. He had grimaced as pebbles skittered to the ground, praying that the sound wouldn't carry. But the loose dirt had been no more than a surface layer.

What had happened to that determination?

He had spent an hour in the shower alcove. It offered the only direct openings to the outside world. He had peered up into the beetle-infested crevice from which water flowed, even tried to brace himself against the walls and climb closer. He had received only a soaking for his efforts. Like the sinkhole below it, the crack had been too narrow to squeeze through.

The Selachians brought more food, at last. The diluted nutrient paste was grey, almost tasteless and insubstantial, as always, but it warmed Paterson's stomach and made him feel that some of his old vigour was returning.

He was disabused of that notion when he spotted his reflection in the curved surface of his dish. He looked old and pale. The half-light glinted off a long scar at the top of his forehead, as if to remind him that it was still fresh.

In a poignant, unexpected moment, he understood Zoe's disillusionment. He had been a brave man, once. Resourceful. Capable. He could see no trace of that man now.

Zoe came back, eventually. Of course she did. Mere words could never have quelled her enthusiasm, her hope.

'They don't teach you how to deal with this,' reflected Paterson, sitting beside her and using his fingers to scrape the last of the precious paste from his dish. 'I guess they don't care what happens to us from now on. Why should they? We're no use to them any more.'

'You must have known you could be captured or hurt,' said Zoe.

'I suppose. But you kid yourself. You think your luck won't run out – or, if it does, it'll happen quickly and you won't feel a thing. Perhaps you have to think that, to do this job.'

'But that's silly. As long as you're alive…'

'There's hope, eh?'

'Yes!'

'Look, miss, I know what you're trying to do. But you can see how the Sharks have left me. I can't get you out of here. It doesn't have to be me, does it?'

'Oh, but it does. You can lead these people.'

'I got the impression you weren't too thrilled with my leadership. On the island, I mean.' Paterson looked at Zoe, but she turned away from him quickly. 'I see.'

'You didn't have to kill her.'

'Don't you think I regret that?'

'I don't know. Do you?'

'Well, look at me – look what happened!'

'Is that the only reason?'

Paterson gritted his teeth. 'What do you want from me? I wish I could say I'll remember her, that she'll haunt me. But she won't. I've seen too many deaths on both sides. No, of course I didn't want to kill the Ockoran, but I was doing what it took to keep us both free!'

'Then do it again,' challenged Zoe. 'Don't let her death be for nothing!'

'Oh, that's it, isn't it, miss? You'll go as far as I will for your freedom – but you need someone else to blame for the consequences!'

'What do you mean?'

'I'm talking about the people who'll end up dead if we start a riot in here. Because that's what happens in war, miss: people die!'

'I… I didn't…'

Zoe looked as if she was going to cry. Paterson berated himself inwardly. He had done it again. 'Hey, hey,' he said, nuzzling her chin with his finger, 'don't take any notice of me. I'm frustrated, that's all, and I keep taking it out on you.'

Zoe gave him a brave smile.

'I'm sorry. I just don't see a way out of here, I really don't.' He was trying to speak softly, but his gruff voice was unused to such a pitch. It sounded strained and impatient. 'Even if we could get past the Sharks, we don't know how deep under water we are. Getting out of the internment centre is only the first part of our problem.'

'I know,' said Zoe, 'but we have to try. We can't let them break our spirit!'

'They haven't,' he said definitely. 'They won't. But they've trapped our bodies, for now. Sometimes, you just have to accept that there's nothing you can do.'

'But…'

Paterson forestalled the objection with a look. And, in that moment, he felt the man of old rising within him, undefeated, and knew that Zoe could see him too. 'We'll have our chance again,' he said earnestly. 'I promise.'

John Paterson recalled little of the occupied world into which he had been born. His father had died in a Dalek mine, leaving only a vague impression of a face in his son's memory. But Paterson remembered the hardship that had followed the defeat of the aliens: the rationing, the poverty, the hard and thankless work. Most of all, he remembered childhood games played in ruins that had still yielded an occasional forgotten corpse.

He had joined the Terran Security Forces on his sixteenth birthday. It had felt like the right thing to do: to safeguard others from the creatures that would plot to destroy them. A part of him had even hoped for a rematch with the Daleks.

It had always been more than a job to him. He had felt as if he was doing something important. And he had promised himself that he would do it to the best of his ability.

He wondered when he had lost sight of those ideals; when war had become a way of life, no more than a series of trials that stood between him and another dawn.

He wondered how much good he had really done.

* * *

Zoe had come to a conclusion. 'We have to steal one of their vehicles!' she announced, as if she had solved all their problems.

'You think?' said Paterson, drily.

'Of course, it's the logical answer.'

'They aren't built for speed.'

'Well, we'll just have to make sure we aren't noticed. We have to distract the guards, slip out of the cavern, find a transport and escape before the Selachians know we've gone. There are so many people here, they won't miss a few of us.'

'So, only a few can escape.'

'We only need one to get a message to your flagship.'

'What for? The Sharks have told them about us now.'

'But they don't know precisely where we are.' Paterson could almost see Zoe's mind ticking over, looking for ways to justify her plan. She found one. 'The Selachians' vehicles have weaponry, don't they? We'll be able to defend ourselves.'

'So, how are we supposed to find a transport?'

'They use them to bring in new prisoners. I mean, we were brought right into this cavern.'

'Yeah, along with five guards.'

'Well, I'll bet the Supreme Leader didn't walk here, either.'

'No... but he probably drove out again, hours ago.'

'But it shows there must be a... I don't know... a vehicle park or a depot or something.'

'And, by the time we've found it, the Sharks will have shot us dead.'

Zoe scowled. 'I'm sure I can find it. I've seen around the complex, and I have a good sense of direction.'

For the first time, Paterson felt a glimmer of interest. 'You've seen a depot, then?'

'Well, no... but I know where not to look for one.'

It must have sounded desperate, even to her. Paterson only had to raise one sceptical eyebrow, and Zoe sighed and slumped against the wall.

'Oh, that's it,' she groaned, 'I give up!'

He didn't know whether to feel relieved or disappointed. He hadn't appreciated until now how infectious her hope had been. Even as her insistence had irritated him, he had wanted her to succeed, to come up with a viable plan.

Now, there really was no hope.

Chapter Twenty-One

The village lay in a valley on the ocean floor. Redfern looked down at it feeling, for the first time, lost on an alien world.

At first, he had dismissed the village as a collection of natural, albeit colourful, rock formations. Only the giant, white screens that stood at intervals around and above it had kept him from swimming straight over it. He crouched beside a screen now, trusting it to conceal him from the gaze of the unarmoured – yet no doubt dangerous – natives that swam along the thoroughfares below. He looked at the formations, and knew now that they had been carefully sculpted. The Selachians had built crude dwellings for themselves.

Why did that surprise him? He had seen their technology. Why had he imagined that, on their home world, they would live like goldfish, or like the dolphins to which – according to human scientists – they bore a slight genetic resemblance?

The Doctor had identified the white screens as solar panels: somehow, they tapped into the sun's energy and channelled it towards the village. Redfern imagined that the Selachians' manufactured caves might even contain television sets or communications devices, built for underwater use. And, in a way, the bizarre image comforted him – because it suggested that, even here, his enemies were somehow as out of place as he was, at odds with the beauty of their undersea world.

The village was hundreds of metres in diameter. The solar panels on its far side seemed small and distant. Some of its towers came level with the bases of the panels and Redfern saw that they had large, jagged holes torn into them. He saw only the odd native here and there but there could have been many more, in hiding. He shuddered with distaste at the sight of the Selachians' pink, lithe bodies. And he realised, belatedly, that the openings in the towers were doorways; that the aliens could reach them as easily as he could walk the distance from his office to his quarters on the *Triumph*. He almost envied them that ease of movement, that freedom from gravity's pull.

Redfern was a long way from home; a long way from his circle of friends and the transplanted Victorian mansion that he had been forced to rent out. In his arrogance and impatience, he had not stopped to consider the perils of this mission. The reality was less certain than his plan. He was no longer in control; literally, out of his element. He couldn't even see properly without the aid of technology. Sensors in his helmet sought to duplicate the Selachians' acute night vision, and cast a greenish tint over everything he surveyed.

Still, he was the commanding officer. He had to maintain his confident front, or everything would fall apart.

Why hadn't Michaels talked him out of this? Damn it, what was wrong with the man?

Redfern turned to the others and extended his right hand. They followed suit, laying their hands on top of his. They had all increased the virtual weights of their belts so that the water wouldn't snatch them from this plateau. The Doctor, however, floated around like an out-of-control acrobat. He swam over to join the conference, span awkwardly, reached for the pile of hands and missed. One of the privates caught his arm and pulled him gently downwards like a wayward balloon.

Redfern had ordered radio silence. He didn't want the Selachians to suspect that they had visitors. However, when the unit was in contact like this, their communicators could link up securely through the filaments in their uniforms.

'Our intelligence didn't tell us about this place,' he growled. 'We can't go over it, and I don't like the idea of going around.'

'Why ever not?' the Doctor's voice buzzed in his ears.

Redfern didn't appreciate being questioned in front of the

lower ranks. He bared his teeth in a warning snarl, but the Doctor would have been unable to see this through his respirator. He tried to convey his annoyance in the tone of his voice, instead. 'This internment centre, if there is one, is on the other side of that settlement. If anything goes wrong there, we'll have God knows how many Sharks between us and the T-Mat terminal.'

'Not Sharks,' the Doctor insisted, 'Ockorans.'

'Thank you, Doctor, I'm sure the politically correct term will be a big help to us.'

'No, no.' The Doctor sounded irritated. 'I mean, those beings down there aren't Selachians at all. "Selachians" is the name chosen by the armoured Ockorans, the fighters. Look at them, Commander – they don't have implants, their tails haven't been amputated – they couldn't fit into battlesuits if they wanted to.'

'I thought all the Sela... the Ockorans fought,' said a young private whose name Redfern couldn't remember.

'That's probably what they think about you,' said the Doctor, scathingly. 'But, yes, I suppose most of the healthy, young males will have been drafted into the Corps. Villages such as this one will be populated by females and by the very young or old, perhaps by those who are ready to mate. This is what the Selachians are fighting to protect.'

Some of the privates exchanged uncertain glances: a reflexive gesture, though useless, given that their faces were concealed. The Doctor was undermining their resolve.

'Don't make these creatures out to have human feelings,' Redfern spat. 'Who were the Sharks "fighting to protect" when they massacred the civilians of Regus 4? Or when they tested their sun-stoker on a Martian colony that had refused to sell them arms? Or when they blew up a hotel in Earth orbit? We're here to keep them from taking more lives, and you can save your liberal nonsense until we're done!'

'You are planning to go on, then?' asked the Doctor, mildly.

'You bet I am,' said Redfern. 'But, armoured or not, be aware that those creatures won't exactly be pleased to see us. We need to be on guard!'

'Oh, I'm sure we'll all be very careful.'

'Right,' said Redfern through clenched teeth, 'let's move out!'

He yanked his hand away and broke the connection with the others. As he led the way around the alien village he felt pleased that, even under such trying circumstances, he had been able to assert his authority.

So, how was it, he wondered, that he had done precisely what the Doctor wanted?

Just under two hours later, Redfern stood with his back pressed to a lichen-encrusted rock wall, and peered around a corner at an entirely different Ockoran development.

All he could see was another rock-face, with an opening cut into it. But the pre-programmed tracker on his wrist told him that the Supreme Leader had transmitted its ultimatum from a room some 17.4 metres beyond the opening and a similar distance above it. If an internment centre existed, then this was it.

Redfern strained to see more, but his optical sensors discerned only the first metre or so of an uneven tunnel. An armoured Selachian – the first one he had seen on Ockora – stood guard at its mouth. Its presence supported the Supreme Leader's claim, but didn't confirm it.

Redfern felt a hand against his, then heard the Doctor's voice in his helmet.

'Satisfied?'

'Not until I see some prisoners.'

'For goodness' sake, man, the Selachians don't wear battlesuits under water for nothing.'

'They might, if an attacking fleet had taken up orbit around their planet.'

'But they don't know you've sent people down here!'

'I want to see proof!'

'And how do you propose to find it? By getting yourself captured?'

'Don't be ridiculous!'

'I did wonder. You are aware that the Selachians use organic technology, aren't you? You might be leaning against a sentient alarm system.'

Redfern leapt away from the wall, turned and glared at the mossy, green-yellow patches that clung to it. Belatedly, it occurred to him that the Doctor was simply doing what he did best: disorienting him, making him doubt himself. Transferring his glare to the little man, he realised that they were still holding hands. He snatched his hand away, petulantly.

Suddenly, Lieutenant Klavar was beside him, making sharp, downward motions with her arms: the signal to take cover. Redfern didn't question her judgement. He increased the virtual gravity of his belt and threw himself, face down, into the silt. Klavar and the Doctor dropped beside him; the other soldiers would have obeyed orders already. Without raising his head, Redfern searched with his left hand for Klavar's shoulder.

'What is it?' he asked, as he made contact.

'Selachian vehicle, sir. One o'clock.'

Redfern did raise his head now, a fraction – and he saw something that he had only seen in photographs, video feeds and extrapolated schematics before. It looked like a giant green sea monster at first, but then he saw its caterpillar tracks and observed its slow but confident progress. The transport rolled across his field of vision. Fortunately, its path didn't bring it too close to where the nine intruders lay, barely concealed, flat on the ocean floor. However, Redfern was just able to make out two figures in the vehicle's cab: Selachians in battlesuits.

The transport halted, and the sentry spoke briefly with its occupants. Then the alien stepped aside, and, with a Herculean effort, the transport hauled itself over the lip of the cave mouth and trundled along the dark tunnel, passing out of sight.

That settled it. An attack was out of the question. Redfern had no way of knowing how many Selachians, and what other surprises, might be waiting down that tunnel.

So, he needed another plan. He had to be decisive.

He could do it. He had spent his whole life dealing with situations in which he had felt like an outsider.

His family had been the first. Redfern had had to live with the knowledge that his parents had not wanted him, that his presence had torn them apart. The divorce had left his mother without the funds to send him to a good school. While his brothers had continued their privileged education, he had been entrusted to the mercy of an under-resourced state.

The Dalek occupation had been a bewildering time. He had been evacuated to Canada, robbed of everything and everyone he knew. In its aftermath, he had been equally lost amongst the lower ranks of the army. That was when he had first tried to take control, to shape his own fate. But the ladder of promotion had been long and steep, and Redfern had been too impatient to climb it. He had used his father's contacts, instead, to marry back into the life that had once been his. But, even there, he had been certain that his peers discussed him behind closed doors. He had had to prove his right to live in their world, every day.

Most of all, Redfern had felt out of place in the courtroom. He had stood alone in the dock, a man of principles and breeding, in an environment reserved for delinquents and reprobates.

He had coped, though. He had always coped. He had learnt how to take stock of each new environment, to learn the rules, to take a decision and to trust to his own instincts.

Be decisive, that was the key. Have confidence. What was this ocean, anyway, but one more alien world in a series of many? Why should this be the one to defeat him?

The Doctor crawled over and touched the commander's arm. 'I could try to get in there.'

'You think I'll let you do that? Even if I could trust you, you'd be throwing your life away.'

'Surely that's my risk to take? I can find a way in!'

'No, Doctor.' He felt his lips peeling back into a smile. 'I know what I have to do.'

Wayne Redfern had a plan. He had seen a way to deal with this. To gain control.

They returned to the Ockoran village. Redfern stood and looked down at it, and this time he didn't feel lost or out of place at all.

At his signal, the detachment joined hands again. 'All right, this is the plan. We're going back to the terminal…'

'Oh, but you can't!'

Redfern ignored the Doctor's interruption. 'We're going back to the terminal,' he repeated, 'only, this time, we aren't going around any Sharks.'

He paused, to allow his pronouncement to sink in. The Doctor raised his head to look at the commander. Redfern imagined the sanctimonious horror in his concealed expression.

'We cross the village in double time, cause as much damage as we can. I want the Sharks to know we've been here. Anyone gets in your way, you use your rifle. Saunders, you start by planting grenades on those solar panels, there and there.'

'Yes, sir.'

'You can't be serious about this!'

'We regroup at the foot of that panel over there,' said Redfern, pointing across the valley with his free hand. 'Any questions?'

'I have a question,' said the Doctor coldly. 'Are you all sure you can live with yourselves if you do this?'

'This is for our people's sake, Doctor; for those prisoners you're so fond of talking about. We'll show these monsters we can play them at their own game. For every human life they take, I can take ten of theirs!' They'll pay for standing in my way, thought Redfern.

'Listen to me, all of you,' the Doctor pleaded. 'You don't have to follow his orders.'

'Yes they do, Doctor. This is war, and I'm their commanding officer. It's my job to make sure we survive this!'

Redfern snatched his hand away, denying the Doctor a chance to respond. With a sweep of his arm he motioned his soldiers forward. They obeyed without hesitation.

He followed them, pushing himself away from the plateau and increasing his virtual weight so that he sank towards the buildings below. As he landed, he looked up and behind to see a cloud of dust billowing outwards from where the first solar panel had once been.

The rest of the detail advanced into the settlement. Whether by design or not, they formed a haphazard arc in front of Redfern, protecting him. He watched as two Ockorans swam from a cluster of red coral to attack Private Matthews. They didn't reach him. Streams of bubbles converged upon the pair as six rifles discharged at once. It was a waste of expensive nanites – but at least, unarmoured, these creatures needed only one good bullet each.

Two alien corpses drifted away, and left a violet trail.

Redfern's tactics were proving successful. His enemies were helpless.

He didn't need protecting.

He adjusted his weight again, kicked upwards and sent himself over the heads of his men. His fingers closed around an electro-grenade, and he cast around for a target. He hurled the explosive device towards a high doorway. The force of his throw sent him drifting as the water likewise coaxed the grenade away from its target. It floated out of sight, denied the impact it required to detonate.

Wiry but strong arms gripped Redfern from behind. He was set upon by two Ockorans. They tried to seize his rifle, but he kept hold of it doggedly. Suddenly, there was an explosion of violet and one of the creatures fell away. Somebody must have shot it, from below. Redfern didn't stop to question his luck. He still had his rifle. He turned it around and fired into the stomach of the second Ockoran. He kicked his feet and swam away from its gutted corpse, his heartbeat pounding in his ears.

It felt good.

He returned to the building that had been the target of his abortive attack. He fumbled with a second grenade, working out how to set its timing mechanism. He swam up to the opening and dropped the grenade through it. Then he braced his feet against the wall and pushed himself away. He moved too slowly. For a moment, he feared he had not given himself long enough; that, again, he had not adequately compensated for his environment. Then the building crumbled in a slow-motion explosion and, though Redfern was hit by fragments of coral, the water stole enough of their momentum for them to barely sting him.

'I think you ought to know, Commander, that the Selachians will almost certainly detect this transmission. If I were you, I would break off your attack on the Ockoran village and leave.'

The Doctor. He had broken radio silence.

Redfern's moment of satisfaction was soured. He had been right all along – but even that only gave him cause to feel angry with himself. Why had he allowed an obvious traitor to allay his suspicions? Why had he let him out of his sight? The Doctor was probably with his Selachian masters now. Redfern vowed they would not save him from justice.

In the meantime, he had another decision to make. He was in danger of losing control.

'You heard the man,' he broadcast, 'we've been compromised. Previous orders stand, but hurry it up. Assemble at the rendezvous point a.s.a.p.'

But Redfern found it difficult to obey his own directive. He was tiring, and the deeper he moved into the village the larger it seemed. He sank to the ocean floor so that he could have a surface to push against; resorting to a stumbling, bobbing walk, he was able both to rest his aching shoulders and to keep his rifle poised. The Ockorans now had fewer directions from which to come. He shot three more, but only when it looked as though they would attack. At one point, six of the monsters swam up behind him, and he scattered them with a grenade. Mostly, though, his concentration was reserved for the arduous task of simply moving. His progress was slow, his fear increasing with each step.

How long had it been since the Doctor's treacherous message? He didn't know. Nor did he know where the rest of his soldiers were, how far it was to the edge of the village or even if he was heading in the right direction.

It was with enormous relief that Redfern reached the valley wall, at last. He tucked his rifle into its sling and swam upwards, eagerly, oblivious to the fact that he was leaving his back exposed to the villagers. He found himself at the base of a solar panel, where he bent double and tried to steady his breathing lest he take in oxygen faster than his equipment could extract it from the water. His stomach sank at the realisation that nobody was here to greet him. He had to get his bearings, see where he was. They were probably waiting for him at the next panel, or the one after that.

His palms still pressed against his knees, Redfern looked up – and stared at his own reflection in golden metal.

He whirled around, to find a second battlesuited Selachian

behind him. With arms outstretched, the creatures closed in.

They were going to kill him. Or, at best, they would torture and humiliate him.

He had only a second in which to make a decision. It was all he needed. There was only one way, one desperate way, to regain control.

Wayne Redfern reached for an electro-grenade.

Chapter Twenty-Two

Mulholland perched on the edge of the couch, unable to let herself sink into its cushions. She looked around, nervously. She felt intimidated by the pleasant surroundings of Commander Redfern's office. It was illogical, she knew, but she felt that, somehow, he was still here, watching her. He would have disapproved of her weakness – but, then, he had never faced her demons, had he? He had not felt them clawing at his face, tearing his skin away, or heard their cackling taunts, their accusations that Laura Mulholland had given them power.

Finding a bottle of brandy in Redfern's drinks cabinet, Kent Michaels poured a generous measure into a glass. 'I don't suppose the old man'll miss it.'

'Are you not having one?' Mulholland fought to steady her hand as she accepted the drink.

'Too early for me.'

For me too, she thought, but I need it this morning.

The demons had invaded her sleep again. She had woken with a racing heartbeat and an image of a face in her mind. She had found herself drawn to the bomb chamber, hardly daring to hope that her creations might still be in their housings. They were, of course. She had spent an hour with them, sickened by the same concoction of shame and betrayal and hatred and love which, she thought, must afflict the parents of those who commit monstrous crimes.

'Anyway, I'm on duty.' Michaels pulled a plastic cup from the dispenser by the water-cooler, filled it and took a seat beside her. 'Now, what did you want to see me about?'

'Are you certain I am not disturbing you?' It was the second time she had asked this.

Michaels's moustache twitched with a rare, tiny smile. 'Believe me, there's not a whole lot to keep me occupied in this job.'

Mulholland took a large mouthful of brandy and swallowed it slowly, to give her time to steel herself. Then she asked, slowly, 'Have you ever wondered how the war will end?'

The lieutenant shrugged. 'I think we'll win, if that's what you mean.'

'But how? A Selachian surrender, a treaty, a raid on Ockora, what?' She was aware that a pleading note had entered her voice. Her stomach knotted at the thought of being seen like this. In front of anyone else, she wouldn't have let it happen. Her surroundings disconcerted her, made her feel as though she was baring her neuroses for the world to examine.

Michaels narrowed his eyes. 'The bomb?'

She nodded. 'It was something the Doctor said.'

'Why doesn't that surprise me?'

Mulholland snorted, humourlessly. 'I didn't think anything surprised you.'

'You learn to cope.'

'How do you cope with destroying a world?'

'It won't be your decision, you know.'

'I have to press the button.'

'And that bothers you?'

She stared at Michaels. He had spoken in such a matter-of-fact way, as if he simply didn't care. Had she misjudged him? She had never called him a friend, but he had been a comrade in adversity. She considered him a kindred spirit. They both maintained fronts – hers cold, his indifferent – to rein in the demons within themselves. Perversely, their barriers had often seemed to cancel each other out. She had allowed him to see her true vulnerable self, when she had been most in need of his stoic brand of reassurance. In turn, she had seen through his barriers too, glimpsing anger, uncertainty, despair and even passion.

She had thought they understood each other. Had she been so wrong? His barriers were up now, as impenetrable as ever.

Shaken, Mulholland put down her glass with a clatter, stood up and turned away from him. She felt the itching, phantom pain of talons on her cheeks. 'I simply need to be prepared,' she said, inserting a confidence into her voice that she knew wouldn't show on her face. She was hastily trying to re-erect her own barriers, but they lay in ruins.

She felt Michaels's presence at her shoulder. 'I know,' he said – and did his tone seem warmer?

'You do realise the G-bomb is untested?'

'Could it be dangerous? To us, I mean?'

'It is possible. More likely, the bomb may fail. In my professional opinion, it would be far better employed as a deterrent than as a weapon.'

'You could be right.'

'And yet, as I understand it, you have not informed the Selachians of its existence.'

Mulholland was uncomfortably aware of the incongruity of conducting this conversation with her back turned to Michaels. She was not yet ready to face him, so she masked her awkwardness by wandering around the room. She gazed at the panelled walls, the bookshelves, the cooler, everywhere but at him.

'I guess the CO doesn't want to look stupid if he launches the bomb and it fails,' said Michaels.

'And so, he would rather increase the likelihood of his having to make such a launch?'

'It's his decision.'

'Everything is "his decision", it seems. Does nobody else have a say?'

'Do you really want that responsibility?'

Mulholland thought she detected pain in Michaels' voice. Having found her way to Redfern's chair, she turned to look at the lieutenant across the expanse of desk. 'Can I really absolve myself of it?'

'You could let them replace you.'

'It wouldn't change what is going to happen.'

'Precisely.' Suddenly, Michaels leant forward and placed his hands on the desk. There was an urgent gleam in his eye, a need to be believed. His barriers had fallen. 'Like it or not, it's not up to us to decide what should be done. It's Redfern's choice, his responsibility. Why agonise over something that has nothing to do with us?'

'Just follow orders, is that it?'

'If it keeps us sane, yes!'

'I used to think like that. If I hadn't, I could never have developed the G-bomb.'

'Well, nothing's changed.'

'It has,' Mulholland insisted. She struggled for the words to tell him what she was feeling. 'We are no longer talking about theoretical work, cloistered away in some institute. Since I left Earth, it has become so... real. I feel... exposed, unsure and, yes, responsible.'

She saw an image from the end of her latest nightmare. She had fought off the demons, but they had left her sore and bleeding. She had run to her basin, had splashed cold water on her face, but had felt nothing. Then she had looked up. She had seen her face in the mirror, its flesh stripped away. She had stared into the blank eye sockets of a leering, white skull. The face of death. Her face.

Absorbed in the image, she jumped as a voice came over Redfern's compad.

'Lieutenant Michaels, we have a situation.'

Michaels pulled the microphone towards him. 'What's up?'

'Our "guest" has escaped from the infirmary.'

'Escaped?'

'It struck the guard from behind, sir, knocked him out.'

Mulholland tuned out the exchange, as Michaels began to ask questions. Her gaze had strayed to the photograph on the desk. It featured a smiling couple, dressed in designer casual wear, and a blond-haired boy. It took Mulholland a moment to recognise the man as a slightly younger Wayne Redfern. He seemed incongruous amidst the pastel colours of a forest or an orchard. Still, his smile was as fixed and toothy as ever.

Mulholland had known, somehow, that Redfern had a wife – an ex-wife, rather. She had not known, not imagined, that he had a son too.

'What about Jamie?' Michaels was asking.

'Sir?'

'The young lad, McCrimmon.'

'No sign of him either.'

Then Mulholland saw it. She saw what Redfern was. She looked at his taut skin, his prominent cheekbones and his symmetrical teeth, and she knew.

She saw the face of death again.

She gasped, dropped the photograph and put a hand to her forehead. She felt weak. Did the demons haunt her waking hours now, too?

'Is something wrong?' asked Michaels.

'I'm all right, I just feel a little dizzy.'

The light had taken on a red hue: a ship-wide alert signal, presumably instigated by Michaels. Civilian personnel would be hurrying to the safety of their rooms; security teams would be assembling. 'I'll escort you to your quarters,' said Michaels. 'It's on my way.'

'I can manage.'

'No, you can't – there's a Selachian loose on board. Come on!'

Michaels's long stride looked unhurried, but Mulholland found herself struggling to keep two steps behind him and to maintain her dignity and composure in the process.

'What will you do about the Selachian?' she asked.

'Find it,' he said, without looking over his shoulder.

'Then what?'

He didn't reply.

An intriguing thought occurred to her. 'You are in charge of the mission now. What will you do if Commander Redfern does not return?'

'He will.'

'Will you give the order to employ the G-bomb? Would you take that responsibility?'

Michaels stopped abruptly, and rounded on Mulholland. 'I believe in this mission. I think we're right to be fighting the Sharks.'

'For the sake of Earth's big businesses?'

'For the sake of all the people the Selachians have tortured and killed!'

'You know that is an excuse. You know the real reason for the war.'

'I know, but it doesn't matter. The "excuse" is true enough and reason enough.'

'You haven't answered my question.'

She could almost see the shutters as they sprung up over Michaels's brown eyes and hid the passion within them. 'I have work to do,' he said woodenly.

They had halted at an intersection of corridors. Michaels nodded to his right, to where they could see the door to Mulholland's quarters. 'We have a Stage One alert situation. Lock yourself in and stay by your compad.'

'Yes, sir,' said Mulholland, knowing it would needle him.

The lieutenant turned and marched away. Mulholland walked thoughtfully to her room.

As she entered it, she suddenly felt a presence behind her.

She turned, too late to close the door in front of the black monster that sprang at her.

She fell back on to her table, sending notes fluttering across the room. Long fingers closed around her throat and she stared into round, black eyes and imagined for an instant that she was looking into those terrible, empty sockets again.

Then the monster – the Selachian, she realised, in a water-filled survival suit – was torn away from her. Another figure had followed it into the room, and was now wrestling with it fiercely. 'No,' he cried, 'leave her be. What do you think you're doing?'

Mulholland had a fleeting impression of a young man clad, bizarrely, in ancient traditional Scottish dress. He was even carrying a blade. She didn't stop to question who her rescuer was, nor where he had come from. He had given her an opening. She raced for the door.

But the young man cut in front of her.

He waved the blade beneath her chin, not exactly in a threatening way but leaving her in no doubt that he knew how to use it. 'I'm sorry,' he said, and his expression suggested that he was genuine. 'I don't want to hurt you, but I can't let you leave.'

'Kill it,' the Selachian urged, behind her. 'Kill it and it cannot launch its bomb.'

Oh God, was that what this was all about? Her future, catching up with her.

Perhaps it was for the best.

'I won't do that,' protested the young man.

'Then I shall.'

'No!' He looked confused, almost desperate. 'If… if you kill her, they'll only get somebody else to do their dirty work. If she's alive, we can use her as a hostage. We can get to the bomb and… and make her do something to stop it.'

Mulholland's gaze was rooted to the tip of the young man's blade. But she heard the Selachian padding up behind her, and shuddered as its sibilant voice hissed in her ear. 'You will disable your weapon for us, won't you?'

Mulholland nodded dumbly.

And, although she had never been so terrified in her life, a tiny part of her also felt a sense of relief that the decision had been made for her.

Chapter Twenty-Three

Later, Zoe would not know what had made her do it.

She would remember curling up into a ball on the cavern floor, surrounded by the somnolent or somnambulant forms of the beaten and lost, hating herself for being so useless and longing for the passage of time that sleep would bring.

The worst thing was that Paterson was right. Her plan, such as it was, was both dangerous and destined to fail. She had even begun to question her objective. As Paterson had said, there was no longer any need to contact the flagship – and, even if there had been, it would have been easier to gain access to the communications room than to search for a distant T-Mat terminal. No, Zoe had to admit that she was only interested in her own escape. Was she being terribly selfish?

She couldn't help but feel responsible for the hundreds of other inmates, as if she should be including each one of them in her plans. But how could she?

She drifted into a doze, wishing for the comfort of the Doctor's presence. He knew where she was now. Perhaps he was on his way. But, then, he had had days in which to find and rescue her. What if he couldn't do it? What if he was too late?

Perhaps that thought was still uppermost in Zoe's mind when she woke, shouts ringing in her ears, befuddled by sleep. She sat up groggily, trying to make sense of the raised voices and the scuffling, and concluded that a fight had broken out. She didn't know how or why, or who might be involved. From her sitting position, blinking tiredness from her eyes, she only got a vague impression of people running to – no, in most cases from – the disturbance.

And then the Selachians were there.

She almost screamed as two of the creatures bore down on her. They marched in step with each other. But they were not interested in her. They passed one to each side of Zoe. She wondered if some prisoners had found the nerve to attack their guards. If so, should she join in? She remembered the summary punishments that had been meted out on the warcraft, and her stomach turned. She couldn't face seeing such a thing again.

And then, she saw something else.

The Selachians had left the nearest exit unguarded.

And why not? There was nowhere to escape to. Only the foolhardy or the suicidal would have risked taking advantage of their lapse.

The foolhardy, the suicidal or the desperate.

In the end, Zoe would reflect later, she just hadn't stopped to think.

Instinct kicked in. She scrambled to her feet and made a break for freedom. She literally fell out of the cavern, trying to move faster than her legs would allow. Skidding on a wet patch of moss she scraped her knees, but rose again in one movement and continued to run. Terror was her only motivation now. There was no going back. She had committed herself to an ill-conceived plan; she was in no doubt about her fate, should it fail.

Were there footsteps behind her? The thumping of her heart made it difficult to hear. She didn't dare to look back, couldn't risk slowing down.

She was in an unfamiliar part of the complex. She threw herself down a side tunnel at random. She wished she hadn't done this, wished she had had the sense to listen to Paterson's advice and wait for the Doctor.

The tunnel was dark, devoid of the light-giving fungus. Zoe found herself slowing, reaching out to the ever-narrowing walls to keep herself on course.

And then, the tunnel came to a dead end.

At first, she couldn't believe what she was seeing. She stared at the wall of rock before her, stunned, her mouth open. Then she ran her hands over the walls to each side in case, somehow, impossibly, she had missed an opening there. Then she railed against the unfairness of it all, and felt like crying. Then the certainty of her fate froze the tears in her eyes, as a numb dread enveloped her.

There were footsteps behind her. This time, she was sure.

Zoe forced her reluctant body to turn, while her feet carried her backwards as if in an attempt to propel her through the wall. Her back was pressed against the unyielding barrier.

Three figures came to a halt before her.

They weren't Selachians. Zoe gave a moan of relief.

They sat in a huddle, and conversed in low voices. Zoe had begun to feel relatively safe. Clearly, the Selachians didn't use this truncated tunnel, and she had heard neither alarms nor search parties – nothing to suggest that the absence of four prisoners had been noticed.

'It seems to me,' said Leanne Davidson, 'that we are relying on luck.' She was a tall and heavily built woman, in her late twenties. Chestnut hair fell untidily across her almond-shaped eyes. A large mole was positioned prominently beside her equally prominent broad nose. She sat with her arms folded, exhibiting her habitual expression of down-mouthed cynicism. 'If we move from here, we either run into the Sharks or we don't.'

At this, young Adam Dresden raised his head and bleated, 'We'd be better staying put.'

'Then what was the point of our escape?' asked the Kalarian male, whose name sounded like Kukhadil with the emphasis on the middle syllable.

'At least they can't see us here. They can't hurt us.'

'I would rather risk being recaptured than starving to death unnoticed.'

Kukhadil had spirit, but he lacked Davidson's stamina. It had taken him several minutes to recover his breath after his sprint. He seemed even taller and thinner than his fellow Kalarians, his white hair was depleted and, when Zoe looked closely, she saw that his pink skin was slightly mottled with white. By the standards of his race, he was evidently quite old.

When she had first realised that three other prisoners had followed her in her mad dash, her hopes had soared. She didn't have to do this alone, she had thought.

'We are less likely to starve than to be found and executed,' said Davidson, pragmatically.

'We should go out there and fight!' said Kukhadil.

'We have no weapons, nor any way of getting them.'

'We should have stayed where we were,' moaned Dresden. He pulled his knees up to his chest and buried his face in his arms again, so all Zoe could see was an untidy mop of red hair. She felt sorry for him. Dresden was only seventeen years old. He had been captured on Molinar, during his first combat mission with the Terran Security Forces. If ever he had aspired to a soldier's life, his illusions had been ground out of him. Like the others, he had witnessed Zoe's departure from the holding area, had realised he wasn't under scrutiny and had followed her on nothing more than a rash impulse.

'Kukhadil's right,' said Zoe decisively. 'We have to do something.'

'What's your plan?' Zoe's first impression of Davidson was that she was probably good at following orders, but unprepared to take the initiative.

She had been stunned to realise that the others looked to her for direction. Suddenly, they had become more of a responsibility than a help. But she was also rather flattered.

What would the Doctor have done? Zoe had not yet seen the

prison that could hold him – and, after all, she was more intelligent than he was. OK, so perhaps he was more intuitive, but she would get there in the end. And he might be more knowledgeable, but she had learnt a great deal about the Selachians and Ockora from Paterson.

She was determined. She could do this.

She tried to mimic the Doctor's characteristic confidence. She hoped her efforts would be less transparent than his often were. 'First, we have to find a Selachian vehicle.'

'Aren't they filled with water?' protested Davidson.

'We can drain it out, even if we're submerged. They have systems to let you do that.'

'So, where can we find one?' asked Kukhadil, in an encouraging tone.

'Well, I've been thinking, and I haven't seen any in the complex at all, apart from when new prisoners are brought in. So, I wonder if the Selachians leave them outside, under water. It would make sense – the vehicles probably aren't optimised for land use, and they won't want them to empty whenever they open the doors.'

Zoe paused. The lack of any challenge, any qualification at all, to her theory disconcerted her. She got the impression that the others weren't interested in her reasoning, just in her conclusion. Could she do this on her own?

'Now, there might be an airlock somewhere,' she pressed on – they would all be lost if she faltered – 'but I'll bet there isn't. I should think the entrance to the complex is under water. The Selachians must get out of their vehicles and swim upwards to get in.'

'So, what are you suggesting?' asked Kukhadil.

'We go to the communications room,' said Zoe. 'Don't worry, I can find it. The Selachians' Supreme Leader was there, so it makes sense that it should be nearer to the entrance than the main holding area is. From there... well, we'll have to explore.

Just the passages I haven't seen, of course. And, wherever possible, we'll head downwards.'

'Sounds like a plan to me,' said Kukhadil. Zoe was grateful for his support.

'Davidson?'

'If you think it is our best hope.'

'Adam? How about you?'

The boy looked up. His eyes were red and swollen, but also round and frightened. A teenager's beard of fine hair had grown during his months of captivity. Zoe gave him what she hoped was a reassuring look. At last, he rewarded her efforts with a mute nod.

Zoe smiled, feeling as if she had accomplished something. 'Right,' she said, 'so long as the main passageway is empty I think we should start out.'

They reached the communications room quite easily. There was only one worrying moment, as they took shelter from a Selachian. They pressed themselves against the wall of a side passage, and Dresden shook so fiercely that Zoe was almost convinced that he would be heard.

They found a downward-sloping tunnel, as Zoe had planned. After a few minutes she realised it was taking them, by a circuitous route, to the cell in which Paterson had been tortured. They turned back and tried again.

Partway down the new tunnel Leanne Davidson stopped them unexpectedly. She put a finger to her lips when Zoe tried to ask why. After a few seconds, she explained in a whisper, 'I heard a slithering sound.'

'Look!' Kukhadil pointed at the uneven ground in front of them.

Dresden recoiled, although Zoe couldn't see anything and doubted if the boy could either. She took a tentative step, but the old Kalarian dragged her back. 'Get away from it!'

'From what? I can't see anything!'

'It's right there.'

'Yes,' said Davidson, in awe, 'I can see it.'

Zoe concentrated – and, at last, she saw something too. She didn't know what. Her brain couldn't process the information, couldn't tell her what was happening. It was as if parts of the ground were shifting and changing, although the effect was almost imperceptible.

'What is it?' whimpered Dresden, from behind them.

'A creature,' said Kukhadil. 'It has disguised itself.'

'A Shark thinker weapon!' said Davidson.

'What can it do?' asked Zoe.

'Who knows? Bite, burrow, burn, freeze, shock; it could even be acidic.'

The ripple effect had spread almost to Zoe's foot. Alarmed, she skipped back away from it. Kukhadil and Davidson did likewise. 'Does it know we're here?' asked Zoe.

'I think it's locked on to us,' said Davidson. 'It will follow us.'

'It moves slowly,' Kukhadil pointed out. 'We can easily outpace it.'

'Yes,' mused Zoe, 'it clearly wasn't engineered for pursuit. I'll bet we were meant to step right on it. If it hadn't been for Davidson…'

'We must go back,' said Davidson.

'No. This has to be the way out. Why else would the Selachians have left that thing here?'

'Can we jump over it?' asked Kukhadil.

'I can't see how long it is,' said Davidson. 'Can you?'

'There must be a way to get past it,' insisted Zoe as the group was forced to take three more paces backwards. 'How would the Selachians do it?'

'It probably has some way to recognise them,' said Davidson.

'Perhaps their armour protects them,' said Kukhadil.

Zoe looked down at her bare feet, gloomily. They were cut and bleeding.

Davidson was running her hands over the wall. Finding handholds, she levered herself up and rested her right foot on a precariously narrow ledge. Her left foot hung unsupported.

'What are you doing?' gasped Zoe.

'Let me try this. Keep walking up the tunnel. When I think the creature has passed me, I'll drop down behind it.'

'We can't all do that!' protested Dresden.

'Just do as she says for now,' said Zoe.

'I hope this thing can't crawl up walls,' muttered Davidson.

They moved slowly, constantly checking for the tiny signs that would show that the creature still followed them. It moved at a painstaking crawl, and Zoe began to fear that Davidson would lose her grip and fall on top of it. When she did leap back to the ground Zoe held her breath. But Davidson was unharmed. She straightened up and grinned.

'What now?' asked Kukhadil.

Zoe had been thinking about that. 'I think we should speed up and get out of the creature's range. With a bit of luck, it should forget about us, turn around and follow Davidson – then we can follow them both down the tunnel, until it widens out or forks.'

'We can't go down there,' moaned Dresden. 'What if there are more monsters?'

The following hour was especially harrowing. It wasn't that there was any immediate danger – it was simply that, forced to move at a tortuous pace in the wake of Davidson and the thinker weapon, and with little else to think about, Zoe couldn't help but worry about what might happen. This tunnel had to be in use, she thought – if a Selachian came along it in either direction, either Davidson or the three of them would be trapped.

Fortunately, no Selachian came. The tunnel ended, at last, at a vast cavern the size of the main holding area. Most of its floor area was taken up by a huge lake. Zoe felt a tingle of excitement. 'I was right,' she whispered. 'This must be the entrance to the complex.'

Davidson led the thinker weapon around the lake, then broke into a run as she reached the opposite side, and rejoined her fellow escapees. Hopefully, Zoe thought, she had left the creature behind. She warned everyone to be on their guard, just in case.

The quartet shrank back into the tunnel as the armoured head of a Selachian appeared at the water's edge. The creature hauled itself out into the cavern. Then it marched smartly through one of several more openings in the wall.

Zoe hurried forward, dropped to her knees and peered intently into the beautifully clear water. 'I can see big, greeny-brown shapes down there,' she reported joyfully. 'Selachian vehicles, they must be. And they don't seem too far down.'

'Well done,' said Kukhadil, emphatically. Zoe glowed with pride.

Davidson brought her back down to earth. 'Let's hope they aren't booby-trapped or guarded, and that we can hold our breaths long enough to work out how to operate one.'

'I think just one of us should go down there, to start with,' said Zoe, thoughtfully. 'The Selachians are less likely to notice.'

She looked at the others. Dresden was terrified. Kukhadil was too frail. Davidson had risked her life for the group once, so Zoe didn't like to ask her to do it again.

'I'll go,' she decided, trying not to show her reluctance.

To her disappointment, nobody argued.

Zoe grimaced as she slipped into the water, feet first, remembering her recent aquatic misadventures. She allowed the weight of her overalls to drag her down, not putting too much effort into her strokes and hoping that this would enable her to hold her breath for longer. To her delight, there were at least thirty vehicles below her, parked neatly in a grid pattern.

She kept a wary eye out for Selachians, but saw none until she had settled on to the sandy floor. Then an armoured figure swam overhead. She shrank against the side of a vehicle, and the creature passed out of sight without noticing her.

The vehicle had the same design as the two in which she had previously travelled. Its door opened easily, and she pulled herself into the cabin. She saw nothing that resembled a steering column or a joystick, but there was a recognisable dashboard. Bumpy controls grew out of it like tiny swellings. There were no displays, no labels in any language.

Zoe was running out of time. But perhaps, she thought, she could at least find the button that drained the cabin. Then she could take a breather, have a proper look at the controls and go back for the others with the best possible news.

She touched one of the growths experimentally. It dimpled beneath her finger.

She gasped, as a thin tentacle whipped out of the dashboard and coiled itself around her wrist. She pulled at it, but it held her fast. She gripped the tentacle with her free hand and tried to wrench it free. This, too, was to no avail. Trepidation turned to self-recrimination, and then to panic. She should have guessed the vehicle would have a security system. She should have been more careful.

Her chest began to ache. The last of her air spilled out of her mouth and bubbled away. Her lungs strained for more, and Zoe had to force herself not to breathe in water.

Something buzzed inside her head. At first, she put it down to her brain's initial protests at being starved of oxygen – but there was something else. A presence. It felt as if some sort of worm had slithered into her skull. She blinked fiercely, as if to dislodge it.

Then she realised what it was. The tentacle wasn't a security system at all. Somehow, its touch allowed Zoe to communicate telepathically with the vehicle. Yes, telepathic circuits… she had felt something similar in the TARDIS, but never this strongly.

With desperate hope, Zoe formed an image in her mind: an image of water flowing out of the cabin. She tried to make it as vivid and realistic as possible.

Pain stabbed into her head. She couldn't keep herself from squealing. She took in water and had to suppress the powerful urge to cough. Her vision had misted. But the pain had gone and, to Zoe's surprise, she saw that the tentacle had retracted. Perhaps it had finally responded to her need. Or perhaps, in the absence of any commands at all, it had simply turned itself off. Either way, she was free.

She stumbled out of the vehicle and swam upwards. Her arms and legs felt weak and unresponsive, and the baggy overalls that had aided her descent only dragged her down now. She didn't look for Selachians. She didn't care, couldn't afford to care, if she was spotted.

She could hardly see, anyway, for the black void that crashed in around her.

She wasn't going to make it.

Zoe put a hand to her mouth in an attempt to muffle the sound of her coughs. She had been dragged out of the water by Davidson, who had come in search of her. Or so she had been told; she had no memory of the event. Now, she sat propped up against the wall of another tunnel forcing out, between deep breaths, the tale of her exploits in the vehicle park.

'It seems we have run out of options,' said Davidson. 'We can't drive the vehicles, so we can't leave.'

'Not necessarily,' said Zoe. 'Just because telepathy didn't work… well, the vehicles must have manual controls.'

'Why must they?' asked Davidson.

'You nearly died down there,' said Dresden. 'Shouldn't we

give up now?'

'Anyway,' continued Zoe, ignoring them both, 'I have a better idea. I'm willing to bet that the reason the telepathic circuits didn't recognise my commands is because my brain is so different to an Ockoran brain. But Kukhadil...'

'Kukhadil is not an Ockoran,' said Davidson.

'I know that,' said Zoe, exasperated by her continual scepticism. 'But there is a physical resemblance between the Ockorans and the Kalarians. I don't know why – perhaps they share common ancestry, perhaps it's something to do with the conditions in this system – but there is a similarity.'

'You think the vehicle may respond to me?' asked Kukhadil.

'It's possible.'

Zoe watched as the old Kalarian allowed his head to loll back against the wall. She tried to read the thoughts that passed across his eyes. He wasn't frightened, she could see that, but he was asking himself if this was a wise thing to do.

'I know it's asking a lot,' she said, 'but the vehicles aren't a long way down, really they aren't. I'm sure you can make it. And I'll go with you, so I can bring you out if anything goes wrong.'

A weak smile formed on Kukhadil's face, and he nodded. 'Very well,' he said. 'If you think it is our best course of action, then I shall try.'

Zoe's stomach fluttered as she realised, once again, that the responsibility for this plan lay entirely with her.

She pointed out the button to Kukhadil. He moved a long finger towards it, then pulled it back again. But the water around them allowed no time for hesitation. Kukhadil turned his head from the dashboard, closed his eyes and pressed the button.

The thin tentacle shot out and wrapped itself around his wrist. Zoe crossed her fingers and studied her companion's face intently. She prayed that, should the vehicle's telepathic circuits prove incompatible with the Kalarian's brain, he could find the strength to break the connection, as she had.

Then a beatific expression settled on Kukhadil's face. Zoe allowed herself to hope.

She heard a gurgling noise, as the water began to drain from the cabin.

But then she heard something else too: a strident bellowing, which seemed to come from the vehicle itself, as if it was in pain. The sound was repeated, over and over. As the water level fell below Zoe's face, she gasped and cried out, 'You've set off an alarm!'

'I'm trying to deactivate it,' Kukhadil wailed, 'but it's asking for a password.'

'It's too late for that – we have to get out of here! Can you drive this thing?'

'Are we leaving the others behind?'

Zoe didn't know what to say. In truth, she hadn't thought about Davidson and Dresden at all. They would be on their way down here in a few minutes, expecting her to meet them and guide them towards the liberated vessel. Now, they would probably swim straight into the Selachians instead. Zoe felt a terrible pang of guilt at the thought of abandoning them, but a more terrible fear at the thought of what would happen if she didn't.

She froze, unable to make the only logical choice.

And then, she saw four Selachians through the windscreen. They marched in step towards the intruders, appearing unhurried but approaching quickly. She tried to kick open the door, to escape, but the pressure of the water outside kept it closed.

And then the creatures were at each side of them and reaching out to open the doors themselves, and Zoe could do nothing but scream.

Chapter Twenty-Four

The Doctor had just taken the biggest risk of his life.

He played with his fingers, anxiously, and paced up and down – which, in the unsteady confines of the rear compartment of a moving Selachian transport, was not easy. The additional presence of two guards made it almost impossible.

'You will sit,' ordered one of the Selachians.

'Don't be so ridiculous!' the Doctor returned, petulantly – and unwisely, perhaps, but his thoughts were dominated by a weightier issue.

If his people found out about this...

What was he thinking? That was the least of his problems – of the universe's problems.

He was halted by the physical impediment of a blaster pressed into his stomach. The second creature, on whose arm the weapon was mounted, growled, 'You will obey all Selachian directives or we will kill you.'

'Yes, yes, very pithy, but that wouldn't be an awfully clever thing to do, would it?' The guard didn't react. The Doctor raised a meaningful eyebrow. 'Your leader would be most upset. You'd be spoiling his plans, and I don't think he'd appreciate that, do you?'

The Selachian seemed to think for a moment, before shifting its arm so that the gun was pointed downwards. It fired. The Doctor leapt into the air with a howl. Fortunately, the guard had not intended to hurt him. Its plasma blast melted the sole of his right boot.

'Oh, very well,' the Doctor sighed, defeated, 'if it means so much to you.' He dropped to the floor, with bad grace.

He sat with his legs crossed, buried his face in his hands and thought frantically.

He had met the Supreme Leader in a dried-out reception room, furnished to human tastes with comfortable chairs, a deep carpet, and screens to hide its bare rock walls. Despite this, he had been made to stand. 'I must say, I am impressed by your hospitality,' he had said ingratiatingly, 'although it really wasn't necessary. As a visitor to your world, I would have been quite happy to have met you in your own environment.'

'Air-breathers are not permitted to pollute our waters.'

'Ah, no, no, of course not.' It was a measure of the Supreme Leader's paranoia, the Doctor had thought, that he was more willing to put on a battlesuit and step out of his life-sustaining element than he was to allow a single alien to remain beneath Ockora's waves. Still, after what Commander Redfern had done the Doctor could hardly blame him.

Two guards had been stationed behind him. As if that hadn't been enough, his oxygenerator unit had been taken from him. He had been trapped in the underwater room.

'You intrigue me, Doctor,' his host had said.

'Oh, good,' the Doctor had returned, warily, 'I do like to remain interesting.'

'You are an enemy of our people. Why did you warn us of the humans' attack?'

The Selachians to whom the Doctor had surrendered had been equally nonplussed – and more so, when he had demanded to see their leader, insisting that he was expected.

'I am not your enemy, Supreme Leader. I am the enemy of anything that is wrong or evil in this universe. My responsibility is to the innocent, whoever or whatever they may be.'

'You have interfered with our plans several times in the past.'

'Only when those plans have been wrong.'

'No, Doctor. Our single goal has always been to protect our innocent brethren.'

The Doctor's anger had matched the Selachian's own. 'No matter who else suffers?'

'Perhaps I should tell you of our people's history.'

'Yes, yes, I am well aware of the terrible things the Kalarians did to you – but you can't continue to take out your frustrations on every non-aquatic life form in the galaxy!'

'They are all the same. Given an opportunity, any air-breather will commit great atrocities against our kind. It is in their nature. Your friends have proved that.'

'They are no friends of mine. I am utterly opposed to what the Terran Security Forces did today. Well, that's why I contacted you.'

'But you could not stop the humans.'

'Sadly, no.'

'No. You could not stop them as they rampaged through a peaceful village, slaughtering almost a hundred of our females and young, destroying the homes of many more.' Even through his translation equipment, the Supreme Leader had sounded sickened. But his predominant emotion, at least the one he had displayed, had been cold fury. 'That, Doctor, is what we have been fighting to prevent. Our species needs a defence against your noisome kind. As the Supreme Leader of the Selachian Corps, it is my duty to provide that defence.'

Saddened, the Doctor had tried one more argument. 'Your enemies know only the side of the Ockorans that you choose to portray: the vengeful creatures, the fierce warriors – you've gone to pains to foster the image of yourselves as ruthless sharks. You should be exporting your poetry, your artwork, your beautiful speech-song. The humans don't recognise the difference between your soldiers and the rest of your people, the non-combatants.'

'That is because they are air-breathing animals!'

Raising his voice again and beetling his brow, the Doctor had snapped, 'You ought to recognise their attitude, Supreme Leader – because it is not too different from your own!'

The Doctor had not asked what had happened to Redfern and his unit. Part of him didn't want to know. He had not found it easy to betray them, but he had had no choice. He had not been able to stand and watch as they murdered innocent beings.

And yet, Selachian justice was harsh. What if the Doctor's interference had led to the deaths of the young and naïve Lieutenant Klavar, or of the hapless privates?

He thought of all the monsters – the Daleks, the Cybermen, the Ice Warriors – that he had been forced to kill to keep them from committing greater evils. Sometimes, greed and haste had led them to destroy themselves, but always the Doctor had had a hand in their downfall. Was it so different this time? Was his guilt any greater because his actions might have brought harm to human beings?

No. He had done the right thing. He had saved many, many Ockoran natives. If their would-be killers had died, then he would mourn them. But he couldn't regret what he had done.

Except...

What if the Selachians had killed Wayne Redfern, or even captured him? Left in charge of the mission, the more cool-headed Kent Michaels might see reason. The G-bomb might never be launched; Ockora might be spared. A crucial page of history might be rewritten, and it would be the Doctor's fault. More lives saved, he thought, but at what cost?

He tried to reassure himself. So far, he was only dealing with maybes. Time was good at handling maybes, at confounding probabilities. It would bend, but it might not break.

But his likely effect on Redfern's fate was the lesser of the Doctor's two problems.

He had also done something far worse.

* * *

'You must release my friend!'

'The human female is of use to us.'

'My offer still stands: take me in exchange for her.'

Selachians were incapable of laughter, but the Supreme Leader's derisive snort had sounded very much like it. 'I already have you, Doctor. You have been caught trespassing on my world.'

'But I surrendered to you, I warned you what the humans were doing.'

'You committed a criminal act in accompanying them to Ockora. You obviously planned some form of action against us.'

Aggrieved and angry, the Doctor had forced himself to calm down. He had interlocked his fingers and raised his eyebrows in a gesture of appeal which had been belied by his gritted teeth. 'Come now, Supreme Leader, you don't need to maintain that intolerant façade with me. We are both civilised beings, I'm sure we can discuss this reasonably.'

'There will be no discussion. Our laws are clear.'

'You don't frighten me, you know.'

'Then you should be frightened, Doctor. You should fear justice.'

'I am asking you for one small favour – surely you owe me that consideration?'

'The Selachians owe their enemies only the pain of death!'

'Well, that's gratitude for you!' the Doctor had complained, his patience exhausted.

'You have escaped from Selachian custody before. The human female will be our insurance. She will die if you defy us. However, once the war has ended she will be released.'

'It will be too late by then!'

The Doctor had spluttered the words in desperation. He had regretted them instantly.

'How so?'

'Well, I mean… what I mean to say is… how do I know I can trust you?'

The Supreme Leader had not been distracted. 'What do you know of the humans' plans?'

The Doctor had drawn himself up to his full height, attempting to bluff the Selachian with false confidence. 'They... they don't confide in me.'

'You can tell me now, Doctor,' the Supreme Leader had said, almost sounding bored, 'or I can torture you...'

'I can assure you, that would be a monumental waste of everybody's time.'

'...or I can torture your friend.'

One life. One life against the sanctity of history, the safety of the universe.

The Doctor was familiar with the dilemma. He had heard of it long ago in the stifling halls of academia. It had haunted him since. Even humankind knew its basics.

Could you kill a baby, if you knew that baby would grow up to become an evil dictator? If that simple act could save many thousands of lives?

The Doctor should have let Zoe die. One life for a future. That would have been the logical decision.

But he couldn't always live by the rules of logic. She was his responsibility. He had dragged her into a life of peril. He couldn't abandon her now, any more than he could have put a gun to that hypothetical baby's head.

The Doctor hadn't had time to think: the Supreme Leader's questions and threats had come thick and fast.

He had been painfully aware of time running out. His mind had focused upon Zoe, upon what the Selachians might do to her, what would happen to her anyway if she remained on Ockora.

In the end, he had seen no choice.

'The humans are going to destroy your world.'

'That is impossible.'

There had been no point in holding back, then. 'They've developed a new weapon. A bomb. They should have used it already. I don't know how long you've got.'

'Why should I believe you?'

'Contact the flagship. Ask them outright.'

'That is where the bomb is situated?'

'Yes, yes, now please do as I ask, you may not have much time.'

'And how do you suggest we counteract this weapon?'

'You can't, not in the time remaining. You must surrender!'

'Surrender?'

'You have no choice, Supreme Leader. It's the only way to save your race!'

The Doctor raised his head, gloomily, to look at the staunch figures of his two Selachian guards. Their leader wouldn't want to surrender – but nor would he risk the destruction of everything and everyone for which he had fought. He would follow the Doctor's advice. He had probably contacted the *Triumph* already.

Or perhaps he wouldn't have time. Perhaps the bomb would fall now. Perhaps that would be better, although it meant the Doctor's life would be forfeit.

But what about Zoe?

Even as he had blurted out his information, the Doctor's mind had been ticking furiously. How could he ameliorate the effects of his interference?

He would have to stay in this era, of course. He could broker a peace between Selachians and humans. If Ockora could be sealed off, then its inhabitants would have little influence upon the future. Their survival might not affect the big picture.

The sheer magnitude of the task depressed him. But, short of commandeering the *Triumph* and launching the bomb himself, what else could he do?

He considered that alternative for less than a second.

'Very well,' the Supreme Leader had said. 'In consideration of your service to us, I will release the young female.'

The Doctor had been unable to disguise his relief – but it had been short-lived.

'However, your past transgressions cannot be overlooked. You will be executed. The event will be made public. It will be good for morale.'

The Doctor's face had fallen as, at the Supreme Leader's signal, the two guards had taken his arms. 'No, wait, you can't do this!'

'Fear at last, Doctor? Do you value your life after all?'

'It isn't my life I'm concerned about. It's your life, the lives of all your people, of every sentient being in the universe. I'm begging you, Supreme Leader – I've done something very foolish, and I need to be allowed to put it right.'

The Selachian had turned away from him, uncaring.

'You must forget what I told you,' the Doctor had yelled, desperately. 'Ockora has to be destroyed, or else the entire universe will perish!'

The Supreme Leader hadn't understood, of course – and perhaps that was for the best. 'If Ockora is indeed to die,' he had growled, fists clenched, back still turned to the Doctor, 'then the destruction of a universe would be a suitable atonement.'

The Doctor was on his way to a Selachian prison, there to await execution. But even that predicament seemed inconsequential.

He had dealt Time a grievous wound. He had hoped that, with his attempts at first aid, it could heal. But it had been a desperate gamble, an insane risk.

He very much feared that he had damaged history beyond all hope of repair.

Chapter Twenty-Five

The bomb chamber was sealed by a heavy door which bristled with locks and bolts. It was a comforting image, but a laughable precaution. The weapons within could each destroy a world; they weren't likely to balk at fifteen centimetres of steel.

Right now, though, the door was a palpable obstacle.

'Situation?' rapped Michaels, as he strode up to the three-man security detail who stood helplessly outside the chamber.

'The motion detector shows three people inside, sir, but we can't get in.'

Michaels stabbed at the access button.

'They don't respond, sir.'

'You've tried overriding?'

'They've engaged the voice lock.'

'On whose authorisation?'

'Professor Mulholland's, sir.'

Michaels thought for only a few seconds. In this type of situation his duty was clear. The others just needed somebody to decide what to do and and give the order.

'Do we have an explosives expert?'

'Godwin, sir.'

'Get him down here. We need to blow that door.'

One of the soldiers pulled his communicator from a pouch and began to make the arrangements. Another approached Michaels with a nervous cough. 'Lieutenant Michaels, you do know the G-bombs are in there?'

'It had crossed my mind,' said Michaels drily.

'But, sir, we were warned not to expose them to vibrations.'

'What do you think is happening in there, Private? That

Selachian has taken two hostages, and one of them happens to be the only person who knows how to activate those things. I'm guessing we'll feel a few vibrations ourselves, if we don't act pronto.'

'Yes, sir,' said the private, cowed.

Of course, Mulholland couldn't actually launch the G-bombs, not without the authorisation codes. But, once the Selachian learned that… well, as Michaels had just been reminded, there were many ways in which to detonate the unstable bombs *in situ*.

The corridor began to fill up as soldiers concluded their own fruitless searches and converged upon the chamber. Godwin arrived and set to work. He fixed electro-grenades around the door, making fine adjustments to the direction and force of the output of each one. As Michaels watched him, he couldn't help but wonder if this was where it would end for him. It seemed almost fated. Of all the people on this ship, why had the Selachian had to take Mulholland and Jamie? It was as if he was being punished for breaking his own rules, for becoming involved.

For an instant, the situation became distant and unreal. Michaels seemed to be seeing the door across a black expanse – as if the tunnel had arrived for him, appearing as a negative image to his still-open eyes.

And then, Godwin motioned to the onlookers to move back, although Michaels stayed dangerously close. If anything was to go wrong, he thought, the *Triumph* wouldn't be big enough to escape it.

The grenades took out the hinges and locks of the door, whilst barely buckling its surface. It fell inwards, landing with a nerve-jangling thud. By the time it hit Michaels was already sprinting into the chamber, pulling his rifle from its sling. There was no time to be cautious.

He raised his weapon, blinking as his eyes adjusted to the

dim, red light. He felt the presence of four soldiers at his back. He looked across the array of consoles and saw the Selachian in its life-preserving suit. It was unarmed but it held Mulholland in a headlock, using her as a shield. Jamie stood to one side. He seemed bemused and helpless, but the Selachian was paying him no heed. That could be useful.

Oh, and the impact of the fallen door hadn't set off the G-bombs. That was good, too.

'Let the woman go and get those hands up!' Michaels ordered, trying to forget the woman's identity. 'You can't win, you're outnumbered.'

'I can save my world,' the Selachian hissed. It must have got hold of a translation device, somehow. 'I can prevent you from employing your cowardly weapons.'

'We won't need to employ them if your Supreme Leader surrenders.'

'We will not surrender. We will defeat your weak kind, with your flimsy bones.'

'That's not going to happen.'

'This repulsive piece of plankton has agreed to dismantle the bombs.'

'She can't, she doesn't have the activation codes.'

'I did tell you that,' Mulholland interjected, pointedly.

The Selachian paused, as if disappointed. It must have been testing the scientist's claim. 'Very well,' it said finally. 'You will release the codes, or I will snap her neck.'

Michaels shook his head. 'I'm not giving you the chance to blow us all sky high.'

Unexpectedly, Jamie stepped forward. 'Look, he just wants to shut those things down.' He glared at the Selachian and added, 'Right?' Michaels wondered what game he was playing.

'Enough of this,' the Selachian growled. 'You know my terms. I will give you ten seconds to agree to them.'

And, suddenly, Kent Michaels didn't know what to do.

The feeling frightened him. He had always been able to take decisions before, almost without thinking. His duty had always been clear and logical. But this time it was different. He asked himself what Redfern would have done and concluded that he would have started firing, whatever the risk. Mulholland was expendable: her death would set back the mission, but only for as long as it would take to draft in a replacement, somebody else from the G-bomb project.

'For God's sake,' urged Mulholland, more irritated than scared, 'just let me decommission the bombs. The war's practically won, what do you need them for anyway?'

What indeed? Why sacrifice another human life for so little?

Was Michaels allowing his friendship with Mulholland to cloud his judgement? Doing what he had always fought not to do? Repeating the mistake he had made with Jamie in the Kalarian forest? He knew what his commanding officer would expect of him. He ought to do it: call his enemy's bluff, show the Sharks they couldn't win.

Or was he being too harsh, overcompensating for his personal feelings?

'Well?' the Selachian prompted – too soon, much too soon.

Michaels just stared.

'The female's life is forfeit.'

'No!' Suddenly Jamie charged, shoulder first, at the Selachian. It hadn't expected the attack; it staggered and lost its grip on Mulholland. She immediately dropped behind a console, out of Michaels's sight. He sighted down his rifle, but the Selachian was wrestling with Jamie and he couldn't shoot without endangering the lad.

It didn't matter. The confusion was gone now. He knew what to do.

He ran at the nearest console and vaulted over it, landing heavily but on his feet. He dropped the rifle to free his hands and grabbed the Selachian by its shoulders, tearing it away from Jamie. It fought back, but it was weak without its battlesuit. Michaels unbalanced it easily, and slammed it down on to its back. It landed just as Mulholland climbed back to her feet. Michaels pushed her behind him, protectively.

By now, the other soldiers had circled the room to surround the fallen creature. It made as if to stand, but gave up as it saw four rifles pointed at its head. Far from the hate-filled threats that Michaels had come to expect, the Selachian let out a high-pitched, agonised howl.

Satisfied, if a little disconcerted, he crouched down and reached for his rifle.

It was snatched away from his fingers.

Michaels stood slowly, not believing what he saw. The rifle was in Jamie's hands. He was backing away, but keeping the weapon trained on the lieutenant.

He sounded upset, even frightened, but determined. 'I'm sorry, Lieutenant Michaels – I wouldn't go along with him just killing the professor like that – but I won't let you destroy his world, either.'

'What do you think you're playing at?'

'I want you to do as he says: shut down those bombs.'

More soldiers had entered the room, silently. They covered Jamie with their rifles but, while he in turn covered Michaels, they didn't dare act.

'Am I hearing this right?' challenged Michaels. 'Are you siding with that creature?'

'I'm not taking anyone's side, but you can't just wipe out a whole world – especially not when the Doctor and Zoe are still down there.'

Michaels thought of the soldiers who had died on Kalaya because he had chosen to save Jamie's life. He had allowed his emotions to overrule his intellect; now, it seemed that those emotions had been misplaced. He felt a dangerous anger rising in his stomach and chest. It was the anger he had felt with himself, but now it had found a new direction. It defied him not to release it.

'So, Redfern was right about you – you and the Doctor are Shark sympathisers!'

'No, I swear, I'm still on your side – but if you just knew about the Selachians...'

'The Sharks are our enemies,' growled Michaels, beginning to move forward.

Jamie's eyes widened. He shifted his grip on the gun. He had backed up all the way to the wall. 'Don't come any closer, I'm warning you, I'll shoot!'

He had made a mistake. He was offering Michaels a familiar choice: life against duty.

Michaels leapt at him. Jamie fumbled with the rifle, made his own decision too late, turned it around and used it as a stick to fend off his attacker. By now, Michaels's hands were on the rifle too. He forced it back towards Jamie's throat. The lad was stronger than he had thought. They glared at each other as they struggled. Jamie was sweating, his determination showing in the set of his jaw. Michaels was aware that he had bared his teeth, that anger had twisted his expression. He tried to detach himself, to think clearly. He pushed down hard, surprising Jamie and sweeping the rifle on to the floor. Before the lad had recovered, Michaels followed through with a solid punch to his stomach. Jamie crumpled, and Michaels kicked the rifle away from him.

The other soldiers moved in. The lieutenant raised a hand to stop them. He didn't turn, didn't want to look at any of them. They couldn't see his eyes.

'I'll deal with this myself.'

'Sir?'

'It's over, Private. Take that creature to the brig and get out, all of you! And take the professor with you.'

He heard the scuffling of movement behind him. Blood

rushed through his ears, amplifying his heartbeat. He felt the anger inside him; with deep breaths, he began to form a shell around it, controlling but not extinguishing it. Jamie looked up at him warily, his expression mutinous but his eyes regretful. When Michaels's ears told him that they were alone he stooped, gripped the lad by his shirt and hoisted him to his feet. Noticing the long dagger in its scabbard at Jamie's leg, he seized it and tossed it aside.

'I trusted you,' he snarled, in a low voice.

'Look, I didn't mean to go against you. I thought you'd agree with me. If you'd only listen to the facts…'

Still holding Jamie's shirt, Michaels threw him against the wall and pinned him there. 'You turned a gun on me!'

'Aw, come on… I was trying to save lives!'

'To protect the Sharks, you mean.'

'Them and everyone else on Ockora!'

'I saved your life!'

'Aye,' said Jamie, 'and I saved yours too.'

'You don't know what it cost me!'

Five soldiers. Five soldiers had died on Kalaya because Michaels hadn't done his duty. And he knew all their names, much as he tried not to remember them. He had broken his own rules, and for what? For the life of a traitor.

Michaels must have been pressing too hard because Jamie began to squirm as if in pain. 'Look, get your hands off me!' he protested.

His defiance only hardened the lieutenant's resolve. 'Why?' he spat as Jamie pulled at his hands, trying to break his grip. 'So you can report back to your masters? I was stupid enough to think you were my friend!'

'Then you've a funny way of treating your friends,' asserted Jamie. He lashed out with a foot, and caught Michaels by surprise with a sharp kick to his knee.

As Michaels recoiled Jamie pressed his advantage. His fists

flailed, striking wherever they could. The blows were almost ineffective against Michaels's padded uniform but the lieutenant lost ground to the sheer energy of the attack. He tried to defend himself and hit back at the same time, which resulted in him catching Jamie's chin with his arm. Jamie saw the futility of punching his foe and tackled him instead. He buried his head in Michaels's stomach and sent them both crashing into a console. Michaels winced as he felt its sharp edge in his back. But it gave him leverage. He flung Jamie away from him. Jamie went with the motion, dropped to the floor and rose again with his blade in his hand. But Michaels was already upon him, seizing his wrist and twisting it so that he lost his weapon again.

The dam had burst now, and a torrent of anger had been released. The more Michaels fought, the more he revelled in it. He began to see Jamie through a red haze – and then he wasn't seeing him at all, he was seeing William Butcher. He was fifteen years old again and fighting the bully of his childhood, the boy who had hospitalised him.

He fought his way through Jamie's defences, punched him three times and, with an almost feral cry of triumph, threw him backwards. Jamie hit the wall hard... but it wasn't the wall...

A sobering fear crept over Michaels as he saw what he had done. He had hurled Jamie into the transparent shield at the front of the housing of one of the G-bombs. As the lad rebounded from the plastic it vibrated alarmingly. The red haze lifted, the world snapped back to normal and something cold twisted in Michaels' stomach as he waited for the explosion.

Jamie had seen the threat too. He was doubled over and breathless, but his fearful gaze was fixed on the bomb. He backed away from it until he was at Michaels' side.

There was silence, for a second.

They both jumped at the sound of a furious voice, from the doorway behind them.

'What the hell is going on in here?' bellowed Commander Redfern.

Chapter Twenty-Six

Zoe's stomach dropped and she almost fell as the Selachian vehicle launched itself off the seabed and shot vertically upwards. She wanted to cry out to Kukhadil, to ask what was happening, but she was too short of breath. And then the answer became obvious.

She was pushed down, almost crushed, as the transport decelerated rapidly. It emerged from the water and bobbed placidly on its surface.

'I didn't know it could do that,' gasped Zoe, putting a hand to her chest and feeling the quickened rhythm of her heart.

Kukhadil's pink face was flushed. 'I told it to get us out of there – there was only one way left unguarded.'

Zoe needed to think quickly, but the continuing bellow of the alarm disrupted her concentration. 'They'll be following us.'

The vehicle rotated slowly, presumably at Kukhadil's instruction. The old Kalarian surveyed the cavern through the windscreen. 'I can't see Davidson or Dresden.'

'This wasn't part of our plan. They must think we're Selachians – they'll be hiding.'

'I'll take us to the edge of the water.'

'That way,' said Zoe, pointing. 'That's where we left them.'

Kukhadil nodded, and lines of concentration appeared on his face. As he flexed and unflexed his hand the tentacle that was coiled around it pulsated. The vehicle began to move, painfully slowly, trembling as if it had extended legs or flippers and was paddling. Zoe found herself wondering how intelligent the Selachians' organic machines had to be before they could be considered truly alive.

As the transport hit the rocky bank Zoe pushed open the door and yelled out the names of her missing friends. Her voice was drowned out by the vehicle's cries. She shouted again, scrambling through the door and on to dry land.

Davidson appeared at the mouth of the unfinished tunnel. At the same moment, Zoe heard a tremendous splash behind her. She turned to see that another transport had broken the water's surface. A third emerged beside it.

'Quickly!'

Davidson had vanished but she returned immediately, dragging Dresden by the hand. Zoe ran back to the transport, but halted and gaped as she saw that it had turned so that the open door had drifted away from the bank. She resigned herself to the idea of swimming for it – until she saw what Kukhadil was doing.

He had reoriented the vehicle so that it faced them. It whirred and groaned – but still emitted its raucous siren – as its caterpillar tracks came into play and it hauled itself, with difficulty, from the water. It shuddered to a halt and Zoe leapt into its cabin. Davidson pushed Dresden after her then ran to the far door, yanked it open and took her place at Kukhadil's left.

They couldn't see behind them now. Zoe wondered how close the other vehicles were.

'What do I do?' Kukhadil shouted over the siren.

'You can't turn back,' Davidson pointed out.

'Take us down one of the tunnels,' ordered Zoe. 'Not that one,' she added quickly, 'it doesn't go anywhere!'

'Back into the complex?'

'We'll have to hope there's another way out!'

She expected a complaint from Dresden, but it didn't come. Stealing a glance to her right Zoe saw that the boy was pale and shaking. His eyes were wide and staring. He was evidently too frightened to speak.

The transport trundled into a passageway. Zoe winced as she heard it scraping the walls and worried that it might become trapped. Certainly, there was no way the doors could open here.

'Straight ahead,' she directed, unnecessarily.

'There's a Selachian vehicle,' Kukhadil reported, 'ten metres behind us – and another one behind that.'

'How can you tell?'

'The transport can see them.'

The vehicle bucked and threw its occupants forward. Something had slammed into its rear. It stalled for a second, then resumed its slow but steady pace.

'They're firing on us!' cried Davidson.

'Is there anything we can do?' Zoe asked Kukhadil, urgently. 'Can we fight back?'

'I'm planting a grenade. It might slow them, but that's all. These things have tough hides.'

'Fortunately for us,' muttered Davidson, just audibly.

'We're coming to a junction,' said Kukhadil. 'I can try to shake them off.'

'No. They're too close – and if we turn off the main tunnel, we risk driving into a dead end. Keep going!'

'We'll never escape that way,' insisted Davidson. 'It's just a matter of time.'

'Do you have to find fault with every decision I make? I haven't heard any suggestions from you!' Zoe surprised herself with the angry rebuke; it was most unlike her. But she was even more surprised to find that her words silenced her companion.

Now, if only she didn't know that Davidson was right...

'Selachians!' screamed Dresden, pointing ahead with a trembling finger. 'Selachians!'

Zoe almost screamed too – and probably would have done, had the others not been depending on her. She bit her lip, gaped at the two armoured figures that had stepped out in front of the vehicle, and tried to think of a plan. The best she could manage was to grab Kukhadil's shoulder and cry, 'Do something!'

The Selachians brought up their weapons.

A jet of clear liquid erupted from the front of the transport. It looked like water, but as it hit the Selachians they threw up their hands and fell backwards. The vehicle rolled closer and Zoe was agog to see that the creatures' battlesuits were dissolving, molten rivulets rolling down their surfaces. Kukhadil had hit them with strong acid.

One of the Selachians threw itself at the transport. Zoe squealed as it hit the windscreen, spread-eagled, centimetres from her face. But holes were appearing in its armour and water was flooding out. Weakened, it couldn't retain its grip. It slid to the ground and the transport rolled over it with a bump.

The tunnel opened out and, to Zoe's surprise, they emerged into the main holding area. Their entrance had been heralded both by the blaring alarm and by the second Selachian, which was on its knees in front of them, evidently in pain. Kukhadil steered around it. Prisoners drew back from the vehicle, then gaped in surprise as they saw its operators.

Two more sentries had left their positions. They fired at the transport and the windscreen blistered and cracked beneath the heat of their flaming plasma. Kukhadil couldn't fire back; there were too many prisoners in range. He twisted the vehicle around but, wherever he turned, there were more Selachians.

'Go to the left!' shouted Zoe, directing the Kalarian towards the passage down which they had originally escaped. Perhaps they could double back to the exit.

But then, another Selachian jumped on to the windscreen and, with a powerful punch, put its fist through the weakened shielding.

Zoe screamed and recoiled. Kukhadil wrenched the transport around violently so that the creature was dislodged. Davidson shouted something that couldn't be heard over the clamour.

Dresden howled, elbowed the door open and jumped from the transport.

He was shot before he landed.

The image of the teenager, briefly suspended in mid-flight, surrounded by a corona of fire, his skin blackening, his mouth open in a silent scream, branded itself in Zoe's mind.

Kukhadil pulled the transport around. Still paralysed, Zoe almost pitched headfirst through the open door.

Then the door on the other side of the cabin was wrenched open from without. A Selachian reached in and seized Davidson's arm. She struggled and swore but it pulled her from the vehicle. Zoe didn't see her again after that, but she knew what must have happened.

'No, no, no,' she whimpered to herself, eyes bulging with tears.

Kukhadil let out a shriek. He arced backwards so that Zoe feared his spine might break.

'No, no,' she cried helplessly, 'not you too. What's wrong? What are they doing to you?'

He slumped to the floor, the control tentacle pulling at his wrist so that his arm remained raised even as his body went limp and his eyes rolled back into his head. The effect was somehow gruesome.

'Terminal psychic feedback,' replied a gravelly voice behind her. Zoe whirled round to see that John Paterson had swung himself easily into the cabin. He pushed past her, took Kukhadil's place at the dashboard and began to operate the controls expertly 'The Sharks've stuck neuro-blasters on this thing, but it should still work on manual.'

'Have they killed him?'

'Don't think about it. Here, lend me a hand.'

'What?' Zoe blinked, dazed. This couldn't be happening. How could things have gone so wrong, so quickly?

It was her fault.

'I mean, literally.' Paterson reached over, took Zoe's wrist and pulled it towards one of the bumpy controls.'Keep your finger on that.' She did as he instructed.

A moment later, he was pushing her out of the door. 'OK, miss, we're out of here!'

Zoe stumbled out of the transport into a scene of carnage. The noisy arrival of three vehicles and the unprecedented slaying of two Selachians had stirred the prisoners into revolt. They attacked their guards with rocks, dishes and bare hands. Sheer numbers gave them an advantage. She felt a surge of elation as she saw that a group of soldiers had prised a Selachian's helmet from its head. Another group had commandeered one of the pursuing transports. But she also felt disgusted as alien weapons spat fire and people died in agony. Acid burst from the third vehicle and killed at least twelve prisoners on contact. To Zoe's astonishment, two Selachians were also caught in the indiscriminate blast. It said something about the creatures' desperation to contain the situation. But that came as little comfort.

Her companions were dead, and it was all her fault.

As, to an extent, would be the fates of everyone who suffered in this riot.

It was too much to take in. Tears rolled down Zoe's cheeks. She could hardly think. But now Paterson was here. He could tell her what to do.

The abandoned transport lurched towards the centre of the cavern, apparently on a random course. The tone of its alarm had changed, becoming higher in pitch and even more strident. Zoe saw that the Selachians avoided it and she realised what Paterson must have done.

'Get out of the way!' he yelled to those humans who thought they saw an opportunity to capture the vehicle for themselves. 'It's going to explode!' His warning delivered, he rounded on Zoe. 'How do we get out of here?'

She stared at him, her lower lip quivering.

Paterson held her by the shoulders and shook her, roughly. 'Which way?'

She pointed towards the opening through which she had made her entrance. Then, thinking again, she said, 'No, there might be more Selachians following us.' She knew she had to concentrate to stand a chance of surviving this – it was just that she couldn't stop thinking about what had happened to Davidson, Dresden and Kukhadil. 'Down there,' she said, indicating her original escape route.

Paterson took her by the hand and dragged her across the cavern.

The distraction he had created earlier worked against them. They were forced to change direction as the transport – beginning to smoulder now – cut across their path.

A Selachian loomed before them. It gave them no warning. It raised its guns and fired. Paterson pushed Zoe to the left, simultaneously diving right. Zoe hit the floor, feeling heat from the plasma stream but mercifully untouched. She rolled and made to climb back to her feet but the Selachian had trained its weapons upon her again. She froze in a crouch, knowing she couldn't avoid it this time.

A whirling, black-uniformed ball span into the Selachian and unbalanced it. It took Zoe's fatigued brain a second to accept what she was seeing. By then, the Doctor was clinging to the Selachian's back. His arms were wrapped around its neck, his knees were clamped to either side of its chest and his eyes were closed as he held on for his life.

Zoe cried out his name, in disbelief and joy.

There was a fierce crackle, a brief smell of ozone and a blue flash. The Doctor wailed as he was flung to the ground. The monster turned towards him.

'No – leave him alone!' shrieked Zoe, running at the Selachian with little regard for the fact that its armour might still be electrified. It wasn't, but her charge didn't budge the creature. It turned its head towards her and raised its arms so that one gun threatened Zoe whilst the other was pointed at the Doctor. He was on his knees, looking up at his would-be killer with a helpless expression.

The transport ran into the Selachian's back and exploded.

Zoe screamed and turned her eyes away from the brilliant flash. When she looked again she saw that the Selachian had fallen, its armour cracked and leaking. But, elsewhere, the explosion had caused more fear and confusion than damage.

Paterson cannoned into Zoe and pushed her onward. She hesitated, pulling away from him and turning back to look for the Doctor.

He was right behind her. She ought to have expected that.

The passageways beyond the holding area were full of prisoners, some limping, others lost or looking for places to hide. Paterson ignored them all, racing faster than Zoe would have thought possible with his injuries. He paused only at junctions, where he turned to her with a questioning look and awaited directions.

Zoe stayed at the Doctor's side. 'Where did you come from?' she asked as they ran. 'How did you get here?'

'The Selachians brought me.' He grinned. 'They led me to believe it would be a little more relaxing than this.'

'You've caught us in the middle of an exercise period,' said Paterson over his shoulder.

'You were in one of the other transports,' Zoe realised.

'I'd say I arrived here in the nick of time, wouldn't you?'

The trio stumbled to a halt outside the communications

room. The light had changed and it took Zoe a moment to realise that the circles of fungus had turned red.

'What's happening?'

'An alert signal, I should think,' said the Doctor.

'We've got to get out of here!' insisted Paterson. 'Which way now?'

Zoe was about to answer, when the Doctor interrupted. 'What's happening?'

Impatiently, the soldier explained. 'Those so-called lights are explosive. The Sharks can detonate them with radio waves. They're gonna bring this complex down around our ears!'

The Doctor's eyes widened in almost pantomime alarm. 'We've got to get out of here!'

Zoe was already making for the exit tunnel. Then she stopped as the sight of it reminded her of another problem. 'Wait, there's a creature down there – it's almost invisible – it took us ages to get past it!'

The Doctor and Paterson exchanged glances. 'How long do we have?' asked the Doctor.

'Two minutes, from the time those things turned red.'

'Follow me!' The Doctor turned, and broke into a sprint.

'Doctor, where are you going?' cried Zoe.

He shot the answer back over his shoulder, without slowing. 'Up.'

He faltered at a four-way junction, assessing each of his choices before he led them along the steepest upward-sloping passageway. After a few hundred metres he stopped to allow Zoe to catch up. He hopped impatiently as she approached, then propelled her ahead of him with a push. 'If this complex is about to collapse, then we have to make sure there's as little of it as possible above our heads.'

'We've got about ten seconds,' warned Paterson, from behind them.

'Down here!' cried Zoe, skidding to a halt as they passed the mouth of a dark tunnel. 'It's a dead end – there won't be any lights!'

The Doctor followed her directions without question. She was about to follow him – but Paterson had stopped. He was pulling at a disc of fungus on the wall beside the opening. 'We stand a better chance if this isn't here,' he grunted.

'There isn't time!'

'You go!'

Zoe almost did – but the light clung tenaciously to the rock. She rushed to Paterson's side and clawed at the edges of the fungus with her fingernails. It was uncomfortably warm and was heating up as its red hue deepened.

At last, it came free. Paterson squeezed it into a ball and hurled it back the way they had come. Zoe ran for the opening and collided with the Doctor as he returned for her. They clung to each other, found their balance and fled, hand in hand, Paterson behind them.

The explosions began, distantly at first but approaching with heart-stopping speed. Zoe thought the Doctor was shouting something, but she couldn't hear him.

The walls began to fall in.

The passageway was shorter than she had hoped. They reached its end and knew there was nothing more they could do. Zoe turned to see a thick, black dust cloud rolling towards her.

And then, the roof collapsed.

Chapter Twenty-Seven

It had felt like the longest walk of Mulholland's life. And yet, now it was over, now that she actually stood at the hastily repaired door to the bomb chamber, it seemed as though only a few seconds had passed since Commander Redfern had paged her.

It hadn't been long enough. She hadn't had time to decide.

She had tried to discuss it with Kent Michaels. He had been too absorbed by his own problems. Redfern had returned from Ockora alone, in a foul mood, and Michaels had taken the brunt of his wrath. But this had been nothing compared to the lieutenant's own self-recrimination. It was that which threatened to consume him.

'You saved my life,' she had reminded him.

'No. Jamie saved your life.'

'I hardly think he had my best interests at heart.'

'It was my fault,' Michaels had said, surprising Mulholland with the bitterness in his voice. 'I brought him on board. I shouldn't have trusted him.'

'Listen to yourself,' she had snapped. 'You cannot help what has passed – how many times have you said that? You are allowing it to affect you. You ought to pull yourself together!'

Even as she had spoken so harshly she had known what she was doing. She had thrown up her icy front, pushing Michaels away as surely as he had pushed her away in Redfern's office; perhaps for the same reason.

The war had taken its toll on both of them. It had shattered their barriers and pricked at their emotions. When Mulholland had looked at Michaels she had seen a reflection of herself. He was a walking, hollow reminder that she too was falling apart.

When Redfern's summons had come, Mulholland had glimpsed sympathy in Michaels's face. Perhaps he had seen how her cheeks had paled on hearing where the commander expected to meet her. Perhaps he had been ready to reach out then, to comfort and help her. It had been too late. She had left his quarters with neither a word nor a backward glance.

She had embarked upon the longest walk of her life, alone as she had always been.

Mulholland reached for the unlocked door but couldn't touch it. Her muscles wouldn't respond to her instructions. She imagined that, as the door opened, it would release the demons. They would stream from the aperture to taunt her and bite her and tear at her skin.

She swallowed and told herself not to be so stupid. She had to think about what she would say, how she would respond to Redfern's inevitable demand. After all the nightmares, all the times she had dwelt on this moment, she still didn't know.

She had thought of herself as a strong-willed woman, one who knew what she wanted and took it. But when she looked back on her life, it told a different story. Oh yes, she had worked hard at college, she had earned her grades, but then she had drifted into the first job that had been offered. She had been lured to Earth by her present employers because they had come to her with more money. She had set herself to whatever work they had provided, not questioning what they asked. She had found herself in charge of the G-bomb project without ever having voiced such an ambition; sent to oversee its culmination, without having quite conquered her fear of space travel.

She had never had to make a big decision before. Was it any wonder, then, that she was unable to make this one?

Mulholland had delayed for too long. The commander would be waiting. She steeled herself, placed her palm against the door and pushed. But she closed her eyes as she did so.

When she opened them Redfern was standing less than three metres away, his arms folded impatiently. She started, imagining the skull face of death imposed over his lean features.

Death was here. In the bomb chamber. At the heart of the *Triumph*.

Her nightmare had begun.

'I paged you ten minutes ago, Professor.'

'I'm sorry,' she mumbled, looking down at her feet.

'We'll discuss it later. I'm here to release the activation codes.' Redfern strode to a console, then turned back to Mulholland in irritation when he saw that she hadn't moved from the doorway. 'Is something wrong, Professor?' he asked, in a dangerous tone.

'You intend to use the G-bomb?'

He bared his teeth. 'I thought I had made that clear.'

'But…' She had rehearsed this conversation in her mind a hundred times. Not once had it occurred to her that she would be unable to force out more than one word.

Redfern raised a warning finger. 'Don't tell me you've gone soft on me, too. I've had my orders questioned about as often as I'll stand for, Professor.'

Mulholland still couldn't move. Nor could she face him. As much to cover the embarrassing silence as anything, she stammered, 'The hostages… didn't you find any hostages?'

'The only thing I found on Ockora was an ambush. Your Doctor friend lured me down there while McCrimmon tried to destroy this ship, or have you forgotten that?' Redfern clenched his fists, and his chest heaved as he took short, angry breaths. 'Those shark-faced bastards killed seven good soldiers – and, if they hadn't been good soldiers, you could have counted me as dead too. They saved my life, and I swear that's going to count for something!'

Had her own emotions not been in turmoil, Mulholland

could almost have laughed. Redfern had had his first taste of actual combat, of being under fire, of watching comrades cut down in front of him. He was handling it badly, already beginning to crack. Just like everybody else aboard this ship, it seemed.

He was almost ranting now; he could well have been oblivious to her presence. 'I've contacted Earth and they're in full agreement with me. I'm going to avenge my people, and everyone else the Sharks have killed. I'm going to show them what happens when they mess with humanity. I'll ram one of those bombs right down the Supreme Leader's throat!'

Then Redfern fell silent and, when Mulholland looked at him, he turned away as if embarrassed.

She shifted uncomfortably, realising that it was her turn to speak again.

'Might it not have been better,' she had wanted to ask Michaels, 'if you had given in to the Selachian and the boy?' But the question had never been vocalised.

'Is the Doctor still on Ockora?' she asked – another delaying tactic.

Redfern's lips parted and stretched into a humourless smile as he nodded. 'That, Professor Mulholland, is something that will give me a great deal of satisfaction!'

'Oh,' she mouthed voicelessly. She had no other words left.

She remembered what Michaels had told her. This was Redfern's responsibility. She would just be the tool he used. Why tear herself apart over a matter in which she had no say?

'Get over here, Professor,' said Redfern, 'and let's get this bomb launched.' This time there was no threat in his voice. He was simply issuing an order.

And, as always, Mulholland nodded dumbly and obeyed. Because, sometimes, the easiest decision to make was no decision at all.

Chapter Twenty-Eight

Jamie should have been used to prison cells by now. But the idea of being trapped and useless still caused a plunging sensation in his gut. He paced up and down the tiny room, pulled at the door to confirm that it was immovable, tried to wrench the solid bars free from the small window that looked out on to the corridor and finally surrendered and sat on one of the two beds, only to stand up again and repeat the entire process seconds later.

His cellmate was no help. The young Selachian stood at the back of the room, turned to the wall and staring at his clenched fists. He had not spoken since they had been brought here.

Before, Jamie had at least been doing something, no matter how poor his chances of success had been. Now, he could only think of Zoe and the Doctor and pray that nothing bad would happen to them – nothing that he could, and should, have prevented.

'There must be a way out of here,' he complained. He turned to his friend. 'Come on, your lot are pretty strong, aren't you? Can't you try working on these bars?'

'Our strength is in our battlesuits,' the Selachian growled, without turning. 'The air-breathers know this, that is why I have been stripped of mine. They fear me.'

'But the two of us might manage it together,' persisted Jamie.

The Selachian turned to him. 'You think I would work with you again?' he asked, bitterly. 'You have proven to be as treacherous as the rest of your plankton-sucking kind!'

'Eh?' said Jamie, confused.

His cellmate took two steps towards him, trembling with

rage. 'You betrayed me. You chose to sacrifice the lives of nine million Ockorans in return for that of the pathetic air-breather who will murder them!'

'Now, look, I've got friends on Ockora too, you know.'

'Air-breathers do not have friends. You are too primitive.'

'Hey, it was me who knocked out the guard outside the hospital, remember? Me who got his keys from him and took your handcuffs off. Me who held a gun on Lieutenant Michaels.'

'You attacked me,' hissed the young Selachian. 'You prevented me from saving my people.'

'Och, that was because you were going to kill Professor Mulholland.'

'She deserved far worse!'

'But it wouldn't have…'

'I will kill you!'

The Selachian threw himself at Jamie, taking him by surprise and knocking him into the wall. The young Highlander almost blacked out as he took a punch to the head. His attacker wasn't strong, but Jamie was still weak from the thinker weapon's assault and his brawl with Michaels. His legs began to shake, and he knew he had to end this fight quickly or lose it.

What had he done that was so wrong that he was hated by both sides in this war?

Nothing, he concluded. He had done precisely what the Doctor would have done, and with the same results. The thought brought a smile to his face, despite the situation.

He fended off the next punch with his arm and struck at the Selachian's stomach. His fist sank into the padded black suit and he heard the squish of water beneath it. Unhurt, the Selachian punched him again. Then he took hold of Jamie's head and drove it back into the wall behind him, three times. Jamie's eyes defocused. He felt sick. He braced his foot against the wall and thrust himself forward, eyes closed, emitting a primal scream as if to drive the pain away. His opponent's grip was broken as Jamie lowered his head and butted his midriff. He stayed with the Selachian and the pair grappled, until Jamie slipped a foot behind his opponent's leg and tripped him. The Selachian hit the ground heavily, on his back, and Jamie leapt on top of him. He delivered punch after punch, praying that some would get through the Selachian's protection. For long seconds he couldn't see anything and lashed out blindly, knowing he couldn't take another blow, couldn't give his opponent time to recover.

When his head cleared Jamie was sitting astride the unmoving body of his former friend. He was cold, sweating, light-headed and trembling in the aftermath of an adrenaline rush. He looked down at the blank mask between his knees and the staring eyes beneath it, and suddenly he was repulsed by what he had done. Could he blame the Selachian for being angry? His family, his race, his whole world, were about to die. But he had given Jamie no choice. He had forced him to fight, but only in self-defence.

Jamie shivered as he felt for the floor behind him and dragged himself off the Selachian with his hands. His arms couldn't support him for long. He fell backwards and didn't move for several minutes. He stared at the uneven ceiling, listening to his own frantic heartbeat and waiting for the cell to stop spinning.

Eventually, he detected the quiet gurgling sound of bubbles forming. The Selachian was still breathing. Until that moment, it hadn't occurred to Jamie that he might not have been. He felt cold and nauseous all over again.

He rolled over, raised himself on to his hands and knees and looked at his recumbent cellmate. In his desperation he had overestimated the strength of the unarmoured Selachian. What if he had really hurt him?

He called out for help, but his voice was weak. With difficulty he clambered to his feet and lurched towards the window, clutching at its bars to support himself.

'Help,' he called again, into the corridor. 'Is anybody out there? Help!'

Nobody responded. Jamie closed his eyes and leaned forward against the cold metal of the bars, allowing them to cool his brow.

He heard footsteps.

'Hey,' he called hopefully, 'is somebody there? We need a doctor in here. Hey!'

The footsteps drew closer. They sounded unnaturally heavy.

Jamie leapt back, startled, as the owners of the footsteps came into view. Belatedly, he flattened himself against the door where they wouldn't be able to see him.

He felt the hairs on the back of his head prickling, as four battlesuited Selachians passed the window and marched briskly along the corridor.

Chapter Twenty-Nine

Kent Michaels lay on his back, on his bed, and thought about the future for the first time in months. After so long, it seemed incredible that the war was just minutes from its end. Perhaps the G-bomb had been launched already. Perhaps the enemy were no more. Perhaps Redfern had given the order to turn around the *Triumph* and its fighters, to head back to Earth. Perhaps, elsewhere, the celebrations had begun.

Michaels could have found out what was happening. But it didn't seem to matter.

Redfern had removed him from his position as second-in-command. He had also threatened him with a court martial for his reckless actions in the bomb chamber. The commander had been letting off steam; he probably wouldn't go through with it. Even if he did, it wouldn't change much. Michaels might be busted to NCO rank, even private, but he was unlikely to be expelled from the TSF. Manpower was at a premium; too many soldiers had died. And there would be another mission, perhaps another war to fight. Life would go on as normal.

Or would it? How could he rebuild his barriers? How could he deny the feelings that he had kept trapped behind them for twenty years? How could he be sure he would never lose control again? Kent Michaels had only ever been afraid of one person, and that was himself, his real self. The self that, after its years of imprisonment, had only become stronger.

Suddenly, the room was awash with red light. From somewhere outside a siren whooped three times. Michaels was already pushing his feet into his boots, reaching for his rifle. He had to report to the bridge.

The siren gave three more whoops as he ran out into the corridor. It would continue to sound at intervals of one minute. This was a Grade Four alert situation, the most urgent. The flagship was in imminent danger. Perhaps something had gone wrong with the G-bomb.

Michaels rounded a corner, and found himself staring at a Selachian.

It must have heard his approach for it swung around to face him and fired. Fortunately his reflexes had already kicked in, overriding his doubts. He didn't stop; he transferred the momentum of his run into a leap. He collided with the far wall as burning plasma scorched the carpet at his feet. He ignored the pain in his shoulder, dropped into a crouch, raised his rifle and returned fire. Two bullets exploded as they hit metal, releasing their nanites. Seemingly unaffected, the Selachian took aim again. Michaels performed a forward roll in the direction he had come from and put the corner between them.

He raced back along the corridor, wishing he had made time to visit the armoury since his return from Kalaya and his assignment to the *Triumph*. He had replaced his combat uniform, but he had not restocked it. With no combat missions imminent, he had not seen the need. The rifle was all he had – and, for a lone soldier, it was a poor weapon. It would take at least seven or eight shots to kill a Selachian. They could kill him with one.

He took a left turn at the first junction he came to, even as his pursuer rounded the corner behind him. He came up short. There were three more Selachians ahead of him.

Michaels doubled back on himself again, figuring – in the split second available – that his only hope lay in taking the first creature by surprise. He charged at it, loosing off three shots in quick succession. Bewildered, it only fired once and, misjudging his speed, missed. Michaels dived to its left, feeling a surge of elation as he succeeded in passing it. One of the first things he had learned about Selachians was that, although they were faster than they seemed, their battlesuits limited both their peripheral vision and their manoeuvrability. By the time this one had lumbered around to face him again he had raised himself to his knees and shouldered his rifle. He pumped three more bullets into it.

Damn it, why wouldn't it fall?

He ducked instinctively as the Selachian reached for him. Its right hand gripped his left shoulder and squeezed it. Michaels winced, feeling as though it had driven a blade right down to his left thigh. He dropped his rifle and grabbed an armoured finger with each hand, trying to prise them free. At the same time, he scrambled to raise his knees from the floor, to push himself up with the balls of his feet, to use his leverage.

The Selachian's free hand found Michaels's other shoulder. It pushed down hard and he fell back on to his knees, painfully. He took advantage of the movement to drop further and faster than his attacker expected. He lurched forwards, on to his face, and pulled the creature's hands down with him until, unable to bend too far in its battlesuit, it let him go. Sprawling between its feet Michaels fumbled for his rifle, but knew instinctively that the Selachian had turned its weapons on him again, and that it wouldn't miss this time.

He felt a wet sensation as something heavy hit the small of his back. He let out a scream of defiance, thinking this was it, that his brain was simply not registering the all-consuming pain as blood erupted from his body. But the Selachian hadn't fired. It had fallen. The nanites had done their work at last, and its battlesuit had split open. As water flooded on to the carpet a scrawny creature flopped out of the ruptured shell and made one final attempt to take its enemy with it. It fought frenziedly, its weak fists pounding him in desperation. Michaels drove his elbow backwards, into its gut. As it toppled, he dragged himself from beneath it, scooped up his rifle and stood up, expecting another attack.

The creature flapped helplessly as it suffocated to death.

The other three Selachians had just stepped into the corridor.

Michaels evaded three blasts, more by luck than by reflex. He sprinted around the corner again, and took two more turns at random as he tried to formulate a plan.

If there were four Selachians in this part of the ship, the chances were that there were more on board. He could not guess how they had got on to the *Triumph* undetected – the flagship was protected by fighters and by early warning systems; it was supposedly unassailable – but it didn't matter now. They were here, and he had to deal with that fact.

He was running out of options. One human against even one Selachian was a decidedly uneven battle – Michaels had already been lucky once – so whenever he saw the creatures he had to turn back. And as he had surmised there were many Selachians in the corridors.

After several detours he concluded that all routes to the bridge were blocked. He abandoned his plan to reach it. The area had evidently been targeted; it was scarcely likely that anybody would be left alive there. Michaels had seen several other soldiers on his travels, but each one had been lying, mutilated and unmoving, on the ground, his blood soaking into the carpet.

How had this happened so quickly?

The armoury, he thought. If he had to fight alone, then at least he could fight prepared. He raced down to the ship's lower level, hoping the Selachians hadn't reached it yet. But again he was confounded and forced to run, blaster fire ringing in his ears.

He sprinted up a flight of stairs with two persistent pursuers on his heels. It led him into the main atrium, where he glanced at the paintings, the statues and the enormous chandelier but saw nothing he could use. From here, two more staircases led up to Redfern's office and a corridor that would ultimately return Michaels to the officers' quarters. He raced up the one on the right, taking four steps at a time – or rather, he tried to. His battered and war-weary body betrayed him. He had a stitch and felt as if the plastiflesh in his side was working itself free. He missed a step, his ankle turned beneath him and he crashed heavily on top of it. He hauled himself up again and leant on the banister, cursing as he tried to put weight on his right foot and felt a stab of pain. He looked down. The Selachians were on the lower staircase.

He had to delay them. He raised his rifle and fired at the chandelier's mounting. It was a difficult shot, and he missed twice. But his third bullet struck the metal chain that supported the elaborate crystal structure. Michaels turned and limped, as fast as he could, up the stairs as nanites burrowed into the unprotected metal. As he reached the top corridor, he turned. The Selachians had reached the atrium. The first of them was aiming its guns at him.

The chandelier crashed down on to the creatures, and exploded into fragments. It would hardly scratch them but, hopefully, it would confuse and blind them for a moment. Michaels couldn't run, so he made the only choice left open to him. He stumbled towards Redfern's office and pressed the access button with his thumb. There was just a chance…

The door slid open. He had been lucky again. Evidently, Redfern hadn't had time to advise the computer of his demotion. He could still override all systems. 'Lock!' he ordered, as the door closed behind him. Not that it would help. The door was not reinforced and there was no other exit. He had cornered himself. He could only pray that the Selachians hadn't seen him and wouldn't look in here.

At least he could find out what was going on. He crossed to

the desk and drove his fist down on a large, red button on the compad. Nine monitors sprang out of the wall to his left; a tenth emerged from the desk itself. Michaels punched up the ship's schematics on this main monitor, overlaying them with sensor information to chart the positions of everyone on board. There ought to have been over ninety human beings on the *Triumph*, although he had lost count of the exact number. The computer informed him that there were twenty-eight. It had also detected thirty-six alien life traces. As he watched, one of the red, square alien icons moved into the personal quarters of one of Redfern's accountants. The white square representing the room's hapless occupant disappeared, and the computer amended its count of the ship's personnel to twenty-seven.

Michaels found himself short of breath. It was a massacre.

He tried to contact the fighter ships, but communications were jammed. He couldn't even put out an all-frequencies distress signal. By the time anyone knew what was happening on the *Triumph* it would be too late. And the Selachians had climbed the stairs now. They were standing outside the office, as if discussing where their prey might be hiding.

This was it. This was the end.

Michaels looked at the schematics again, and his heart dropped into his stomach at the sight of four red icons in the bomb chamber. No human traces were present. Was Redfern dead? And Mulholland? Had they managed to complete their task?

He could think of no more useful action to take, so he satisfied his curiosity. He called up a situation report on the G-bombs, and frowned as the information appeared in red letters that blinked urgently.

The activation codes had been entered, and a bomb had been primed for launch in thirteen seconds. But there was one final check. The computer required a password. If it didn't receive it before the countdown reached zero it would abort the procedure.

It seemed so unfair. Redfern and Mulholland had come so close.

And, Michaels realised with a prickly, queasy thrill, he could finish the job for them.

If Redfern hadn't rescinded Michaels' override authority, he probably hadn't changed the password or erased the lieutenant's voiceprint from the system either.

He could barely believe what he was doing. It was as if somebody else had taken control of his body: somebody who forced him to grip the spindly stem of the compad's microphone and patch his voice through to the bomb chamber. Somebody who wasn't afraid to make one of the most important decisions in history.

The password caught in his throat. He remembered Mulholland's misgivings. But the Selachians were on the flagship, they were killing its occupants, and it was conceivable that they had found a way to turn the tide of the war. How many more would die, if they had?

The countdown had reached two seconds.

With a tremendous crack, the wooden door splintered. Michaels could see a Selachian through the new, jagged gaps. It stepped back, orienting itself for a second assault.

If he was to do anything at all, it had to be done now. So he did what felt right.

'Solution,' he rapped into the microphone.

The door exploded inwards. Two Selachians marched into the office. Michaels didn't have time to duck behind the desk or unsling his rifle. He straightened up, his hands raised.

'Gravity bomb launched,' announced the clipped tones of the computer, to Michaels's grim satisfaction. 'Monitoring progress towards Ockora.'

'Good evening,' the lieutenant said evenly. 'I'm afraid you're a little bit too late.'

The Selachians fired, simultaneously.

An inferno flared in Michaels's guts. He was dimly aware of banging his head as he was flung back into the wall. But darkness descended too rapidly for him to suffer much pain. He gave in to it with a feeling of resignation, almost of gratitude.

Until, with a lurching, sickly terror, he realised that the darkness was absolute.

The tunnel hadn't opened for him.

Chapter Thirty

The Doctor was shouting something, but Paterson couldn't hear him over the howling wind. He concentrated on running, and on trying to ignore the stinging sand that was whipped into his face, the water that weighed down his overalls.

When he had first felt the wind he had dismissed it as a natural breeze, forgetting what the Doctor had told him. But the strange little man – the man whom Paterson had known for only a matter of hours, but whom he now trusted implicitly – had known better.

Zoe succumbed to the constant buffeting, and fell. Paterson faltered, but the Doctor was already there to catch her and to take her hand. He cast around, looked lost for a moment, then pointed – not quite decisively – and set off inland, his head down.

It had always been Paterson who had taken the lead when things had gone wrong. Only hours earlier he had asked himself why people couldn't look to somebody else. And now he had found somebody. He was injured, lost and helpless, and only the Doctor kept him going. He followed the little man without question. But he thought of the people who had died in the prison to give him his freedom, and he wondered if he could do this any more.

It had been the Doctor, of course, who had saved them from the cave-in. They had sustained only scratches and slight bruises from the falling rocks – nothing compared to what Paterson had already suffered – but they had been trapped. The soldier had foreseen only two possibilities: they would run out of air or the Selachians would find and kill them. The temperature had risen and breathing had become difficult. But the Doctor had refused to give up. He had produced a long, thin, silver device, which he had called a 'sonic screwdriver'. It had given off a whining sound which had oscillated as the Doctor adjusted the instrument. The sound had dislodged the rocks above them, and Zoe had shrieked as another shower of dirt had fallen. A heavy boulder had thudded into the ground between them and the Doctor's expression had been regretful – and also relieved that worse hadn't happened.

The fact that he had been able to see the Doctor's expression had been a surprise in itself. Looking up, Paterson had been astonished to see daylight. It had only been a sliver, but it had provided warmth, air and, most of all, hope. Galvanised, he had followed the Doctor's instructions, allowing the slighter man to stand on his shoulders and hoisting him upwards so that he could work on widening the crack. Paterson had taken his turn at doing the same, although he had soon become tired. The Doctor had used his sonic screwdriver twice more, vibrating obstructions into dust. And finally Paterson, the Doctor and Zoe had hauled themselves up through the hole and on to the white sands of a beautiful Ockoran island.

'I suspected as much,' the Doctor had said, with a smugness that would have been infuriating had he not just saved their lives. 'The Selachians must have hollowed their complex out of the base of this island. Fortunately, and thanks to Zoe's quick thinking, we weren't too far below the surface when they demolished it.'

By then, Paterson had been deeply fatigued. But the Doctor had sprung back into action. He had scurried and hopped about like a hyperactive pixie, driving his companions to further efforts and frequently stressing the urgency of their situation. Under his directions, in surprisingly short order, they had cobbled together a serviceable raft from driftwood lashed together with creepers. They had dragged it on to the beach, and Paterson had all but collapsed on top of it as they launched it on to the waves.

'Professor Laura Mulholland has created a gravity bomb,' the Doctor had explained, reluctantly, when pressed by Zoe. 'As it hits the surface of Ockora, it will begin to collapse in on itself, becoming a powerful gravitic force.'

'How powerful?' Zoe had asked, doubtfully.

'At first, it will feel like a soft wind. But as the g-force increases the wind will become stronger. Soon, it will be as if the planet has two centres of gravity. Everything on it will be pulled in two directions at once. Then, eventually, the bomb will exert more force than the planet. Plants and buildings will be uprooted, landmasses will be torn apart and the sea will be dragged from its bed. Of course, by then, everybody on this world will be dead.'

The Doctor had become caught up in his explanation. He had stopped paddling, to gesticulate ever more wildly. When he had seen the worried look on Zoe's face, he had let his hands fall into his lap, seeming abashed. 'Of course, we can worry about that when... I mean, if... the TSF decide to use their weapon.'

'That's hardly likely,' Paterson had scoffed. 'Even Redfern's not that insane. It's just a deterrent.' The Doctor's expression had left him in no doubt that he believed otherwise.

Zoe had looked up at the sky, fearfully, as if expecting a bomb to fall on their heads at any moment. 'How long do we have?'

'I don't know,' the Doctor had confessed. 'It should have happened already, but I'm afraid I have rather disrupted things.' Crossing his fingers he had added, under his breath, 'I only hope I haven't caused too much damage.'

It had almost sounded as if he wanted the G-bomb to be dropped.

The wind was becoming unbearable now. It blew at right

angles to their course, and Paterson had to fight not to be knocked aside. They came to the ruins of a Kalarian holiday resort, as the Doctor had said they would. This, at least, was a relief. Despite his attempt to feign confidence, the Doctor had seemed by no means certain that he could retrace the route from the internment centre to the T-Mat terminal. Indeed, he would have led them in the wrong direction had Paterson himself not had a vague idea of the terminal's location, based on recollections from a long-ago briefing. 'Ah, yes, yes, of course, well done,' the Doctor had said, as if his mistake had merely been a test.

Their raft had capsized as they reached the resort. They had had to wade ashore through the turbulent water. Paterson had feared then that it was already too late.

Rubble skittered across the ground. Chunks of masonry were torn from half-standing walls. A small piece whistled into Paterson's left ear. He lost his footing and was carried for over two metres before hitting the ground on his side. He dragged himself forward on his elbows and knees. He couldn't stand again, and doubted if he would be able to move at all for much longer. The horror of his situation was only beginning to sink in. His own people had dropped a bomb. An entire world was dying, and it would take him with it.

His left ear was bleeding.

The Doctor came back for him. Somehow, the little man was still standing, although it felt as if the wind had reached almost hurricane proportions. He gripped Paterson's arm and hauled him to his feet, managing to anchor him as he ploughed determinedly onward.

The terminal was nearer than Paterson had thought. Two crumbling walls protected the cubicle but it was still lashed by debris, and it creaked and groaned as its top half threatened to splinter away. The Doctor left Zoe clinging to the separate console. The wind had caught her legs and pulled her feet from the floor. Paterson made a lunge for the console, too, and leant over it scrabbling for a grip with his fingers. Only now did it occur to him that somebody would have to stay behind to operate the controls.

'Take Zoe to the cubicle!' the Doctor shouted in his ear.

Paterson shook his head. The Doctor had brought them this far – now it was his turn to do the only thing he could, to give the only thing he had left. 'You'll be more use than I will up there. Go. You can bring me up after you.' The Doctor hesitated. 'No time to argue!' yelled Paterson. 'I'm not budging from here. Stay with me, if it'll make you happy!'

As if to underscore the urgency of the situation the cubicle slid a short way, protesting loudly. The wires connecting it to the console emerged from the debris and were pulled taut.

The Doctor nodded and a faint, awkward smile of gratitude flickered across his face. Then he bundled Zoe into his arms. He had carried her halfway to the cubicle before she realised that Paterson wasn't following. She looked at him with a helpless expression, as if she wouldn't know what to say even if there was a chance of him hearing it. The wind was full in his face now, and the effort was tremendous, but he managed to force a smile.

The cubicle slid again, even with the additional weight of two bodies inside it. The Doctor and Zoe would be lucky if the connection held long enough for Paterson to send them on their way. They certainly wouldn't have time to operate the controls at the far end, and anyway he couldn't have reached the cubicle unaided.

He couldn't keep his eyes open. He fumbled blindly for the controls, crossed his fingers and prayed he had been successful, even as the console began to shift beneath him. Water lashed his face, blown in from the ocean. He was battered by another hail of rubble, and the console was ripped from the ground altogether.

He clung to it for as long as he could, but it twisted beneath him and he was hurled free. He expected to fall, but the wind kept him aloft. He couldn't breathe, but the experience of flying was exhilarating. He forced his eyes open, wanting to take one last look at life. He was caught up in a maelstrom of bricks and trees and earth and water, as if the entire island had been torn apart and tossed up into the air.

Then his head was snapped back and his eyes were forced closed, and he felt as if the pressure was squeezing him out of his body.

John Paterson's penultimate thought was of a sixteen year-old boy, signing up for the Terran Security Forces and wanting so hard to make a difference.

He died, clinging on to the hope that he had at least saved two lives from this carnage.

And that that would be enough.

Chapter Thirty-One

The young soldier had only vague memories of what had happened.

He had fought with the treacherous human. He ought to have known better. Weakened by his experiences, neutered and almost smothered by the air-breathers' suit, he had not stood a chance. And the human had flown into a berserk rage, snarling and brawling like the lowest specimen of bed-crawling animal. How typical of its kind.

The sound of rending metal had disturbed his dreams of home. He remembered being carried from his cell by two of his own people, briefly noticing how the door hung limply from its one remaining hinge. He had attempted to stammer an apology for his weakness, but he had not been able to find his voice.

When next he had woken, he had found himself back in the hospital of the humans' flagship. He had wondered for a moment if the events of the past day had been no more than a fevered hallucination.

The door was thrust open, and in strode three of his armoured brethren. The foremost of them wore the blue stripe of a Selachian leader, so the young soldier levered himself off the bed and, dismissing the throbbing pain in his head, snapped to attention. It was a response that had been drilled into him, but the hydraulic legs of the human suit were less efficient than those he was used to, and they lurched together gracelessly.

The leader came straight to the point. 'You allowed yourself to be captured,' he said. He spoke in the Ockoran tongue, but it was mutilated by the speaker system necessary to project his words across the waterless void. The young soldier's joy at being rescued dissolved under the fear of what his own superiors might do to him.

'No, Leader, I swear, I tried to activate the termination protocol. But the air-breathers attacked me from behind. They left me too injured to perform my duty.'

The leader stared at him, angrily – or so he assumed. The officer's helmet masked his true expression but was fearsome enough in itself. The young soldier couldn't even tell which of his fathers was beneath the disguise. That was part of the image, of course: air-breathers were encouraged to think of the Selachians as homogenous troops with one single-minded purpose. They had to believe that the death of one Selachian meant nothing, because another would only rise to take his place.

The young soldier had not experienced the full psychological impact of a battlesuit before. He trembled, feeling exposed and humiliated in the clothes that the air-breathers had made for him. In an attempt to fill the silence, he allowed more justifications to tumble from his mouth. 'They starved me and tortured me, Leader, but I was strong, I didn't tell them anything. I tried to take my life again, but they prevented me. Then, I discovered a threat to Ockora, and I knew it was my duty to deal with it.'

'Indeed?'

'Yes, Leader. The humans have developed a powerful bomb. They plotted to destroy our world. I almost killed the creator of the evil device...' He faltered, realising how the Leader would view the sorry end of his tale. Certainly, he couldn't tell him of his dealings with the human; he would bring shame upon himself. He hung his head and concluded, 'But I was unarmed, and they defeated me with their weapons.'

He wondered what had happened to the creature with which he had so foolishly allied himself. His comrades must have found it in his cell. The leader must have wondered why the young soldier had been imprisoned with such a thing. And yet, he had said nothing.

'I accept your explanation,' said the leader, after a pause, 'and it is a shame indeed that your valiant attempt was unsuccessful.' Had a note of awkwardness entered his voice? 'We know of the humans' bomb. Ockora is no more.'

At first, the soldier couldn't take in the news. He couldn't equate such a devastating truth with the dispassionate manner in which it had been imparted. An awful dryness crept over him. The strength drained out of his body, and only his rigid, artificial legs prevented him from falling.

'Fortunately, the Supreme Leader was forewarned of this atrocity.'

Forewarned? Then surely he would have done something...

'The despotic commander of the human forces had invaded our world. He was allowed to flee, so that we could discover the method by which he achieved such an intrusion.'

No, what was he thinking? He already knew the end of this story. The leader was talking as if something, anything, could compensate for that tragedy. But Ockora was gone.

'He led us to a concealed transmat terminal. It allowed the Supreme Leader to bring a platoon here, to the humans' flagship.'

A platoon? Just forty Selachians? Were they all that remained of a bright civilisation?

The young soldier thought of his sister and, suddenly, a deluge of misery crashed down upon him. The fate of a whole world had been too much for his mind to encompass, but the death of one special, sweet, innocent female unleashed his emotions. But then he thought of his mother, too, and the misery was compounded. And his brothers, and his cousins, and the fields in which he had played and the coral mountains that he had once painted and the songs and the tales that were no more. And, suddenly, it was too much again, and his insides were in turmoil and he ached with helplessness.

A stricken wail rattled in the back of the young soldier's throat.

The leader clenched his fists. 'Do not mourn for Ockora. Our noble people have shown that, even in death, they will not submit to dictators. They can be sure of a glorious reward in the true Second World. And we shall have our revenge, in this one.'

'No. You should have surrendered.'

The young soldier didn't know what had torn the damning, imprudent words from his chest. The Supreme Leader had executed troops for such insubordination. But, in that second – and just for that second – he had believed what he said; believed that the pride of the Ockorans was not worth the terrible price that had been exacted for it.

The leader remained surprisingly calm. 'I will forgive you that outburst, soldier, because it is a difficult time for us all.'

'Yes, Leader,' the young soldier stammered. 'Thank you, Leader. I... I know, of course, that death is preferable to oppression.'

'Granted, it is unfortunate that we could not have arrived in time to save our world, as we had hoped. However, honour will yet be satisfied.'

'How so, Leader?'

'The air-breathers are inefficient and stupid. They furnished their ship with two bombs.'

'Yes. Yes, I have seen them.'

'The Supreme Leader has captured this vessel and turned it around. Already, it is out of the range of the humans' fighters. We are heading towards the planet Earth.'

'Yes,' breathed the young soldier, in excitement. 'Yes!'

'We will avenge our fallen brethren,' said the leader, his voice swelling with righteousness. 'We will destroy the humans' world, as they have destroyed ours!'

Chapter Thirty-Two

The siren ceased in mid-whoop. The lighting lost its red tint and Jamie wondered if the emergency was over, if the Selachians had been defeated.

Then, the lights went out altogether.

Blinded, he was startled by a half-rumbling, half-whooshing sound, which came from all around him. It lasted for only a second, and then there was silence. Jamie felt exposed in the corridor, so he reached out for a wall and felt his way along it until his questing hands encountered empty air. Only then did he realise that the strange sound had been that of a dozen doors sliding open as their electronic locks disengaged.

As Jamie stepped through the doorway he felt a chill on his back. The heating had been turned off, too. The Selachians had to be behind this. He made a bet with himself that they didn't feel the cold. And they could probably see in the dark.

His own vision was beginning to adjust. A hulking shadow loomed over him, and he saw now that it was a rack of shelving. He was in a storeroom. He wondered how long he could avoid detection if he stayed here; how long he would last if, instead, he kept moving.

The situation appeared hopeless, but only because Jamie hadn't found a way out of it yet. After all, he had survived so far. He had concealed himself beneath his bed in the cell as two Selachians had torn open the door. His nose had been inches away from their golden boots. He had held his breath as they had stooped to lift his unconscious cellmate. But they had not considered that their enemies might have imprisoned one of their own kind as well.

Everywhere he had gone, for the past half-hour, he had

encountered the burnt remains of people who had been less fortunate than him.

By touch, more than sight, Jamie found that the nearest shelves contained fresh combat uniforms, folded and stacked. He pulled one free, hoisted it by the shoulders – or by one leg, as it turned out – and let gravity unfurl it. He patted it down, hoping to find a leftover weapon in one of its pouches. There was nothing. But there were many more uniforms, and Jamie had a plan now – so he pursued it. He moved along the shelves and ran his hands over their contents, looking for anomalous bulges.

Then he heard something, and froze.

Somebody was breathing.

No, not just breathing – sobbing, softly.

Ever since the blackout, Jamie had kept as quiet as he could. It had been an instinctive reaction – he had not even been fully aware of it – but he was glad of it now. Whoever else was in the room might not have heard him.

Could it be a Selachian? He doubted it. It sounded like a woman.

Jamie followed the sound on tiptoe, wishing he still had his dirk. The room was smaller than he had imagined. He reached the fourth and furthest of the parallel, free-standing racks, and peered around it. It took him a moment to spot a hunched-up figure on the floor, in the furthest corner from the door. The figure's head was buried in its knees, so he couldn't make out who it was.

He crept a little closer, straining to see through the darkness.

The woman must have heard him, or sensed his presence – for, suddenly, she looked up, saw his face a few feet from hers, gasped and then screamed.

Jamie rushed to her side. 'Hey, shush, shush,' he coaxed her, urgently. 'There's nothing to be scared of.' He laid a steadying hand on her shoulder, and thought about clamping the other hand over her mouth – but that would have been discourteous.

He recognised her, at last, although the skin around her eyes was red and blotchy and her blonde hair hung in clumps which partially concealed her face. Professor Laura Mulholland fell silent at his bidding, but she shrank against the wall in a feeble attempt to distance herself from him.

'I'm not going to hurt you,' he promised. 'That business before…'

'You were right,' Mulholland blurted out.

'Eh?'

'What we have done is an abomination. I only wish you could have stopped it.'

Jamie didn't know what to say. 'Aye, well, good,' he began. Then he frowned. 'Hey, what are you saying? Do you mean you've already used one of those bombs?'

Mulholland's face crumpled, and Jamie began to panic. Taking her other shoulder, he shook her impatiently. 'Come on, tell me, have you dropped a bomb on Ockora or not?'

'I… I don't know,' Mulholland stammered, through tears. 'I had to do it, don't you see? It wasn't my responsibility. I can only follow orders.'

She was staring at Jamie with a fanatical gleam in her eyes, as if the most important thing in her life was that he should believe her. But he was not interested in her excuses, just in the Doctor and Zoe. 'What do you mean, you don't know?'

Mulholland shook her head, as if to clear it of extraneous thoughts. She swallowed and composed herself. 'Commander Redfern instructed me to come to the bomb chamber. He had decided to launch the first G-bomb. The target was to be Ockora. I… I completed my part of the operation. The countdown began.' She took a deep, wracking breath and her eyes defocused. 'Like a heartbeat,' she whispered.

All of Jamie's nerve endings tingled with dread. 'What happened then?'

Mulholland turned her gaze back on him, as if seeing him for the first time. 'The alarm sounded. Redfern dismissed me. My part was done. It was not my responsibility. He stayed. He had to wait for a prompt from the computer, to enter the final password.'

'He might not have had a chance,' said Jamie, wanting to believe this, wanting to believe that the Selachians had found Redfern – and killed him? – before he could commit genocide.

Fresh tears rolled down Mulholland's cheeks. She closed her eyes and began to tremble. 'He will have done it. He was always the one. He is the demon, the bringer of death.'

Jamie shook his head, stubbornly. 'The Doctor will have done something.'

Mulholland had drifted off again. 'My best hope is that I may never know for sure. The demons may stay locked in my mind, if only I can die before I know for sure.'

'Hey, we'll have none of that talk. I'm taking you back to the TARDIS.' The Doctor would be there, he had to be. But what if he wasn't?

A new fear crossed Mulholland's face. She turned to Jamie, and gripped his arm so tightly that it hurt. 'What if he didn't complete the launch? Commander Redfern entered the activation codes. The Selachians will have the bomb – both bombs.'

A few hours earlier, Jamie had been able to think of nothing more terrible than the destruction of Ockora at human hands. This new possibility was almost too much to take in.

Nor did he have time to react to Mulholland's warning. From the doorway, across the room, he heard the unmistakable sound of a heavy footfall. He turned but, of course, he could see nothing. Perhaps, if they were quiet, they wouldn't be detected. More likely, it was too late.

'They've found us!' cried Mulholland.

Jamie grimaced, leapt to his feet, took her wrist and pulled her up beside him. She was like a dead weight as he dragged her along the row of shelves. They reached the wall and Jamie saw that the route to the door, at its far end, was clear. He drew Mulholland to his side, put a finger to his lips and crept forward.

He checked to the left. The aisle between the first two racks was empty.

A Selachian stepped out of the second aisle, immediately in front of him.

Jamie made to run, but Mulholland fell and he stumbled into her and lost his balance. He froze in a semi-crouch and raised his hands. The Selachian's guns were aimed at him.

'You!' the creature exclaimed.

As Jamie and the Selachian stared at each other through the darkness Mulholland crawled between their feet. Whimpering like a frightened child, she tried to bury herself in the uniforms on the nearest, lowest shelf. It was a risible attempt at concealment, but the Selachian ignored her.

'It's... you, isn't it?' said Jamie. The idea was ridiculous – he saw nothing of his erstwhile cellmate in this armoured monstrosity – but what else could explain its outburst? He straightened, slowly, but kept his hands visible.

The temperature in the room was still falling. He suppressed the urge to shiver.

'Now, you will pay for your betrayal!'

'Look,' said Jamie, trying to remember what – who – was beneath the fearsome disguise, 'I don't blame you for being upset, but you know I was only trying to help.'

'It is because of your "help" that my world no longer exists.'

Jamie's jaw dropped open. He had been thinking hard, putting together arguments, looking for anything he could say to save himself. Now, all his carefully chosen words fled from his mind and he could only stammer the beginning of a question before his throat dried up.

The Selachian stepped closer and thrust its left fist against Jamie's throat, so that the barrel of a gun was an inch from his nose. 'Our race has been wiped out,' it rumbled, 'but enough of us remain to eradicate the vermin that is humankind!'

Jamie retreated, but the Selachian only followed him. 'Hey, two wrongs don't make a right, you know.' He had been trying to emulate the Doctor, to stir the emotions of his would-be killer with a profound truth – but his friend would have come up with something more original and undoubtedly more effective.

'We are travelling to your world. We will destroy it with the remaining bomb – your own weapon. It will be an apposite punishment. As for you, plankton...'

'If you want to punish somebody,' said Professor Mulholland, 'then punish me.'

She was at the Selachian's shoulder, standing again, although she leant against the shelves for support. The revelation of Ockora's fate had had a strange effect on her. The red rims around her eyes had darkened. She spoke calmly and distantly, even coldly, but Jamie detected a dangerous undertone to her voice.

The Selachian had to turn its entire body to look at her. Jamie took a deep breath as its guns swung away from him.

'I created the gravity bomb. I launched it. I am responsible.'

'Yes,' hissed the Selachian. 'The Supreme Leader has plans for you.'

Remembering the Cloak that he had used under water, Jamie seized a uniform and hurled it over the Selachian's head. As his opponent dealt with this brief distraction, Jamie reached past it, took Mulholland's arm and dragged her back the way they had come, between the final rack and the wall. They reached the end of this passageway and turned right, even as a plasma blast illuminated the room and scorched the wall behind them. They kept on running, to the far corner. From here, there was a straight path to – and through – the doorway. They could see the tempting patch of lighter darkness that indicated its position.

Jamie came to a halt. He was faster than any Selachian, but if the creature had covered only half of the distance that he had run it would have cut him off already. Where was it?

He steadied his breathing, and wished Mulholland would do the same. He listened for any sign of movement, but heard nothing. Was the Selachian lying in wait somewhere? Or was it sneaking up on them, moving stealthily down one of the aisles?

What if it had already summoned reinforcements?

He couldn't afford to wait. 'Stay here and keep quiet,' he whispered into Mulholland's ear. She nodded. He tiptoed towards the door, bent almost double and keeping as close to the shelves as he could. Perhaps, if the Selachian did appear in front of him it might not see him right away. Perhaps, just perhaps, he might have time to run.

He froze as he reached the end of the rack. He still couldn't hear anything. He convinced himself that the monster was around the corner, waiting, just inches away. As soon as he took another step it would kill him. He could make a dash for the exit, but he might not be quick enough – and what about Mulholland?

At least she would know where the Selachian was. Perhaps it would follow him, and give her a chance to escape.

It was his best plan, his only plan. Jamie steeled himself to take the risk.

An armoured hand erupted from the uniforms to his right. Steely fingers closed around his arm. The Selachian was on the far side of the rack, reaching through. Jamie cried out in alarm, and then in pain as sparks flew from the hand and an electrical charge ripped through his body. He tried to break free, but his attacker was too strong.

Mulholland rushed to his side, hesitated, then wrapped a uniform around her hands for insulation and strove to pull Jamie and the Selachian apart. The creature lost its grip, although Jamie felt as if it had taken a handful of flesh with it. He slumped backwards into the wall. He was drained, but he couldn't falter now. He took Mulholland's hand and ran for the doorway, and through it.

He could barely make out the shape of the corridor. He ran on, faster than was safe, trailing a hand along the wall until he found a corner and rounded it. A short flight of steps took him by surprise: he tumbled down them and was lucky not to injure himself.

After two more turns, they stopped and rested by mutual, unvoiced consent. 'I think we've lost it,' whispered Jamie gratefully.

'Why should it pursue us?' There was a hysterical edge to Mulholland's voice again. Evidently, her surge of bravery in the storeroom had been fleeting. 'There are many more of them on board. We can't run for ever. They'll kill us!'

'No. We have to do something. They've got the second G-bomb.'

'What can we do?'

Jamie repeated the question to himself as he struggled to find an answer. Of course, there was only one. The usual one. 'The Doctor. I reckon he'll have a plan.'

'I thought your friend was on Ockora.'

'He'll have got away in time. He must have done.'

'You're deluding yourself!' Mulholland had probably meant to sound scornful but her words emerged with a sob, reminding Jamie of a defiant child who couldn't get her own way. He couldn't imagine how she was feeling but he knew that, in this state, she was unpredictable and potentially dangerous.

He felt a sudden, hollow pang of loneliness. He shuddered and tried to dismiss it.

The cold bit through his shirt. He could see his breath.

'Where are we?' he asked. Mulholland didn't answer. Jamie took her by the shoulders again, staring into her eyes in what he hoped was a reassuring way. 'Look, I know you're upset about this Redfern chap using the G-bomb, but getting us both killed won't change anything. You heard what the Selachian said, they're taking the other bomb to Earth!'

'You don't have to tell me what I've done!'

'I'm not blaming you!' In his frustration, Jamie had raised his voice too high. He took a deep breath, and whispered, 'But you don't want them to destroy another world with your weapon, do you?'

Mulholland looked as if he had dealt her a mortal wound. Jamie cringed inwardly at his own tactlessness. 'What I mean is,' he amended, 'things might be bad, but we're probably the only people who can stop them from getting worse. Will you help me?'

A few long seconds passed. Then Mulholland's face softened and she turned away from him. 'The bomb chamber will be guarded,' she said dully.

'I reckon we should find the TARDIS first – the blue box. The Doctor said it was just behind the hospital.'

'The blue box, yes. Redfern had me examine it. What is it?'

'It's where the Doctor will make for, if he is back on the ship.'

'And if he isn't?'

'We'll have to think of something else. Can you find it? The TARDIS, I mean?'

'I believe so. It's not far.'

Jamie grinned. But the grin turned into a look of alarm as his keen hearing suddenly told him they were not alone.

He leapt at Mulholland, knocking her out of the way and simultaneously trying to see where his enemy was. Fire ripped through the air, almost close enough to singe his shirt, and

Jamie cursed as it destroyed his night vision. 'Which way?' he yelled, a negative imprint of the blast trail blocking out his sight. He heard the sound and felt the heat of another shot as Mulholland took his hand. His remaining senses told him that, fortunately, the Selachian was still a good hundred metres away. Under Mulholland's guidance he stumbled around one corner, then another. He ran as fast as he could, but it wasn't fast enough. He was slowing them down; his carelessness would kill them.

Mulholland came up short and Jamie heard her gasp. Though her vision was still blurry he saw two vague figures. They were right in front of him, too close to flee from this time.

With a cry of useless defiance Jamie tackled the nearest figure, expecting to hit hard metal. Instead, his victim wailed and collapsed beneath the young Highlander's weight.

Confused, Jamie blinked and tried to focus on the pale blob of the figure's face, beneath him. Gradually it gained definition, and became very familiar indeed.

'Yes, Jamie,' spluttered the Doctor, 'I'm very pleased to see you too.'

Chapter Thirty-Three

'So, the Selachians gambled – and lost – their world, for the chance to steal the second G-bomb. I ought to have known.'

The Doctor was sickened, sad, relieved and worried, all at once. He had believed in the Supreme Leader's better nature, but he had been unable to reach it. He had failed, just as he had failed with Redfern. But, because of that failure, Ockora had been destroyed after all. Its inhabitants had been wiped out, along with every one of their prisoners. That was a cause for mourning – but history had been saved, and that was more than the Doctor had expected. Except that, because of his interference, a platoon of Selachians had survived to seize one of the deadliest weapons ever devised. He had placed Earth in peril. How much more guilt would he bear if, instead of shattering the time stream by saving a world, he shattered it by causing the destruction of another?

Most of all, he felt resigned. His adventures in history always had to end this way: with everything to lose and nothing more to gain than the slim chance of extricating himself from the chains of time. When would he ever learn?

At least he could spare his companions further suffering. 'Jamie,' he said, fishing in his boot, 'I want you to take Zoe and Professor Mulholland to the TARDIS. It's just around that corner and to your left, you can't miss it.'

He grinned triumphantly as he produced the key to his ship and handed it over. Jamie accepted it, suspiciously. 'What about you?' he asked. Just for once, the Doctor wished he could have been less predictable.

'I'll join you as soon as I can, but I have a mistake to rectify first.' He held up his hands to forestall the inevitable objection.

'And, as the mistake was mine, it's my responsibility to deal with it.'

'You're going to sort out the Selachians, aren't you?'

'It would be rather remiss of me to allow them to destroy Earth, wouldn't it?'

'Then I'm coming with you!'

'No!'

'You can't fight those beasties on your own.'

'I don't intend to fight them, Jamie.'

'What are you going to do, Doctor?' asked Zoe.

'I'm going to find a way to launch the second G-bomb. If it detonates in space, then the Selachians can't cause any harm with it, can they?'

'Aye,' said Jamie, 'well I can help you with that.'

'No, Jamie. I... I need you to make sure that Zoe gets back to the TARDIS safely.'

The tactic worked, as it always did. Jamie gave a disgruntled nod of agreement.

'However, you do need me to accompany you,' said Professor Mulholland.

'I can assure you...' began the Doctor.

'Do you know how to operate the controls in the bomb chamber?'

'I've seen them,' he hedged. 'I'm sure I can work out...'

Mulholland interrupted him again. 'You are unlikely to have time.' She brushed her hair back from her face and regarded the Doctor with an icy stare. She had composed herself, regained control, over the past few minutes. He wondered how long it would last.

'Even assuming the launch codes are still active,' said Mulholland, 'you still need to solve the problem of how to bypass the final password.'

'And do you know how to do that?'

'I have one or two ideas. You may be able to do this alone,

but I can greatly increase your chances of success.'

The Doctor sighed. To his chagrin, she was right.

The bomb chamber was guarded.

The Doctor had expected this, but it was still frustrating. He peered around the corner at the two motionless sentries, then returned to where Mulholland was waiting. He paced aimlessly and tugged at his lower lip. 'We need some kind of distraction. If we can just get into that room, we can seal the door and that might give us enough time to...'

'The door has been damaged,' said Mulholland. 'It won't protect us.'

'Eh? Oh. Oh, that's unfortunate. Well, in that case, we'll need a bigger distraction.'

'Weren't you issued with weapons when you were given that uniform?'

'Yes, yes. I'm afraid I disposed of them. Terrible things. Although...' The Doctor patted himself down, found something, reached into a pocket and produced an apple core. He frowned at it, put it back, tried again and grinned with delight as he discovered an electro-grenade tucked into a belt pouch. 'Aha!'

Mulholland took it and inspected it doubtfully. 'It won't do much.'

'No... but, with the right timing, it might make the Selachians look elsewhere for a while.'

'What do you intend to...?'

Mulholland didn't complete the question. The Doctor raised an inquisitive eyebrow, then realised that her gaze was fixed on something behind him.

He whirled round, expecting to see a Selachian.

Instead, he saw Wayne Redfern.

The commander's face was red, his grey hair was plastered down with sweat and his uniform was torn and spattered with the blood of two species. His mouth twitched as he glared at the Doctor, and his lips peeled back from his teeth. He held a long blade, which the Doctor recognised as Jamie's dirk. Redfern raised the dagger and advanced, slowly and menacingly.

The Doctor raised his hands in an urgent warding-off gesture. But Redfern's expression twisted into one of fury, and he let out a roar as he broke into a run. Abandoning his caution, the Doctor drew breath to cry out, to tell Redfern that he was not his enemy. But then his attacker was upon him and the blade was whistling towards his neck.

The Doctor wailed, squirmed and somehow managed to drop beneath the arc of the weapon. He tried to run, but Redfern seized him by the collar and hauled him back.

The Doctor threw up his hands, and accidentally knocked Redfern's wrist back into the wall so that the dirk clattered from his fingers. Seeing an opening, he made another attempt to speak reason, but Redfern was snarling like an animal and didn't want to hear.

The Doctor's main concern had been that the skirmish would attract attention, but he realised now that the commander was maniacally strong and a palpable threat in his own right. Now, Redfern's hands fastened around his throat. The Doctor tried to yell for help, but his words were stifled and he couldn't even see where Mulholland – his only hope – was. His legs felt weak, but he was determined not to fall. At least, standing, he could gain leverage. His hands found Redfern's face, and he strained ineffectually to push it away.

He couldn't breathe at all now. He felt his windpipe being crushed as tears were coaxed from his eyes. His vision blurred, but not so much that he didn't detect a flash of gold. The Selachians were here, but Redfern didn't seem to care.

The Doctor spread his feet to brace himself and gave one final, desperate push. He managed to tear one of Redfern's hands free. It flailed for an instant before attaching itself to the Doctor's shoulder. The pair span, in a gruesome parody of a waltzing couple.

Then Redfern screamed as a jet of burning plasma ripped into his back.

He took a long time to fall – long enough for the horrified Doctor to appreciate that, had his executioner fired a second earlier, it would have found a different target. Redfern slid to the floor and revealed, behind him, the impassive figure of the Selachians' Supreme Leader. He was flanked by two of his troops.

Belatedly, the Doctor thought about running. He turned to find another creature behind him. He raised his hands slowly, although he didn't expect the gesture to help him.

'At last, Doctor, you will pay for your crimes.'

The Doctor rolled his eyes. 'Just get it over with, can't you? I'm a little tired of listening to your threats.'

Then, to his surprise, the Supreme Leader and his entourage turned and hurried back the way they had come. The fourth Selachian brushed past the Doctor as it followed them.

It took him a moment to link the creatures' strange behaviour to the fact that they were heading towards the bomb chamber and that Mulholland had disappeared. He ran after them, and froze in the doorway to the chamber.

Mulholland had used the distraction afforded by Redfern's attack. She had reached the housing in which the remaining G-bomb hung. And she was surrounded. The quartet of Selachians had joined three others to form a circle around her.

But she had the electro-grenade and, therefore, the Selachians' attention.

She held the grenade above her head, so that it was clearly visible. 'I have set the timer of this device to its lowest level.' She was trying to sound confident. It would have been almost convincing, had the Doctor not known that her voice was normally a tone lower. 'My finger is on the activation button. It's unlikely that you can kill me before I press it. The grenade will detonate four seconds after I have done so. You can probably deduce what the explosion will almost certainly do to the gravity bomb.'

She needed some support, the Doctor decided. He stepped into the room and cleared his throat loudly. 'I should do as she says, if I were you.'

None of the Selachians moved. They didn't even look at him.

'Oh, for goodness' sake!' he cried. 'You can't intend to risk firing those weapons. Have you learned nothing at all from what has happened today?'

'Selachians do not surrender,' growled the Supreme Leader.

'That attitude has already lost you your entire world!'

'But it will win us our revenge!'

'Supreme Leader, you have my word that Professor Mulholland and I don't mean you any harm. We only want to dispose of the G-bomb.'

'The bomb will be our instrument of vengeance.'

'But it isn't worth risking extinction for!' the Doctor shouted, with the petulance of a child who couldn't understand why the world wouldn't comply with his reasonable requests.

'The possibility of victory,' said the Supreme Leader quietly, 'against the certainty of defeat and humiliation.'

'Doctor.' Even the pretence of confidence had fled from Mulholland's voice. 'I think you ought to get out of here.'

It had occurred to him that she had considered, even wanted, this to be a suicide mission. He could see now that, even if he had been right, she didn't want to die any more.

Laura Mulholland had been destined to take her own life. Instead, thanks to him, it would be taken from her as she fought to redeem herself by saving a world. Was it a better fate or a worse one?

The Doctor hesitated – and, in that second, a silent signal must have passed from the Supreme Leader to his troops. They fired simultaneously. Mulholland's body was incinerated in the crossfire of fourteen weapons.

And, with that image seared into his mind, the Doctor turned and fled.

At the first corner he stooped and gathered up Jamie's dirk, knowing how highly his companion valued it as a memento.

As he straightened, an explosion shook the floor beneath him and blew a cloud of debris out of the bomb chamber. A gentle breeze began to blow down the corridor.

The Doctor did what he should have done when he had first landed on Kalaya.

He ran back to the TARDIS with all the speed he could muster.

Chapter Thirty-Four

The streets of New York City were strewn with the remnants of civilisation. Miraculously, the Empire State Building still stood proudly, its status as the city's tallest skyscraper restored. Zoe thought it a fitting monument to human achievement; to the indomitable spirit that had driven the invaders away.

'Be careful,' warned the Doctor. 'Some of the debris is still unstable. One misstep and it could shift beneath you.'

'Why are we here, Doctor?' she asked.

'Well, when I saw where we'd landed, I thought you might like to see something.'

'And Jamie?'

'Oh, I shouldn't think there's any need to wake him. I think he's better off where he is.'

Zoe was curious, she had to admit it. But she hated being here. The Doctor had spoken of the invasion many times, but it belonged in her future. In her time, the people of Earth still had to know this tragedy. She could console herself with the knowledge that the Daleks would be defeated, but only if she didn't think about it too hard. The reality of this terrible aftermath made her ache for all the people who had been – who would be – lost.

Downtown, refugees made homeless by the invaders had found shelter in crumbling buildings. Red ticker tape sealed off a block. The Doctor ducked beneath it without a qualm, and Zoe followed. They stood and watched as soldiers sifted through rubble.

'A tenement collapsed last night,' explained the Doctor. 'They're searching for survivors.'

'Excuse me, sir, madam… you shouldn't be here. It could be dangerous.'

Zoe turned, to see that the speaker was a young man in army fatigues. He couldn't have been more than seventeen years old. He was tall and wiry with full, blond hair and a haunted look that suggested that his eyes were buried deep within his head. His southern drawl and the prominent bone structure of his face were somehow familiar.

The Doctor drew himself to his full height, clasped his hands behind his back and looked down his nose at the young soldier. 'We are government observers, Private, here at the request of your General Howard. You are?'

The soldier snapped to attention. 'Wayne Redfern, sir. 287-472-692.'

Zoe stifled a gasp. Of course she had not recognised him – she had seen him only once, on a monitor screen, and he had been much older then – but she knew that name.

'May I suggest, Private Redfern, that you concentrate your efforts upon…' The Doctor gazed around, thoughtfully, before pointing '…that area over there.'

Redfern looked briefly puzzled, but quickly concealed his bewilderment. 'As you wish, sir.'

'Well, then – get to it, will you, there's a good chap.'

The young soldier saluted smartly and hurried away.

Zoe couldn't take her eyes off him. Memories swam to the surface of her mind. She remembered how elated she had felt at the sight of the TARDIS, a safe haven after her long ordeal at the Selachians' hands. But, only minutes later, she had stood in its console room and stared at the scanner screen and her happiness had given way to an aching, hollow sensation.

She had watched as the second G-bomb had detonated, causing the *Triumph* to fold into itself like a sheet of paper being crumpled into a ball.

'Fortunately,' the Doctor had said, still out of breath from his desperate sprint, 'we are a long way from any inhabited worlds. The presence of a new miniature black hole in this sector of space shouldn't impact unduly upon history. Well, no more than it can cope with.' He had clapped his hands together gleefully, but his face had fallen when he turned to Zoe and saw her expression – as if he had only then remembered that lives had been lost.

It wasn't that he was uncaring. He had been as saddened as she was. It was just that, somehow, he could accept it. Jamie, too, seemed able to acknowledge that he had done his best, and that things could have been much worse.

But Zoe's dreams were haunted by Paterson, Kukhadil, Davidson, Dresden, and even the Selachians and Redfern. The TARDIS had taken her to new places, new times, and there had been other problems, other monsters. Sometimes, she could push her experiences on Ockora to the back of her mind. But the memories always resurfaced, eventually.

'Well?' The Doctor's voice took her by surprise, jolting her back to the present. He had waited until Redfern was out of earshot. 'Do you still want to do it?'

'Do what?'

'Change history. Put a gun to his head. Take his life.'

'Doctor!' she protested, appalled.

He interlaced his fingers and gave her a look of pure innocence. 'Not even to save nine million lives?'

'Of course not.'

'Good,' he said simply. He turned around and began to trudge away.

'No,' Zoe called after him. 'No, wait!'

The Doctor turned back to her, an eyebrow raised.

'I just couldn't do it. But… but it would be logical. Wouldn't it?'

'Logical, perhaps. But would it be fair?'

She shrugged, voicelessly. The Doctor gave a sad sigh, and

swung an arm to encompass the devastation around them. 'Look at the world he's been brought into. Is it any wonder that, as an adult, he won't be able to think of a better solution to his problems than the use of force?'

'We could say something,' suggested Zoe, hopefully. 'Warn him.'

'It didn't work in the future. It won't work now.'

'Then why have you brought me here?' she asked, irritation colouring her voice.

The Doctor's expression became mournful. 'I thought you wanted to learn.'

'Learn what? That everything we do is predestined; that we can't make a difference?'

'You can believe that if you like. But Time is remarkably resilient, you know. Oh, of course we mustn't change the broad course of events, but we can tamper with the details. We can improve things in a million little ways, and that can add up to an awful lot.'

Zoe nodded slowly, as she mulled over his words. She was beginning to see things from a different perspective. Whether that made them better or not, she didn't yet know.

She was distracted by a shout. 'Over here – I've got someone!'

Private Redfern was gesticulating wildly to his colleagues. 'It's a young girl,' he reported, excitedly. 'She's unconscious, but still alive!'

The soldiers began to dig into the pile of masonry, under Redfern's directions. Zoe watched, with a bittersweet smile, until she felt the Doctor's hand on her arm.

'I try not to believe in predestination, if I can help it,' he said quietly, as she allowed him to guide her away from that place. 'I'd rather believe in hope.'

THE EIGHT DOCTORS *by Terrance Dicks* ISBN 0 563 40563 5
VAMPIRE SCIENCE *by Jonathan Blum and Kate Orman* ISBN 0 563 40566 X
THE BODYSNATCHERS *by Mark Morris* ISBN 0 563 40568 6
GENOCIDE *by Paul Leonard* ISBN 0 563 40572 4
WAR OF THE DALEKS *by John Peel* ISBN 0 563 40573 2
ALIEN BODIES *by Lawrence Miles* ISBN 0 563 40577 5
KURSAAL *by Peter Anghelides* ISBN 0 563 40578 3
OPTION LOCK *by Justin Richards* ISBN 0 563 40583 X
LONGEST DAY *by Michael Collier* ISBN 0 563 40581 3
LEGACY OF THE DALEKS *by John Peel* ISBN 0 563 40574 0
DREAMSTONE MOON *by Paul Leonard* ISBN 0 563 40585 6
SEEING I *by Jonathan Blum and Kate Orman* ISBN 0 563 40586 4
PLACEBO EFFECT *by Gary Russell* ISBN 0 563 40587 2
VANDERDEKEN'S CHILDREN *by Christopher Bulis* ISBN 0 563 40590 2
THE SCARLET EMPRESS *by Paul Magrs* ISBN 0 563 40595 3
THE JANUS CONJUNCTION *by Trevor Baxendale* ISBN 0 563 40599 6
BELTEMPEST *by Jim Mortimore* ISBN 0 563 40593 7
THE FACE EATER *by Simon Messingham* ISBN 0 563 55569 6
THE TAINT *by Michael Collier* ISBN 0 563 55568 8
DEMONTAGE *by Justin Richards* ISBN 0 563 55572 6
REVOLUTION MAN *by Paul Leonard* ISBN 0 563 55570 X
DOMINION *by Nick Walters* ISBN 0 563 55574 2
UNNATURAL HISTORY *by Jon Blum and Kate Orman* ISBN 0 563 55576 9

THE DEVIL GOBLINS FROM NEPTUNE *by Keith Topping and Martin Day*
ISBN 0 563 40564 3
THE MURDER GAME *by Steve Lyons* ISBN 0 563 40565 1
THE ULTIMATE TREASURE *by Christopher Bulis* ISBN 0 563 40571 6
BUSINESS UNUSUAL *by Gary Russell* ISBN 0 563 40575 9
ILLEGAL ALIEN *by Mike Tucker and Robert Perry* ISBN 0 563 40570 8
THE ROUNDHEADS *by Mark Gatiss* ISBN 0 563 40576 7
THE FACE OF THE ENEMY *by David A. McIntee* ISBN 0 563 40580 5
EYE OF HEAVEN *by Jim Mortimore* ISBN 0 563 40567 8
THE WITCH HUNTERS *by Steve Lyons* ISBN 0 563 40579 1
THE HOLLOW MEN *by Keith Topping and Martin Day* ISBN 0 563 40582 1
CATASTROPHEA *by Terrance Dicks* ISBN 0 563 40584 8
MISSION IMPRACTICAL *by David A. McIntee* ISBN 0 563 40592 9
ZETA MAJOR *by Simon Messingham* ISBN 0 563 40597 X
DREAMS OF EMPIRE *by Justin Richards* ISBN 0 563 40598 8
LAST MAN RUNNING *by Chris Boucher* ISBN 0 563 40594 5
MATRIX *by Robert Perry and Mike Tucker* ISBN 0 563 40596 1
THE INFINITY DOCTORS *by Lance Parkin* ISBN 0 563 40591 0
SALVATION *by Steve Lyons* ISBN 0 563 55566 1
THE WAGES OF SIN *by David A. McIntee* ISBN 0 563 55567 X
DEEP BLUE *by Mark Morris* ISBN 0 563 55571 8
PLAYERS *by Terrance Dicks* ISBN 0 563 55573 4
MILLENNIUM SHOCK *by Justin Richards* ISBN 0 563 55586 6
STORM HARVEST *by Mike Tucker and Robert Perry* ISBN 0 563 55577 7

SHORT TRIPS *ed. Stephen Cole* ISBN 0 563 40560 0
MORE SHORT TRIPS *ed. Stephen Cole* ISBN 0 563 55565 3

THE BOOK OF LISTS *by Justin Richards and Andrew Martin* ISBN 0 563 40569 4
A BOOK OF MONSTERS *by David J. Howe* ISBN 0 563 40562 7
THE TELEVISION COMPANION *by David J. Howe and Stephen James Walker*
ISBN 0 563 40588 0
FROM A TO Z *by Gary Gillatt* ISBN 0 563 40589 9

PRESENTING

ALL-NEW AUDIO DRAMAS

Big Finish Productions are proud to present all-new *Doctor Who* adventures on audio!

Featuring original music and sound-effects, these full-cast plays are available on double cassette in high street stores, and on limited-edition double CD from Forbidden Planet and other good specialist stores, or via mail order.

The adventures begin with
THE SIRENS OF TIME

A four-part story by Nicholas Briggs.
Starring Peter Davison, Colin Baker and Sylvester McCoy.

The Fifth, Sixth and Seventh Doctors, together for the first time!

Gallifrey is in a state of crisis, facing destruction at the hands of an overwhelming enemy. And the Doctor is involved, in three different incarnations – each caught up in a deadly adventure, scattered across time and space. The web of time is threatened – and someone wants the Doctor dead.

The three incarnations of the Doctor must join together to set time back on the right track – but in doing so, will they unleash a still greater threat?

if you wish to order the CD version, please photocopy this form or provide all the details on paper if you do not with to damage this book. Delivery within 28 days of release. Send to: PO Box 1127, Maidenhead, Berkshire. SL6 3LN.
Big Finish Hotline 01628 828283.

Please send me [ ] copies of The Sirens of Time @ £13.99 (£15.50 non-UK orders) – price inclusive of postage and packing. Payment can be accepted by credit card or by personal cheques, payable to Big Finish Productions Ltd.

Name...

Address...

Postcode...

VISA/Mastercard number...

Expiry date...Signature...

For more details visit our website at http://www.doctorwho.co.uk